DRAGON WAR

Also by Laurence Yep

Laurence Yep

DRAGON WAR

HarperCollins*Publishers*

J
(1)

Dragon War
Copyright © 1992 by Laurence Yep
All rights reserved. No part of this book may be used or reproduced in any manner
whatsoever without written permission except in the case of brief quotations embod-
ied in critical articles and reviews. Printed in the United States of America. For infor-
mation address HarperCollins Children's Books, a division of HarperCollins
Publishers, 10 East 53rd Street, New York, NY 10022.
Typography by Joyce Hopkins
1 2 3 4 5 6 7 8 9 10
First Edition

Library of Congress Cataloging-in-Publication Data
Yep, Laurence.
    Dragon war / Laurence Yep.
        p.   cm.
    Summary: The dragon princess Shimmer and her companions fight a war against
the evil Boneless King in order to rescue their friend Thorn and restore the dragons'
underwater home.
    ISBN 0-06-020302-1. — ISBN 0-06-020303-X (lib. bdg.)
    [1. Dragons—Fiction. 2. Fantasy.] I. Title.
PZ7.Y44Dqp 1992   91-28921
[Fic]—dc20   CIP
                                                                               AC

To Bill Morris,
who has been through some wars himself

A dragon was Shimmer—
A princess royal.
A human was Thorn—
Her companion so loyal.

Together they made a vow
To restore the Inland Sea.
So to the dragon king
They went so hopefully.

There they met a human girl—
She was of the Kingfisher clan.
Indigo was her name.
And she helped them with their plan.

The Monkey Sage was there too.
And even Civet the Witch;
For though she'd been their enemy,
She now had made the switch.

A cauldron was the prize
To boil away a sea,
But then its side got cracked
In their urgency.

So toward the mountains they went
Where the Smith and Snail Woman dwelt,
For they could fix the cauldron—
Or so old Monkey felt.

But Civet was possessed
By a Witch deceased.
Strange prophecies she made
Before she was released.

Right away one came true—
Though that wasn't their intention.
They freed the Boneless King
Through Thorn's clever invention.

"I need a stronger body,"
The Boneless King, he said.
And so he found the Butcher
And on his soul he fed.

And in the Butcher's form he ruled—
His wealth, his land, his army,
And with his magic restored,
No country could stay free.

The world was in desperate plight—
The worst it's ever been.
And so to free the others
Civet died—just as she'd foreseen.

To the Smith and Snail Woman
Went the dragon and her friends.
To make a weapon against the King
Into the cauldron Thorn blends.

But Pomfret, Shimmer's brother,
Was more than her match.
From his sister's very paws,
Thorn he did snatch,

And to the Boneless King he gave it.
Dragon, Monkey and girl,
Though torture now they face,
Defiance they still hurl.

—*Old Song from the Festival of Waters, popularly
ascribed to Monkey*

CHAPTER ONE

Did our heroes despair?
Did Monkey dum-de-dum . . .
Did he even care?

No, I needed something about myself. I could feel the
rhyme teasing around in my mind as the snow
sprayed upward from the runners of the makeshift
sled. Ahead of us a company of imperial guardsmen
toiled through the snow, their white cloaks flapping
in the wind. The same wind picked up the snowflakes
that had been kicked up and swept them into our
faces, where they stung like dozens of little needles.

I would have given a chunk of my tail if I could
have wiped the snow from my face fur; but chains
had been wrapped around me so tightly that I

couldn't even raise a pinkie, and the chains themselves had been fastened to the huge bed of the sled.

It had to be large to accommodate the royal bulk of Shimmer the dragon, princess of the clan of the Lost Sea. To restore her home, we had "borrowed" a cauldron from Shimmer's uncle, Sambar, the High King of the dragons; and in our . . . uh . . . hasty departure, the cauldron itself had gotten broken.

Then we had accidentally let loose a wicked creature who called himself the Boneless King. That had been bad enough, but he had been able to take over the body of the King of this land, a cruel man aptly named the Butcher.

Worst of all, we had been trying to repair the magical cauldron—first to use in restoring the Lost Sea and then as a weapon against the Boneless King. For the sake of protecting the world, a human boy, Thorn, had sacrificed himself, letting his soul be made part of the material of the vessel itself. But the Boneless King, with the help of Shimmer's renegade brother, Pomfret, had captured us and stolen Thorn from us.

For maybe the hundredth time, I tested my chains as quietly as I could, but whoever the blacksmith was, he had done his job. They were proof against all the marvelous muscles of my fabled might.

I couldn't see the human girl, Indigo, when she spoke, because she was on the other side of Shimmer. "I just wish I knew what the Boneless King plans to do with us. We seem to be heading toward Egg Mountain." Egg Mountain was where the Boneless

6

King had been imprisoned for thousands of years.

I felt sorry for the girl. She had spent most of her life confined to menial jobs in the kitchen of the dragons' undersea palace; then, during what time she had spent on land, she had been chased, drowned and otherwise entertained by all sorts of villainous creatures. The least we owed her was some reassurance.

"Well," I said, trying to sound cheerful, "if he meant to kill us, he would have done it already."

Orphaned, Indigo had learned quickly to rely only on herself, so she was almost as tough as the chains that bound us. But the prospect of having to fight a ghost and the army he had taken over—well, that was enough to make anyone lose a little confidence. "I just know it's something slow," she said. "Something slow and horrible."

A huge black shadow suddenly covered us; and I looked up to see Shimmer's brother, Pomfret, the former King of the Lost Sea. He kept pace with slow, steady beats of his wings that sent more snow puffing up all around us.

He tried to smile encouragingly, but he had become such a mean and sly creature that his smile was like a cheap tin imitation. "I've been waiting for this opportunity to speak to you alone. You know," he said to his sister, "I could use my influence with the King to see that you meet a quick and relatively painless end—if you were to give me the dream pearl."

Chains had been wound around Shimmer, so all she could do was hang her head. "Uncle Sambar took it." Sambar was the High King of the dragons in whose palace Indigo had labored.

"If he had, you would never have left until you had gotten it back." Pomfret hung just a little lower in the air, his claws arching menacingly over my head toward his helpless sister. "I think I'll just check."

Listen to my two rules in life and you might live as long as I have: Never eat fried foods before you go to sleep, and never get caught between two feuding dragons. The first rule even I haven't kept, but I always thought I'd be able to keep the second.

I tried to duck down as Pomfret swept in, but the chains wouldn't let me, so I wound up being squeezed between the leathery bulk of two dragons.

Shimmer tried to avoid Pomfret's paws, but he managed to seize her throat just below her chin. "You always were a crafty one—always sneaking extra desserts." He took the pearl—the source of all the magic she knew—from beneath the fold of flesh in Shimmer's forehead.

"Ah, I knew you had it." Even in the bright light reflected from the snow, rainbow shafts of light flickered through the cracks between his paws. Although she had told me that she had the pearl, this was the first time I had seen it. Now, I've seen quite a lot of magic in my time, but even that little glimpse of its lovely light made me gasp.

Shoulders sagging, Shimmer mumbled despairingly, "Go on then, like a good little pet. Give it to the Boneless King."

"I won't believe your lies. Will you quit pretending he's not the King of this land?" Pomfret clapped another paw over the pearl so that its beams were hidden. "He's the Butcher, and he'll make me High King of the seas."

Shimmer snorted. "Now who's pretending?"

"But I've already paid for my throne with the cauldron." And picking up a flap of flesh on his forehead, he popped the pearl beneath it so it was hidden. "I was just waiting for my chance to recover this."

"Thief, traitor!" Shimmer tried to throw herself at him, but her chains caught her up short.

Each of them was a mass of bone and muscle, so it was like being caught between colliding mountains. "Have a care," I wheezed. "There are innocent bystanders. Or rather," I added, "in-between-standers."

Pomfret smirked at me. "From what I've heard about you, Monkey, I don't think you were ever innocent."

Shimmer spat angrily at him, "You've doomed our whole clan and now the entire race of dragons."

Pomfret pressed in so tight that I couldn't even breathe. "You're a fine one to call me a thief. Who stole the dream pearl to begin with?"

I might have been turned into a furry pancake, but at that moment the sled gave a lurch. "Go slower. We don't want the sled tipping over," Pomfret shouted to the long lines of guardsmen hauling the makeshift sled up the snowy slope of the mountain. "The King wants them there in one piece."

"What about the quick and merciful end you promised in exchange for the pearl?" Shimmer grumbled.

"You always were gullible," Pomfret said, gloating.

He might have rubbed it in more, but the sled continued bumping along, much to Pomfret's annoyance. "I ordered you to slow down," he shouted to the officer in charge of the hauling.

However, the lieutenant, a man named Crusher from the capital, ignored Pomfret. Neither the duty nor Pomfret were any too popular with the lieutenant and his men. First they'd had to make the sled and then they were freezing their tootsies slogging through the snow.

"I said slow down." Spreading his wings, Pomfret darted over the lines of startled guardsmen. Whatever the lieutenant might have thought privately of dragons, he ought to know it wasn't the wisest thing to pick a fight with one.

I settled back against Shimmer's familiar bulk. "You know," I said, "it might help matters if you tried to win him over to our side instead of insulting him."

Shimmer glanced at her brother and then swung her neck around. "This," she grunted, "from the master of tact."

Up ahead, we could hear Pomfret arguing with the lieutenant. "This is a strange time to do calisthenics," Indigo said.

However, Shimmer was too busy straining her head forward to answer. She stretched and stretched until the joints in her neck cracked, and still she tried to extend her head. Suddenly she raised a hindpaw.

"How'd you get free?" I gasped.

Still Shimmer said nothing until, with one last snap of her vertebrae, she managed to touch her forehead against the hindpaw. Wriggling her claws, she worked a quick muttered spell.

"I wish," Shimmer murmured, "that I could see his face when he finds he has an illusion. But I probably won't."

Suddenly, there was a second image of Shimmer on the sled, so real and solid-looking that it was hard to tell which was which.

I squirmed gleefully but couldn't move very far because my chains were secured to the sled itself. "You made a copy of the pearl."

Shimmer gave me a wink. "You're not the only one who's good at playing tricks. I managed to do that when we were captured. And later I fooled them into thinking they had bound all of me. The timing was tricky. I had to scratch just before they started to chain my hindleg."

"Then we could have escaped anytime," Indigo said accusingly.

"Yes, but I wanted to wait until we were near the Boneless King again. Wherever Pomfret is, the King is bound to be close-by. I'd even wager the pearl that he's at Egg Mountain preparing our punishment." And with the same joint-popping noise she bent her forehead forward. The next moment, I was looking at

11

the spitting image of myself.

I blinked. "If I didn't know I was me, I'd say that I was over there."

"Yes, gruesome, isn't it? Is the world ready for two Monkeys?" Shimmer then repeated the motion so that, I suppose, there was an imitation of Indigo on her other side. "And where the Boneless King is, he'll have Thorn."

Indigo immediately seized on the advantage Shimmer's guile had gained for us. "Clever. Now the King will be lulled into a false sense of security."

"Exactly." With her hindpaw, Shimmer freed her other limbs and quietly slid meter after meter of chain behind us like a long, dark trail behind a giant snail. The sled had slowed in pace as Pomfret himself marched at the rear of the guardsmen.

"Watch out," Shimmer warned as she extended a paw toward me. "This may pinch a little."

As her claws closed around the chains, they pulled them even tighter. "You aren't joking," I gasped. Fortunately, her strong paws made short work of the chain that bound me, and in the next moment she had snapped Indigo's.

"We'll have only a little time," Shimmer said as she fell.

I plopped backward into the soft snow. "That's cold," Indigo grunted as she joined us.

When I sat back up, I saw our fake selves still bound to the sled. "The chains must be weighing down the sled."

12

"But they're bound to notice the difference in the weight soon." Shimmer plucked Indigo from the snow, snapped a link, slid the chains from her as if she were unwrapping a package, dusted off some of the snow and set the girl upon her back. "We can cut around the ridge and get to Egg Mountain ahead of them."

I shivered, thinking of that strange, cruel creature. "I'd rather go in the other direction."

"And where would you flee?" With a flap of her wings, Shimmer rose into the air. "Anyway, I'm not leaving Thorn in their hands a moment longer."

No one could have asked for a better or braver companion than Thorn, and the thought of his being forced to do the will of the Boneless King made me angry. "You're right," I said, and somersaulted up into the air as if on invisible steps, the way I usually did.

CHAPTER TWO

The icy winds whipped at us as we put the ridgetop between us and Pomfret. The brown cliffsides rose out of the snow like ribs breaking through white flesh. And below us, snow sprites leaped and whirled in a mad dance.

We swung around Egg Mountain, where the Boneless King had been imprisoned. The glare from the snow was almost blinding, but I managed to pick out three specks. As we swept in, I could see Horn, the little wizard with the corkscrew goatee. The Boneless King pretended to work his magic through Horn so that no one would suspect he wasn't the Butcher. Horn was cautiously sniffing the jar of needleweed juice he had taken from Indigo. "It seems harmless," he said, corking it. Indigo had made it when we had camped by the strange crypt under the lake, because she had thought it would come in handy.

Next to him was the barrel shape of the Butcher himself. The Boneless King had taken over his body—though so far we had been unable to convince anyone of that fact. "The odor is familiar," the Boneless King mused, "but where have I smelled it before?"

Standing faithfully by the king's side was Snowgoose, the huge white dog that was the Boneless King's pet. Something glinted on its back, and as we darted in, we saw the coppery sides of the cauldron that now housed Thorn's soul.

Instinctively I started to reach for the staff that I kept shrunk behind my ear, and not for the first time I regretted that it had been taken from me when we had been captured. I felt like I'd lost an arm.

"The Sea! The Sea!" Shouting the war cry of her clan, Shimmer seized Thorn. However, when she tried to rise, she lifted Snowgoose at the same time.

Twisting, the huge dog sank its fangs into her leg. Startled, Shimmer banked sharply, but there wasn't enough clearance, and she thudded into the snow. Indigo went flying through the air to land at the feet of the Boneless King.

The little wizard, Horn, swung at Indigo with the first thing in his hand—which happened to be the jar of needleweed juice—but Indigo managed to grab his wrist. While the two of them wrestled, I began to somersault toward the King.

I was too quick for him to work any magic, but the Boneless King thought fast—I'll give him that much.

Reaching into his sleeve, he held up what looked like a metal toothpick with a little gold ring at either end.

"Looking for this?" he asked, and before I could say anything, he had pitched it through the entrance to the mountain.

With a cry, I leapt after it, trying to pick it up as it clinked and skittered along the tunnel. Suddenly I saw beneath me a narrow slot opening onto the cavern inside the mountain. In the glowing light cast by the minerals, I could see the river below. If my staff fell into the water, I knew I could spend a lifetime searching for it.

"Shimmer!" I heard Indigo scream from behind me.

With a final lunge, I just grasped the staff. "Hold tight," I called back to her. "I'm coming." I kicked out my feet and managed to stop, but the tunnel here was a straight drop into the cavern.

Pebbles rattled against my back. "Tsk, tsk, don't you know better than to litter this pristine landscape?" I whirled around to see Indigo struggling in the grasp of the Boneless King. "I trust you'll find your stay as comfortable as I did. I've added a few of my own refinements." And saying that, he pitched Indigo at me.

"Help," she cried as she fell through the air. In her hand she had the juice jar.

I caught her. However, her momentum knocked us both backward, and the next moment we were falling through the air, and I lost my grip on her. And as we fell, I heard the Boneless King's taunting voice floating down after us. "I'll check on you in a few thousand years."

"I've got you." Tucking my staff safely behind my ear, I somersaulted toward Indigo. It wasn't my best set of acrobatics, but I leapt up through the air and caught her.

"Look out below," Shimmer cried. I barely dodged a kiloton of falling dragon, bound in chains that glowed with a magical blue light. He must have bound her in new ones. The wind from her passage tumbled me around so much that I almost lost Indigo again. It took me a moment to right myself.

In the glow from the minerals in the cavern, I saw a huge white circle break the smooth, black waters of the river where Shimmer must have landed.

Stowing the jar away in her sash, Indigo clung to me tightly. "Where's the island?"

I looked down. The island with the strange, glowing fungus and the forest of mushrooms was gone.

It had been the prison of the Boneless King after he had lost the Great War to the Five Masters. Unable to destroy him, they had stripped him of all magic by taking away his shape and leaving him on an island from which almost nothing could leave. We might have all still been stranded there if Thorn hadn't worked out our means of escape. The one exception to the spell was clay, or else the island might have silted up over the centuries. Since pottery was fired clay, we had managed to float off on a raft of earthen jars. However, unbeknownst to us, we had helped the

Boneless King to escape at the same time.

I looked from the surface of the river toward the ceiling. Over us, the stalactites grew in strange shapes—not just fanglike cones, but long strands like noodles curling down, or even in sheets like flags waving.

I tugged at my ear. "Funny, the cavern seems smaller than last time."

On one wall of the cavern was a narrow ledge about two meters above the river's surface. Dropping through the air, I deposited Indigo there and went over to the spot where Shimmer had sunk.

In the dim light, the water looked black as ink. I hopped over the area where the falls had been. Though the water there had once foamed and frothed, it was now as smooth and calm as the rest of the river, which had risen high enough to cover it. Hovering over the surface of the river, I could feel the icy cold, and I didn't much enjoy the idea of diving into the water.

The river was so dark that anything white stood out in stark contrast. At first I thought there was a floating chunk of ice that had fallen into the river somehow. But then I took a second look. It was a fish floating belly up, the white flesh gleaming like a giant grain of rice. About ten meters beyond it another bobbed to the surface. In fact, dead fish bobbed up and down all around us on the river.

Suddenly I began to realize what some of the "refinements" were that the Boneless King had made in his former prison. He had blocked up one end of the cavern so that the river could enter but not leave. Then he had poisoned the river.

"Shimmer!" I shouted with new urgency.

The next moment the dragon rocketed to the surface, drenching me in a sheet of spray. "Brrr, that's freezing," she gasped. Glowing chains still bound her legs to her body. Even so, she could wriggle like a sea snake.

"We've got to get you out of the water. It's poisoned. Maybe I can break these chains," I said, and gazing fondly at my magic staff, I shouted, "Change." At once, it lengthened to an iron rod about two meters long with a gold ring at either end. And as my sweet little toy stretched itself, I gave it a twirl, delighting in its strength, its beauty and its speed. It almost seemed to hug my fingers as I twirled it from one finger to another, making the loops form a golden circle.

"Careful," Shimmer barked.

No one ever understands me. "I'm always careful." I was just going to try to slip a loop under one chain when the magical links themselves just seemed to melt away. Apparently the Boneless King didn't want Shimmer dying any too soon.

Treading water, she spread her wings. "I no sooner sat up than the Boneless King had bound me with the chains. And then he used his magic to lift me up and dump me into the cavern."

"Save the tales of woe for later. Get out."

Shimmer spread her wings stiffly. "They're numb from the cold."

"Grab hold." I held out one end of the loop toward her. She eyed the golden loop uncertainly and then grabbed hold of it with her fangs. "On the count of three," I said.

Dragons, though, are never big on patience. Shimmer began flapping her wings and sending up sheets of spray. Digging my heels into the air, I began to haul at my staff. Between the two of us Shimmer began to rise, dripping, from the river. As she rose above the water, her wings began to move more quickly and strongly. "Now let's pay another visit to our friends." And once the blood started pumping into her wings, Shimmer was rumbling along like a big green wagon.

However, when she reached the ceiling, she spread her wings and halted. Hovering in confusion, she lowered her long neck so she could scratch her head with a forepaw. "That's odd. I could have sworn the opening was here."

The goldlike minerals gleamed with their own light like miniature stars, casting a soft light over the circling dragon. When I joined her by the ceiling, I studied the area where the opening should have been. "Yes, it was right there." I pointed toward where the stone was darker than the surrounding area.

Shimmer pounded a frustrated paw against a stalactite. "It's been fused together."

"What's wrong?" Indigo shouted anxiously from the ledge. Down below, the human girl looked like a small, pale worm on the rocky ledge.

"We need to find a new exit," I said to Shimmer. "Some tiny sliver of a crack that the the Boneless King missed. Indigo could help us search if she weren't in that inconvenient human shape."

"I'll see if she's willing to change," Shimmer said, and glided down in a wide, easy spiral toward Indigo. I noticed that she was moving sluggishly, as if her brief immersion in the poisoned water had already affected her. If the water could poison her, I didn't see what hope Indigo and I could have.

On the ledge Indigo was looking cold and miserable, huddling with her knees drawn up to her chest. "Did you find the way out?"

It was only then that I noticed that the river had already risen almost to the lip of the ledge on which we stood. The dark water sucked hungrily at the ledge as if it were alive. When we had gone to a higher and wider ledge, Shimmer broke the news to the girl.

"You mean we're trapped?" Indigo asked.

She looked so glum that I patted her on the shoulder. "No magician is good enough to seal off an entire mountain. But we'll need help, so Shimmer will change you into a dragon like herself. And a handsome one you'll make. You might never want to change back."

Indigo stiffened as if we had asked her to become a pile of garbage. "Do I have to?"

"Most creatures would give their right claw to be a dragon," Shimmer said snippishly.

21

"Nothing personal," Indigo said hastily when she realized she had offended her friend. "I mean, it's not like I have anything against *you*. If all the dragons were like you, I wouldn't have any problems."

"It's quite all right," Shimmer said, but everyone can tell when dragons lie. They get a funny look in their eyes. "Tell me this. Did any dragon ever mistreat you in Sambar's palace?"

"Well, no." Indigo shrugged her thin shoulders. "It was the other servants."

"I understand your distaste about becoming a puffed-up lizard," I said, ignoring Shimmer's glower. "But let's be practical. It's not like we're asking you to *stay* a dragon."

Indigo tugged at a spike of her blue hair. "As long as it's only temporary."

Shimmer snapped a pair of claws at me, then turned back to Indigo. "You'll make a fine dragon. You won't look like Monkey, with that mashed snout of his."

When Shimmer glanced my way, I turned around with a sigh, because I knew she didn't want me to see her work her spell. However, from the corner of my eye I saw Indigo's nose lengthen into a snout and her skin change to green before it turned into scales. Shimmer, though, must have been feeling the effects of the poison still, because Indigo's greased blue hair became a ridge of blue spines down her back, and the jar became a large gray wart on her hip.

I pivoted with a dancelike step. "How original."

Curious, Indigo craned her neck over the water to study her reflection. "Hey, why do I look so funny?"

Shimmer flopped back against the rock wall. "It's function, not form, that counts." She wagged a claw at us. "Now remember. Check out every crack in the rock—no matter how small."

I began pulling hairs from my tail, spitting on them and changing them into monkeys. "Go, children. Find a crack that leads to the outside world." I changed the hairs as fast as I could until my tail was quite bald.

Indigo had been trying to catch sight of her new wings. She looked at me now. "Do you know that without hair, your tail looks like a worm?"

I whisked my tail out of sight. "It looks like a tail without hair," I insisted, as a cloud of little monkeys scattered themselves upward toward the the gleaming roof of the cavern.

We searched the ceiling for hours, until Shimmer became so desperate that she even shrank herself to mouse size and began to search about in the ceiling. However, after a while she wriggled out of a crack off to my left. "This is a dead end, too," she called in a tiny voice that I could barely hear over the rushing river. "The Boneless King has sealed up this mountain tighter than an egg."

Wearily I sat in midair. All around me I could hear the little monkeys chattering to one another, the echoes of their high voices carrying down to me through some trick of the cavern. It seemed as if there was a lot less cavern and more of that ominous, black water upon which the minerals in the ceiling were reflected like stars in an oily sky. And the water kept lapping ominously as it relentlessly climbed the rock walls toward us.

Taking off my cap, I scratched my scalp inside the gold circlet I wore and let out my breath in a baffled sigh as I had to admit defeat. "That is some spell the Boneless King cast."

CHAPTER THREE

Indigo came over, but her inexperience with flying showed as her wings dipped first to the left and then to the right. "I'm sorry. If you had Thorn here instead of me, you would have gotten out already."

A small green head rose from a minute crevice. "What makes you say that?" Shimmer squeaked.

"Thorn is the one who's clever." Indigo flapped her wings miserably. "He would have found a way to escape, just like he did from that island. It should have been me who went into the cauldron and not Thorn."

Shimmer buzzed out of the ceiling like a long, slender mosquito. "If anyone should have gone in, it's me."

It's a funny thing with people like Indigo. They're like wild creatures who are barely tamed. One moment they're sitting in your lap, and the next moment—and for no apparent reason—they're trying to take a chunk out of your ankle.

Her blue spikes bristled impressively up and down her back. "You have your clan. I have no one. And I'm of no use to anyone. So I'm sorry that I'm not Thorn, all right?"

Shimmer swelled into her usual length. "If there's anyone who should apologize, it's me. You trusted me just like Thorn did, and I've done nothing but disappoint you. I promised to take you to your forest and your clan, and now I've condemned you to death."

Indigo, though, was sealed within her misery like some little creature locked inside a box. Sometimes the people who seem the toughest have the most doubts. "No, no. It's not your fault that the Green Darkness wasn't what I expected. And you couldn't help it that my clan had dissolved." Indigo's back softened a bit. "I don't know how much time we have to live, so maybe I ought to thank you now for letting me tag along."

It was one of the few times that I've ever seen a dragon speechless. I couldn't help laughing. "Considering that you've been drowned, frozen and burned, among other things, I don't think thanks are due."

"But I saw stars for the first time." Indigo glanced up at the sparkling ceiling as if she needed a reminder. "And I've seen a hundred other things I thought I'd never see." She looked back at Shimmer earnestly. "And it's all thanks to you."

Shimmer glanced at me for help, but I could only

shake my head. I knew how to raise trouble, not human children. "But it wasn't anything."

"Maybe not to you." With a clumsy flap of her wings, Indigo tried to turn her back on both of us. However, instead of doing a 180-degree turn, she wound up doing a full 360, so she wound up facing us again. "But I thought I'd live and die stuck in that kitchen in the palace." She gave a little embarrassed cough. "It was like being born again when you took me away."

Shimmer and I looked at one another, both of us thinking the same thing. Indigo's life must have been truly awful if she was grateful for our little jaunt. Indigo was usually so tough and unpleasant—let's be honest, snotty—that it was easy to forget that it was only armor, and that underneath all that cynical armor plate was a child.

Shimmer swallowed, an elaborate sight given her long neck. "I'm not really much good at this sort of thing."

"Neither am I," Indigo admitted.

"I mean, I've lost the only other friend I've ever had." I knew Shimmer was thinking of Thorn. "I've lived most of my life by myself."

Indigo's head dipped thoughtfully. "Yes, I know how that is."

Shimmer said, considering her own words carefully as if each were made of fragile crystal, "When we first met and I heard how you'd been orphaned, I thought, 'Here's someone who's lost her home and family too.'"

Indigo licked her green lips with a long pink tongue. It was a natural human gesture, but her new form made it seem ferocious. "And when I heard about you, I thought the same thing."

Shimmer's voice had a note of wonder—as if she had been lost and had suddenly stumbled upon a path. "You think you're so strong because you have so much armor."

"Yes," Indigo agreed in excitement and surprise. "But then you realize you're also trapped inside." Her eyes swept over the ceiling. "It's like being inside this cavern and trying to find your way out.

"The way out. That's it. The openings into the cavern." Indigo swung around in an exuberant celebration, but she wasn't used to maneuvering her long tail, and she wound up bowling me over. To my chagrin, Shimmer caught me neatly.

Climbing from between her forelegs, I looked dubiously at the dark, poisonous river. "There's a spell on the exit that won't let anything out." I pointed toward the spot in the cavern where the underground river once again exited from Egg Mountain. Debris from the island and dead fish had quickly piled up there.

"And he probably put the same spell on the river entrance." Shimmer nodded toward the place where the river entered, where the waters thundered through a gap in a rock wall that hung in folds like a curtain flapping in the wind. "Nothing will get out through that opening."

Indigo gleefully snapped off a small, wandlike stalactite. "There has to be one exception to the spell on the entrance: It has to let the water come in."

I must have been getting stupid in my old age. "Of course. If water can get in through the opening, then maybe water could get out."

Shimmer rubbed her snout as she considered the possibility. "There are all sorts of problems to a transformation spell like that. That's going from solid to liquid, and that's a kind of change only for expert mages; and even then, they would prefer to use some magical object like Civet's mist stone. Still, even if we could, would we be able to fight the current?"

Indigo chucked the mineral icicle into the river, where it made a loud splash. "What if we were made of frozen water?"

I held up a fist on either side of my head and knocked my head against one and then another. "Yes, what if we were made of ice?" I paused as a new thought occurred to me. "But what about the poison? Would it still affect us if we were made of ice?"

"I don't think so. Flesh has pores that let it in, but ice shouldn't." With new hope, Shimmer began muttering to herself, her claws sketching at the air as she worked out the spell. At the same time, I summoned all the little monkeys and restored them as hairs to my tail.

Then, as Shimmer and Indigo spiraled slowly down, I somersaulted toward the entrance. The water thundered even faster through the gap beneath the rock wall. Right at the mouth of the entrance, I could see that branches and other debris were piling up into a dense tangle. As we had suspected, the spell kept everything out but water.

The next moment Shimmer and Indigo halted their downward spiral with beats of their wings right behind me, and the gust of sudden wind sent me against the rock wall. Fortunately, I got my feet under me and bounced off the stone. "Hey. Watch out."

Indigo's spines seemed to droop a little. "Sorry. I got carried away."

I was more inclined to take it easy on a beginner. "Forget it," I said, and lay on my side with my back to Shimmer. Then, with a wiggle of my nose and a muttered spell, I began to change. I felt the cold penetrate my fur and my arms and legs begin to grow numb. And then my teeth began to ache. I couldn't even feel my tail.

When I tried to move my arms, they felt as stiff as if they were carved of wood, and when I looked down at my paws, I could see right through them to the river. "Finished?" I asked over my shoulder.

"Yes," Shimmer acknowledged. "It feels awfully hot, doesn't it?"

"That's because we're made of ice." Curious, I turned to look at my companions. In the dim light their transparent sides shone like diamonds, and the glittering minerals overhead reflected off their icy scales, so there seemed to be hundreds of stars shining under their skin. By squinting, I could just make out the outlines of heart, lungs and other icy organs, but it was like trying to see a glass globe in a bowl of water.

30

Indigo raised a paw. "You look funny. I can see right through you."

"Then there are no secrets between us." I wiped at a drop of water on my nose. "Are we melting?"

"I think it's just moisture condensing from the air." Shimmer tested the water and grunted as if she were pleased. "It feels lukewarm."

The water looked dark and uninviting, but we didn't have much choice. Holding my nose, I let myself splash into the river, and since ice is lighter than water, I found myself bobbing back up to the surface like a big cork. Next to me Shimmer and Indigo floated just as easily.

"Here goes nothing," I said. Raising my arms and kicking my legs, I began paddling toward the entrance. However, nothing could beat a dragon in the water.

Shimmer shot past me, straight toward the debris that formed a wet, dense cluster at the mouth of the cavern. At the last moment she swung to her right and stretched out an icy paw. The frozen limb easily passed through the invisible barrier. "Indigo was right," she exulted.

Swinging her tail like a giant, icy club, Shimmer began to make a hole through the thicketlike mess at the cavern entrance. Branches snapped and twigs went flying. "I want to see the Boneless King's face when he sees us."

"I just want to see the sun, period," Indigo said fervently.

CHAPTER FOUR

"I'll take the lead." I cut in ahead of Shimmer so I could be first out into the open.

The tunnel was so dark that I couldn't see anything, but with my free paw, I followed the rocky wall. The real problem was that the tunnel ceiling narrowed at certain points. When we had first passed through it, there had been room for us as we had floated on trees; but something must have happened since then to increase the flow—either through some sort of sudden melt or through the Boneless King's magic.

In any event, I found that I had to submerge, which took a lot of effort because my icy body wanted to float. The river was like a giant hand trying to shove me back toward the cavern, and my own lightweight body seemed to fight me. By kicking with my legs, I managed to to shove forward, but I soon found myself beginning to flounder in the inky black waters. I almost panicked, remembering the time when I had been trapped under an entire mountain as a punishment. So I was glad when I couldn't feel the rocky tunnel scraping against my head. As I wondered if I had lost any fur, I turned and raised my mouth out of the water. "Shimmer?"

"I feel a century younger already," she boasted from the darkness.

"Is it safe to talk?" Indigo inquired. She was ahead of Shimmer.

"I think so," Shimmer reassured her. "Even if that magical barrier wouldn't keep the poison inside the cavern, the river current would."

"What happens when the mountain fills up?" Indigo halted when she felt me treading water in front of her.

"The water will build up pressure inside until neither stone nor magic can contain it." Shimmer bumped into Indigo. "What's wrong?"

"Take the lead," I panted.

"Ha!" Shimmer gloated. I felt her swim underneath me and surface in the lead. "Bit off more than you could chew, didn't you, you little fur bag?" Nonetheless, her groping paw took hold of me gently, as she said to Indigo, "Grab hold of my tail."

The promise of freedom really seemed to make Shimmer as frisky as a yearling, because she swam with her strong, confident, joyous kicks. "How can you see?" I asked her.

"This is no worse than swimming on the bottom of the sea."

There was only one more tight squeeze, but she managed to wriggle through it just like an eel— though I heard the stone rasp against her icy hide.

And suddenly over our heads we saw a gleaming disk of light. It seemed to be made of blue and white tumbling snakes as the river water thundered through a hole in the side of the mountain. Shimmer began kicking toward it as if she were hungry for the light. Her long, powerful body undulated and her legs kicked. Even so, the river kept trying to shove her back. When stray branches got in her way, she simply butted them to the side.

The currents must have gotten to Indigo too, because I could see her splashing clumsily in the water. "I don't think I can . . ." she gasped.

"Yes, you can," Shimmer grunted. "Yes . . . you . . . can." With a final kick, we burst headfirst through the surface of the river and were gasping for air above the white, foaming water. The next moment a tired, battered Indigo bobbed up next to us, one paw still wrapped around the tip of Shimmer's tail.

Shimmer and Indigo began to swim at a slant across the turbulent river. I could see over our heads the scrape marks along the steep sides of Cloud Pass where the avalanche had swept us into the cavern that first time.

Snow still clung in patches to the brown sides, but

most of the trees were now gone, as was much of the caravan road.

I wriggled a forepaw free from her grip. "I can manage on my own now." Quickly changing myself to my true form, I tried to somersault out of the water, but my fur and torn clothes were so soaked with water that I felt as if I weighed a kiloton and my somersaults wouldn't have won any applause.

Having reached the calm shallows on the side of the river, Shimmer transformed herself and Indigo back to flesh dragons again. However, when Shimmer spread her wings, they seemed a little stiff, and she rose from the water as inelegantly as I had. Hovering with awkward flaps of her wings, she encouraged Indigo. "Come on."

"Right," Indigo said, and tried to join us. However, her icy transformation had made her twice as clumsy. Her first attempt at flight sent her tilting at an angle that plunged her underneath the surface for a moment. Coughing, she slapped her wings against the water and climbed jerkily into the air.

There was only a thin ledge about a meter wide to mark the road that had once carried camels and horses. However, I noticed a cave just above the track.

"This way," I called down to the struggling Shimmer and Indigo.

At least I thought it was a cave. When I got closer, I could just make out the shape of lips, as if this were the mouth of some giant statue. The stone was worn by time, but as I studied the surface, I could also distinguish large eyes and the bump of a nose.

Perplexed, I scratched under my soggy cap. "Did someone start carving the rock wall?"

Shimmer noticed the head of the statue. "No. When the Boneless King's kingdom was broken up, mountains and buildings got fused together." She shrugged. "Dig far enough anywhere in the mountains and you can find bits of broken pottery or metal. But most people wouldn't have anything to do with the stuff. These mountains are cursed."

Now that I had been told that, I looked harder at the rock walls and thought I could make out bones, turned as dark as the surrounding stones—as if there were skeletons sleeping all throughout the upended country. And in a peak across the river, I could still discern rectangular holes in semiregular rows, as if the peak had been a tower at one time.

I gave a shiver—and this time not with cold. "I'll be glad to get out of here." With water dripping in torrents from my fur and torn clothes, I landed at the edge of the cave.

The next moment Shimmer landed and crept into the cave right away to make room for Indigo. Indigo's landings were as rough as her takeoffs, so she tripped, skidding into Shimmer's tail.

After that I couldn't see anything, because Indigo's wings blocked everything else from view.

I slapped at the leathery membrane. "Fold those things down so that there's some room."

"I can change you back," Shimmer offered.

"Have a human skin in this cold?" Indigo lowered her wings with loud smacks. "No thanks."

"Suit yourself." Shimmer lifted a pawful of rocks and piled them carefully in the center of the cave. Then, touching her free paw to her forehead, she changed the rocks into fiery coals. Heat slowly began to fill the cave. Then, coiling up her long body to make room for Indigo and me, the dragon settled down.

Indigo was careful to copy her friend, so there was still room for me to sit and try to dry myself. Taking off my tiger skin, I laid it across several rocks to dry.

With a sigh, I settled down by one side of the fire and began to wring out the hem of my ragged robe. "What next?" I asked Shimmer.

Shimmer broke off a slender stalagmite from the cave floor, and spreading out the claws of her left forepaw, she began to sharpen them with loud rasping sounds. "Next I find Thorn," she announced.

I got out my staff from behind my ear and lengthened it. "And we can say hello to the Boneless King," I said cheerfully as I checked the staff for signs of rust.

She studied the edges on her daggerlike claws and gave one of them a critical little rub. "Oh, to be sure. We have so much to chat about."

Indigo looked back and forth between the two of us as we prepared for our little visit. "But there are only three of us."

Shimmer transferred her makeshift file to her left paw and began to sharpen the claws of her right one with a slow, deliberate rhythm. "I wouldn't expect you to go."

Indigo squirmed in embarrassment. "I just meant that maybe we ought to find the Smith and the Snail Woman again."

I laid my staff across my lap. "Considering that we let Thorn fall into the Boneless King's hands, I would rather face him than them."

Shimmer looked up for a moment from her filing. "Indigo, this is far too dangerous a trip to ask a friend to go on."

Indigo wriggled her snout. "Then why are you going?"

"Because I owe it to Thorn," Shimmer explained. I think she was feeling a little guilty about what had happened to her other human friend during her quest. "But you have your whole life ahead of you. We'll set you down in some civilized area where you can go on with your life."

I shrank my staff down. "I envy you. You've the whole world to discover. Everything will be new—just like the stars in the sky were. Have you ever seen a rainbow? Have you ever heard the first bird of spring?"

But Indigo was not accepting any of my attempts to ease her exit. "Yes, yes, my father told me all about them while he was alive."

"And now you can see them, hear them, smell them. Go and enjoy them," I urged.

"By myself?" she asked in a small voice.

Shimmer and I exchanged glances as if we both finally understood her reluctance to leave. Laying down the stalagmite, Shimmer leaned forward kindly. "You'll make other friends."

"While you're trying to save the world all by yourselves?" Indigo shook her head as if the whole notion were crazy—well, I suppose it was.

"At least they'll be more sensible than we are," I said, and Shimmer laughed with me.

"Well, yes, they'll certainly have more sense than you two," Indigo admitted, "and yet they'll be . . ." She shrugged. "Kind of stupid too."

I glanced sideways at Shimmer and gave a theatrical whisper. "I think she's saying that we're noble in her own backhanded way."

Indigo thumped her tail on the floor and declared hotly, "There isn't any such thing as nobility. I think you're both being silly." Then she curled her tail around so she could pull at its tip. "But maybe if I stick around you, some common sense will rub off on you."

"Or some silliness might rub off on you," I suggested.

For her part, Shimmer had to chuckle. "A sensible monkey is a contradiction in terms, but wouldn't that be a pleasant difference?"

And humming some dragon tune, Shimmer began to sharpen her hind claws.

CHAPTER FIVE

When we were dry, I draped my tiger skin around my waist again. "Where to? Do we go to the palace?"

Shimmer shook her head. "Let's check the tomb first. He might still be there. The bombs couldn't be his only secret."

I nodded. "I suppose it's disguise time again. Something soldierly should do it."

Indigo was spreading snow on the fire; the flames went out with a hiss and steam filled the cave. "I'm always a servant. Could I be a general this time?"

"Generals attract too much attention." And turning her back, Shimmer began to work a spell.

As Indigo slowly transformed into a guardsman, I asked, "After all we've been through, don't you trust me to see your spells?"

Shimmer didn't even bother to turn around. "When it comes to magic, I don't trust anyone."

I winked at Indigo. "Now you know how dragons pile up so much treasure and so much magic. They're pack rats in leather." And I pointedly worked my own transformation spell in the open, changing myself into a corporal.

Shimmer, though, beat me by turning herself into a sergeant. But when she slowly pivoted, Indigo gaped in astonishment. "Your snout—I mean, your nose."

Shimmer put a hand to her face self-consciously. "I remember the last time, when the soldiers suspected me because of my magnificent snout. Is this one too large?"

I made her lower her hand. Her nose was a mere button. "If anything, it's too small."

She flung up her hands in exasperation. "All human noses look like buttons to me."

Indigo tapped her own nose. "Use this as a model."

As Shimmer studied Indigo's nose intently, I wrapped my white cloak around me. "I am impressed. When a dragon is willing to go with a human-size snout, I know she's really determined."

Showing me her back, Shimmer worked a spell, and this time when she wheeled around, her nose was quite ordinary. At her unspoken question, Indigo made a circle of her index finger and thumb. "You look fine."

Embarrassed by its size, Shimmer felt her tiny nose. "I just hope nobody recognizes me."

"That's the purpose of a disguise." I took her wrist and forced her to lower her hand. "But they will get suspicious if you go around keeping your hand over your nose."

"Here." Indigo helped wind a scarf around the lower part of Shimmer's face. "This will help you breathe in the cold."

"Just don't go inside a house, where you'll have to take off your scarf."

As I left the cave, something wet touched my nose. And when I looked, something equally wet hit my eye. Blinking, I glanced around. Snowflakes were falling. I could hear them melting in my ears with a crisp sizzling sound. What was left of the caravan road was already carpeted with a thick blanket of snow.

"Thunderation," Shimmer grumbled as her head emerged from the cave. "It'll take forever to walk through this stuff."

Grabbing my cloak, Indigo tugged me back into the cave. "Wait. Snow is just frozen water too. So we can use the needleweed." She took out the small jar she had taken back from the wizard, Horn. "It'll make us float."

Fortunately, the juice had thawed as we had sat by the fire, and there was more than enough for all our feet. The next time I stepped outside, it was just as easy as walking on that strange lake back in the barrens had been. I could walk right over the top of the snow.

Indigo followed me gingerly and was delighted to

42

find that it worked. Watching from the cave, Shimmer made sure that we were both all right before she followed.

After a few steps, she beamed. "When this is done, you can make a fortune selling needleweed to caravans," she said to Indigo. "That way they could travel in any season."

"Not just caravans." Getting a running start, I let myself slide over the snow and, with a little twirl, faced Indigo once more. "This could start a whole new sport," I called as I continued to slip backward down the road.

Indigo was still shuffling cautiously along the snowy road with one hand against the rock wall. "That looks like fun. But how do you stop?"

"Well, I . . . um . . ." I scratched my head as the rocks began to whiz by. "I hadn't thought of that one."

"Hit something soft," Shimmer encouraged, and added, "And cheap."

I spun forward again. The road ahead curved sharply inward. If I didn't maneuver correctly, I could wind up back in the river. Deciding that it was better to stop, I tried to follow Shimmer's advice. Unfortunately, the only things to hit were a very sharp-looking bramble bush and a rock.

As I plowed into the bush and hung there, I had to admit, "Of course, every new sport has a few quirks to work out."

"And brambles," Indigo said as she and Shimmer helped to extricate me.

Shuffling more carefully, we continued along the caravan trail. Fortunately, the snowfall began to let up, so we could move even more quickly, and we pushed on as night fell.

Taking the path up to the Nameless One's funeral mound, Shimmer led us at such a pace that the three of us were panting like the Smith's bellows. "It's not going to do Thorn any good if we drop dead," I announced. "I'm taking a rest." And I plopped down rebelliously in the snow. Indigo gratefully sat down beside me, but Shimmer insisted on standing—her one concession to how tired she felt was to put her hands on her knees.

And then all too soon she was starting on the road again. "Come on," she urged us.

"We should never have let her become the sergeant." Standing up, Indigo reached a hand down to me.

I took it gladly and got to my feet. "Next time insist on being a general."

When we reached the mound, we found that all the holes had been resealed as if no one had ever tampered with it, and the campgrounds were a mixture of dirt, mud and ashes from the great fire—now all frozen like some strange painting.

"They must have finished looting the tomb." Indigo skated toward the mound and squatted down near the former site of a pit that had contained companies of stone soldiers. "They've covered up the trenches and pit with dirt."

Shimmer nodded toward the mound. "And sealed the tomb with rocks."

Indigo slid over to the mound itself and felt the smooth stone face. "The Boneless King doesn't want anyone finding out he's not buried inside."

"He carted something out." I pointed to the wagon tracks, still visible under a coating of snow. They must have come in during some thaw when the ground was soft, because we could see the wheel ruts running straight as an arrow toward a narrow gap in the mountains. "What'll we do now?"

Shimmer rose and looked toward the wide stretch of blackened, baked earth where Civet must have been destroyed. I almost thought I could hear sighing, but it was only the wind. "We follow," she said determinedly.

We moved on through the snow. Glancing behind me, I noticed that we left hardly any impression on the snow. Our sliding tracks would probably puzzle any patrol that found them.

The gap opened on a newly made road that wound down the mountain slope toward the barrens. "The Butcher must have been preparing to loot this mound for a long time," Shimmer said. "He made a road and everything."

"I told you that he had some trick up his sleeve when he started the war with you dragons." I rested against the rock wall, surveying the moonlit slopes and beyond.

"It's hardly complimentary to yourself to brag that

you think like that beast." Squinting, Shimmer pointed. "There. They've made camp by the banks of the river."

Not having a dragon's sharp eyes, it took me a moment longer to spot the little pinpoint of light.

Once we were down on the flat barrens, we could race over the snow as fast as we liked. We crouched low, partly to cut down on our silhouettes and partly to reduce the resistance to the wind. "This is almost as much fun as flying," Shimmer observed.

The tiny pinpoint of light steadily grew larger until it divided into campfires spread across the barrens. Holding up a hand, Shimmer pointed her toes inward and gradually came to a stop.

I knew there wouldn't be tents because Civet had destroyed most of them when she had started that fire. However, I hadn't been expecting so many wagons. They stood row after row, and each was filled with crates. The soldiers had made makeshift tents by hanging canvas off the sides of the wagons.

Only they didn't seem to be using them. I saw a lot of soldiers with lanterns rushing back and forth. And beyond the camp were lines of horses, but the horses seemed to be spaced at odd intervals.

Shimmer tightened her scarf about her mouth. "Those crates are all the same size."

They puzzled me too. "They could have been mass-produced that way."

"Those crates can't have more living-fire bombs," Shimmer mused. "Civet must have destroyed them all."

I gave her a nudge. "You're getting a curiosity bump almost as big as mine."

Her elbow shoved mine aside. "You needn't act so smug." Rising, she tidied up her clothes. "Now try to look military."

I tried to march along behind Shimmer, but I must say that the only one who looked very martial was Indigo. I suppose she'd seen enough of the dragon guard in the palace.

I missed being able to skate along the surface of the snow and—truth to tell—my boots wanted to skate instead of stomp. Suddenly a sentry in one of those white camouflage cloaks rose up seemingly out of nowhere. Pointing a crossbow at us, he called, "Halt. Who goes there?"

Shimmer's hand shot to her face to keep the scarf there—as if she were still self-conscious about her undragonish nose. "We were on patrol," Shimmer adlibbed.

"There's been no patrol duty since the spies were sealed in Egg Mountain." And the sentry kept the crossbow steady on Shimmer.

The trouble with dragons is that they have no knack for lying. They have too little imagination and too much pride. Instead of coming up with some good excuse, Shimmer hemmed and hawed and then said, "Well, we got lost."

"What's your unit?" the sentry demanded.

"Well, it's . . . uh . . . Oh, thunderation." Squatting down, Shimmer did a leg whip that knocked the sentry's feet out from under him.

47

"Help," he managed to shout before I could get on top of him. A quick punch knocked him out.

"Duty officer," someone was shouting in the camp.

"The problem with these disguises is that we don't know enough about the guards to pass ourselves off as them," I said.

Lanterns danced in the guards' camp like fireflies. Shimmer plucked at my sleeve. "No one will question horses."

Crouching down, Indigo began immediately skating toward the horse lines. But I couldn't help grumbling, "This is going from bad to worse: first the army and now the pack train."

Shimmer hooked her arm through mine. "Come along. You'll make a handsome horse." And she began to slide over the snowy barrens, tugging me along with her.

Horses jerked their heads nervously as we ran past, but their bridles were tied to a rope strung parallel to the ground. The odd thing, though, was that there were so many horses lying dead on the ground.

"Was it an epidemic?" I wondered to Shimmer as we slid past.

"No," Indigo said from up ahead. We saw her pointing to a collapsible canvas bucket. "I bet they gave the horses water from the river."

"The water in Egg Mountain must have broken through the rock and spilled into the river again." I glanced back at the camp. "And that explains all the commotion we saw in the camp earlier. There were probably guardsmen who drank the water too."

"It's a wonder any of them are alive," Shimmer said. She dragged me to the end of the horse line, where three horse corpses lay. As lights bobbed across the barrens, Shimmer lifted one of the heavy carcasses. "Help me throw them to the side. They won't notice the extra bodies with so many others dead." And she tossed the corpse a few meters to her left.

I helped with a second while Indigo kept an eye on the searchers. "They're coming toward the horses."

"Right." Shimmer heaved the third horse to the side. "You change yourself," she ordered me.

"At least a horse's muzzle should be long enough for you." I took a place by the rope, and with a muttered spell I found myself leaning forward on my paws. My ears and face lengthened, and the next moment I had changed myself into what I thought was a handsome golden horse.

Indigo was standing next to me. "Hurry," she urged.

Having disposed of the third corpse, Shimmer trotted over as a grayish-blue horse. I suppose that was as close as she could get to being green.

"They must be around here somewhere," we heard a familiar voice saying. "Keep searching."

"Hurry," Indigo said in a low voice.

Shimmer shook her mane so that it touched her forehead. The next moment the girl had snapped over in two and her hands fused into hooves, and black hair had begun to cover her body. But her human face looked at us in fright as the lanterns' glow approached us.

She looked at Shimmer as the grayish-blue horse assumed a position in the line. I shook my head for her to stay still. The soldiers weren't examining the animals. They were looking for humans. The end that counted had already changed, and the rest would, too, in a moment.

"I don't see any sign of them, sir." A corporal whom I recognized as Tubs appeared, walking along in a crouch, looking between the horses' legs. "I say it was just more spooks and ghosts around the barrens. Every sentry's reported them. Potsy just got scared, ran and hit his head on a rock."

"Keep looking anyway, Tubs." I recognized the voice of Lieutenant Crusher, who had first captured us. "It might be more dragon spies."

"Think they poisoned the water?" Corporal Tubs grunted. Having reached the end of the line, he came around to the front.

"It was more likely some kind of pollution. This accursed place has never been right since the Great War." The lantern-jawed Lieutenant Crusher strode into view, his white cloak wrapped tightly around him.

Tubs glanced around and then said quietly to his officer, "Some of the boys are saying it's an omen. There's no good will come of tampering with that one." He did not even want to name the Nameless One—which was an earlier name of the Boneless King.

"That's just superstition," Lieutenant Crusher insisted.

"And what about that . . . that thing we saw up there?" Tubs demanded.

"Whatever it is, it's dead," Lieutenant Crusher said. "And His Highness wants this load at his palace. Care to make excuses to him?"

Tubs gave a shudder. "No. He's gotten twice as funny since he was up at the mound."

As we saw the lights moving toward other areas of the encampment, Shimmer lifted her head. Like Indigo and me, she had simply draped her reins over the line. She trotted backward with difficulty because of the needleweed juice still on her hooves, half sliding. "Now, let's have a look at those wagons. If another sentry sees us, he'll just assume we've broken loose." Backing away from the horse line, we followed Shimmer over to the wagons.

When we reached the wagons, Shimmer glanced in the improvised tents of one row to make sure there was no one else there. Then she changed herself back into a dragon and crept up on a wagon. With the tip of a claw, she pried off the lid and searched around among the packing. "It's just one of those stone soldiers from the pit."

I was keeping a sharp watch for other sentries. "What about the others?"

Shimmer checked another crate in that wagon and then crates in three other wagons, but they all contained statues too. I thought again of that vast pit back by the funeral mound. It had been filled with hundreds of the statues. "I'd bet my cap that there is a statue in each crate."

51

Shimmer slid back down beside us. "But what does the Boneless King want them for?"

I wriggled a long, horsish ear. "It could be for magic, but what kind of magic?"

"Whatever his purpose, this wagon train is heading for the palace, and that's probably where the Boneless King is." Touching her forehead, Shimmer changed herself back into a horse. "And wherever the Boneless King is, we'll find Thorn. We'll stay horses."

I stomped a hoof upon the frozen ground. "I'd rather ride on a wagon than pull it."

She butted me with her head. "It's the safest way to go straight to him," she argued. "If we take on any other disguise—like guardsmen again—we'll have to answer questions. This is for Thorn. Remember what he did."

I had to sigh. "Well, if he was willing to sacrifice his life, I suppose I can sacrifice a little of my dignity." I began to scrape my hooves against a wheel to get the needleweed juice off. I didn't want to cause any embarrassing incidents tomorrow by skating along in harness. "But they'd better serve a good breakfast."

They didn't.

CHAPTER SIX

Breakfast wasn't much more than a handful of oats that Corporal Tubs brought us. "Here you are, boys and girls." When he dumped the oats on the frozen ground before me, I snorted at Shimmer. She merely flicked her ears, which was all she could manage for a shrug.

But the corporal stopped and stared. "Here now. What are you doing here?" At first I was afraid that daylight had revealed some flaw in the dragon's disguise. But then the corporal's face flushed a bright red and he began to bawl, "Slowfoot, you idiot. What's *she* doing here?"

And like a man with a vital mission, he set his pail of oats down and marched back along the picket lines, bawling for Slowfoot.

"I wonder what got into his helmet?" Indigo muttered to us.

"Who cares?" With my hoof, I tipped over the can of oats and managed to kick some over toward Indigo and Shimmer. "Eat up. This is as good as it gets at this hotel."

But Shimmer only nibbled at the handful she had been given. "You eat them. It's obvious that he's recognized my thoroughbred qualities. I'm likely to get better feed as an officer's horse."

My mouth full of oats, I just gave a snort in answer. Whether it was my present shape or my hunger, the oats were tasting pretty good.

Corporal Tubs returned, towing by the ear a portly, middle-aged guardsman whom I recognized as Slowfoot. Using Slowfoot's ear as a handle made it very convenient for the corporal to shout into it when he stopped before Shimmer. "Now what's this?"

Slowfoot, his head bent at an awkward angle, squinted at Shimmer. "A horse."

The corporal's mouth couldn't have been more than a centimeter away from poor Slowfoot's ear. "But what kind of a horse?"

Slowfoot's eyes flicked back and forth as he tried to pick out something special about Shimmer and failed. "Uh . . . a four-legged one?"

Shimmer had somehow managed to puff out her chest as she glanced proudly at me. I simply rolled my eyes, knowing that I would never hear the last of this.

In disgust, the corporal released poor Slowfoot. "I didn't know you could count as high as four. Have you been practicing?"

Slowfoot fingered his injured appendage as if trying to see if the corporal had stretched it out of shape. "N-n-no," he stammered.

"That"—the corporal pointed a finger at Shimmer—"is a nag, a plug, a hack. It should have been chopped up for the stew pot. It's not even worth feeding weeds to."

I couldn't help giving a loud whinny of laughter. Shimmer looked so angry that she seemed ready to change back into her proper shape and give both of them a lesson, but Indigo nudged her, and I could see her lips mouthing the word "Thorn."

It's a hard thing to be lectured by your pupil—especially with your own words. But it was a measure of Shimmer's determination that she stayed a horse.

The corporal had finished lecturing poor Slowfoot about the deficiencies of his personal eyesight and intelligence, and had just begun on the flaws in Slowfoot's family tree, when Lieutenant Crusher came along.

"Why haven't you finished feeding the horses?" the lieutenant demanded.

"It's Slowfoot's fault, sir." The corporal saluted. "I told him to weed out the mounts that weren't fit to travel. But this one"—he jerked a thumb at Shimmer—"already has one hoof in the glue factory."

The lieutenant looked at Indigo and then at me.

"These other two are no prizes either, but we don't have much choice. We've lost so many horses, we'll have to use even these."

It was Shimmer's turn to remind us silently about Thorn as the two guardsmen stood with their backs to her.

"But these three won't make it, sir," the corporal protested. "Take it from an old farm boy."

"If they don't, you'll haul the wagons yourself," the lieutenant snapped.

"Fine duty for guardsmen," Corporal Tubs grumbled.

"You're lucky we're still alive after letting the spies escape." And then in a harried manner, Lieutenant Crusher hurried off to see to some other urgent task.

The corporal swore under his breath and then nodded to Slowfoot. "Finish feeding the horses." He started off on some errand of his own, but I just managed to trip him. If looks could send a horse to the glue factory, the corporal's glare would have sent me there express.

As his corporal left, Slowfoot righted the empty tin pail and he patted me on my muzzle, grateful that I had taken revenge for both of us on the corporal. "Don't worry, boy. You may still outlive me—the way the Butcher's been running things lately."

Then, swinging the pail, Slowfoot waddled away to get more oats. "Do you think some of them suspect that the Butcher isn't really himself?" Indigo asked Shimmer.

Shimmer pawed at the frozen ground with a hoof. "Maybe. But then he was never too popular to begin with. And maybe this war with the dragons hasn't made him any more popular."

It wasn't long before Slowfoot and the other guardsman returned to lead us over to the wagons. As we were put into harness, Slowfoot glanced at our cargo. "You mark my words. No good ever came of tampering with the likes of the Nameless One or taking things from him."

The other guardsman adjusted Shimmer's harness straps. "It's the dragons who are in for a surprise." Suddenly he slid a foot back. Raising his hands to cup his mouth, he shouted, "Fire."

Slowfoot took up the cry. "Fire."

Harnessed to the wagon, I couldn't turn around to look. But from a wagon up ahead, I saw blue vapors rising from the back.

"It's coming from the crates." Slowfoot made a sign against evil.

Lieutenant Crusher came riding up on a red horse. "Get back to work," he ordered.

The other guardsman pointed at the crates in the wagon ahead of me. "There's something wrong with the crates."

"Do you see any flames? It's some residue of gas," the lieutenant insisted. "His Highness personally assured the general that it was safe and to ignore anything that might happen."

And then Lieutenant Crusher galloped off, bawling

to the rest of the guardsmen to finish their tasks and to ignore the vapors.

Where other soldiers might have run off, their discipline held the guardsmen to their posts. From all around the camp, I heard the makeshift tents being put away and teams being harnessed to the wagons. A fourth horse was added to our own wagon. And then with a jingling and ringing, the wagons began to roll through the barrens.

As the wagon train rolled along, the blue vapors kept rising from the crates. In some ways the vapor reminded me of the green light that had escaped from the broken cauldron when Thorn became imprisoned in it. But the blue smoke didn't seem able to escape, gathering instead into a cloud that hovered over the wagon train.

Behind us, I could hear Slowfoot say to his friend, "I told you no good would come of tampering with the Nameless One. This cloud is an evil omen. The Butcher's gone too far this time. Folks just won't have him rooting around in that old tomb. Or his war. If he loses, he'll have the whole kingdom rising up against him."

"*If* he loses," his friend said, but he sounded shaken by the cloud.

It stayed with us when we bivouacked for the night, casting an eerie light over the camp. There was no water from the river that night, and Slowfoot and many of the other guardsmen refused to sleep under the wagons, preferring to be out in the open.

And the next day we passed by a ragged line of mounds—all that was left to mark the capital of the Fragrant Kingdom that the barrens had once been. As the wagon train slowly rolled by, a wailing rose from the ruins. I think Slowfoot and many of his comrades would have bolted at that point, but Lieutenant Crusher galloped back and forth, keeping order.

It took us two more days to cross the barrens, two days of sheer torture since we were always in sight of the river but never allowed to drink from it for fear of poison. However, that northerly route took us above the thick forest called the Green Darkness, through which the wagons could not have passed.

And with each kilometer the ominous cloud grew, until by the third morning we were in perpetual shadow. When we reached the first village, the people screamed and slammed their shutters and locked their doors. The little beehive cottages with white-washed sides and thatched roofs sat behind stone walls with everything sealed up.

It was only when the guardsmen drew water from the well that one villager finally ventured out. He was a little man with whiskers and stocking cap, and with much bowing he begged the lieutenant not to deplete their only fresh water. As he explained, something had gone wrong with the river water and anyone who drank it grew sick.

When I heard that, I couldn't help glancing at Shimmer. "If no one's dying, the poison from Egg Mountain is being diluted," she murmured.

"But I'm dying of thirst," Indigo muttered. "Aren't you?"

The road had been long and dry, and water would have been just the ticket.

Of course the farmer's pleading didn't do any good. The guardsmen were feeling just as parched. The lieutenant tried to give him a note to collect money from the government. But the farmer tore up the note and threw the pieces into the breeze. "That's what the note is worth," the farmer said angrily. "You've already taxed us to ruin to pay for this cursed war. How much more are we expected to stand for?"

Lieutenant Crusher put a hand to the hilt of his sword, and there might have been trouble, but just at that moment the door opened in a hut behind the farmer and a little girl stepped out. She was only about five or six, with long hair and a clean though patched dress and a little ragged shawl. Her large eyes seemed even wider as she stared at more people than she had ever seen in her life. As she sidled over to her father, her bare feet slid across the cold ground.

"Go inside, Dawn," the farmer said.

Dawn, though, tugged at his sleeve so insistently that I thought she was going to tear it. "Go ahead. I have children of my own," Lieutenant Crusher said, and let go of his sword.

With an embarrassed nod, the farmer bent low enough for Dawn to whisper into his ear. "No," he tried to say firmly. There was more urgent whispering. Reluctantly, he straightened. "My daughter says we should at least give water to some of your horses."

"They've had it even harder than us," the lieutenant admitted. "They had to do the hauling."

Tubs and Slowfoot brought several buckets of water from the well under the watchful eye of the farmer. In the meantime, though, Dawn had stepped out onto the road. I supposed being around a farm, she wasn't a bit afraid of the huge animals looming over her. "Here," she whispered to Shimmer. "I wish it could be more." From a pocket on her dress she took a dirty lump of rock sugar.

Despite her huge teeth, Shimmer took the lump delicately from the child's palm. There was enough water for several teams of horses, and then we set off again to find other safe sources of water. And as we plodded away, we could see Dawn perched upon a wall waving good-bye.

"People," I muttered to Shimmer. "Just when I could wish all of them off the earth, you meet up with one who makes up for all the others."

"The little girl," Shimmer declared smugly, "just had an eye for beauty."

"Oh, please," Indigo murmured, wincing.

I could only grunt in agreement. At the next village there was a fishpond, so the other horses were able to be watered.

The next day it seemed as if word had gone on ahead, because every village we passed seemed deserted. There was not a soul to be seen—or even an animal for that matter.

However, rumors are like yeast in bread. They swell and grow in the right conditions. As the cloud increased, so did suspicions. By the end of the third day rocks were being flung at us, though the throwers hid quickly enough. And there were angry messages painted on walls that blamed the poison gases from the wagon train for polluting the water and making people and animals sick.

From the dark looks I saw, I began to think that the Boneless King might have gotten more than he had bargained for by possessing the Butcher's body. Win or lose the war with the dragons, he could very easily have a human revolt on his hands.

By the time we reached the capital, the countryside was almost ready to rise in rebellion. Indigo was excited when we finally came in sight of the capital, Ramsgate. The high, gleaming walls rose above the green fields. And beyond the walls rose the red sandstone towers and spires, soaring like strange flowers. She forgot about how tired she was from all the hauling and almost tried to pull the team and the wagon all by herself.

"It was built by King Gem after the War of the Three Sorrows," I whispered to Indigo. "He went to sleep one night in his camp tent, and when he woke, he was riding on a ram that brought him here." I nodded to the rams' heads carved in stone above the gates.

Suddenly there was a crash from up ahead of us. "What's amiss?" Slowfoot wondered.

There was a thudding sound behind us, as if his companion had stood up on the wagon seat to get a better look. "There's some kind of barricade," his companion said. "That's funny. The city gates are shut—and in broad daylight."

A stone whistled through the air, missing Slowfoot but hitting me on the rump. "Go back," someone shouted from the left.

"Take your pollution with you," someone else said from our right. And suddenly farm folk in plain clothes and city folk in silk robes came pouring out of the orchards with clubs and rakes and whatever weapons they had grabbed.

Behind us, Slowfoot and his companion drew their swords out of their sheaths with loud hissing noises. "What are we fighting them for?" Slowfoot wondered. "I think they're right." But he didn't sheathe his sword.

It seemed like there would be a pitched battle right there in the middle of the road, but trumpets bleated from the city walls and the gates swung open to let a troop of guard cavalry gallop toward us.

Under the threat of the cavalry lances and the horses' hooves, the mob dissolved, and when the troop joined us, we could see a hurried consultation between the cavalry captain and Lieutenant Crusher. Then Corporal Tubs jogged back along the wagon train. "The statues are going to the royal gardens, and not to the armory."

Under escort of the cavalry, we rolled up to the capital. There another company of guardsmen stood at attention. The area behind the gate was littered with broken jars and sticks.

"It looks like a riot," Slowfoot said.

"It was," one of the new guards informed him. "The city folk wanted to bar the gates."

Another company escorted a dozen wagons filled with smaller crates in the direction of the wharves. There must have been something special about them.

But even more guardsmen—another two troops of cavalry—joined our escort; evidently our strange cargo was very precious to the Boneless King. And the route itself was lined with still more guardsmen.

The streets were eerily silent as we rumbled along, the blue cloud casting strange shadows that leapt about the street. The houses were locked and shuttered tight, and the guardsmen nervously watched us pass—it looked like this was one duty they would gladly have forgone. I began to notice even armed sailors—it seemed that the Boneless King had summoned every available person to guard the wagons.

More than one of our defenders made a sign to ward off evil or spat at the wagons as we rolled by. Apparently, guarding our cargo wasn't too popular with the Boneless King's own forces.

Ramsgate, like many of the older human cities, had grown up in fits and starts from a dinky little village. As the capital had expanded, newer and larger walls had been built, and streets had been set up between the old and new walls.

As a result, even the main street, Diamond Way, snaked from gate to gate. It was a bit like the shell of a nautilus, with smaller and still smaller circles spiraling inward. At the very heart of the city was the golden dome of the palace. Before the dome were huge golden gates decorated with the chrysanthemum, the symbol of the royal family.

Once the palace had been a fortress, but as the kingdom had grown and generations of kings had prospered, the fort had been replaced by the royal gardens. I had been expecting a park on some vast scale, but this was far more. On either side were woods and lakes and streams, bridges and miniature palaces and even small mountains. But in the area right in front of the gate, the famous chrysanthemums had been uprooted and piled in fragrant mounds to the side—hundreds of many exotic varieties. That couldn't have sat well with the folk of Ramsgate, who took justifiable pride in the garden. In place of the flowers was only a huge pit.

A sloping ramp of dirt led to the bottom of the pit, and one by one the wagons were brought to its edge and the crates unloaded. When it was our turn, I could see the Boneless King himself standing with Horn, his puppet wizard. Next to them was a group of men and women in expensive robes and gold chains of office.

The Boneless King waved to the crates being carried into the pit. "With the crates buried, no more gas will escape. But I can assure you that the gas was always harmless. The crates contain only scrolls and art treasures. My wizards assure me the gas was some preservative device of the ancients."

A woman whose neck was draped with gold medals each as big as my hand frowned at the blue cloud that now hid the sun from the gardens. "As you say, Your Highness," she said doubtfully, "but what about that cloud over the city right now?"

The Boneless King clapped Horn on the shoulder. "My wise and wonderful friend will see to it that it disappears." The Boneless King probably was going to work some magic through his wizard. "And if there is any damage from the gas, I'll pay for it. I trust that will be satisfactory."

The city officials bowed low.

As they backed away, a little man dressed in an even richer robe of yellow silk and wearing various gold chains and jade plaques of office took the opportunity to step up to the King, strutting like a regular little rooster of a man.

"Your Highness," he said with quiet urgency, "as your lord chancellor, I must point out to you that the treasury to pay for the war has been vastly depleted. Where would we come up with the additional money for possible damages?"

"Lord Tower, we will use the dragon gold." The Boneless King laughed.

From all accounts, Lord Tower was a conscientious if proud man who had served the former King and queen and had stayed on when the King had died and the queen and prince disappeared. So far he had managed to moderate the Butcher's excesses.

"I trust that will be satisfactory as well." The Boneless King gave both the lord chancellor and the city officials a thin smile. I knew that smile. Neither the Butcher nor the Boneless King liked to be crossed, so whoever the ruler might be, the future of the capital was at risk. Once the Boneless King had disposed of the dragons, he would turn his attention to the uncooperative citizens of Ramsgate.

At that moment, I don't think I would have liked to have been a citizen either of the dragon kingdoms or of Ramsgate.

CHAPTER SEVEN

"No one's looking," Shimmer whispered. Even Slow-foot had gotten down to supervise the unloading of his cargo.

While I had been distracted, the dragon had transformed herself into a lieutenant of the guard. I would have scolded her for doing it right out there in the open—especially with the Boneless King there—but I didn't dare call attention to myself.

In the meantime, though, Shimmer was stepping out of the harness and going to Indigo to release her.

"Here now. What do you think you're doing?" Slowfoot demanded.

Shimmer fixed him with one of her haughtiest stares. "These horses are needed elsewhere." As Indigo trotted away, Shimmer stepped over and began to release me.

Slowfoot scratched his head in puzzlement. "Where'd the fourth horse go?"

The dragon couldn't resist rubbing it in. "When the general saw it, he wanted to know what that thoroughbred was doing in a wagon harness. He rode it away himself."

"That old nag?" Slowfoot scratched his head in astonishment.

Shimmer led me out of the traces and then got Indigo. "You're not as good a judge of horseflesh as you think," she said, and nodded to the old, beat-up swayback that had formed the fourth member of our team. "But you can keep that old thing. He's suitable for the likes of you."

And without waiting for any further discussion, she led us into a small grove of pine trees that had been trimmed over the decades into the shapes of giant dancers. Within the grove was a charming little pond in the shape of a star, into which a dainty waterfall fell down the slopes of a miniature mountain.

In the wink of an eye I was a captain of the guard—I'd had my fill of being bossed around by Shimmer. But the dragon was one up on me, because she had no sooner changed Indigo into a guardsman than she changed her own rank into that of a colonel.

Indigo eyed the glittering decorations on our armor. "Why do I always have to be just a plain soldier?"

"You'll have to come by your rank the same way we did," I said, buffing some of the lacquer plates of my armor. "By your magical prowess."

"You mean by cheating." Indigo poked her head out of the grove and stared at the golden dome that sat like a small sun among the towers and spires of the palace. "Where do we begin looking for Thorn?"

But Shimmer took hold of the sides of Indigo's head and swung her gaze toward the Boneless King. "We follow him."

Ignoring the angry expressions on the faces of the city officials as they stood under the blue cloud, the Boneless King mounted a white stallion. A shining escort of infantry waited on foot.

The little goateed wizard, Horn, had barely clambered onto a donkey before the Boneless King swept out of the royal gardens. "W-w-wait for me," Horn hiccuped as his donkey bounced along.

"Try to look military now." With a final tug at her cuirass, Shimmer slipped out of the grove and marched over to the tail end of the escort.

Sweating guardsmen were carting the crates down into the pit in the gloom of the blue cloud, while city officials supervised, resentful expressions on their faces.

And then the escort swept through the golden gates carved with the image of chrysanthemums.

The area around the palace was filled with city mansions of the noble families. They were only a little less splendid than the palace itself. The next ring held the houses of minor officials and rich folk, as well as shops catering to the court. In a sense they were the beehive huts of the farmers, but on a grander scale. Every house had to have its dome, and each house owner vied with the others to have the prettiest or most interesting dome. Though gold was reserved for the King, many were of silver inlaid with designs of semiprecious stones. Others had mosaics in brightly colored tiles, while others were done in pastel bricks. The effect made the city of Ramsgate seem like a vast tub of gigantic bubbles, each with its own colors and designs.

We had to jog along to keep up with the Boneless King's escort. Every house along the route was shuttered up tight, and the shops were boarded up as if everyone were in hiding. As we followed a street that snaked downward, Shimmer whispered to us, "He's heading for the harbor."

Indigo, used to the splendors of the dragon palace under the sea, had not been overly impressed by the royal palace nor by the palaces of the nobility. But all the houses and shops filled her with a kind of awe. "I've never seen so many stores," she said in a low voice.

"You can buy anything you want in Ramsgate," Shimmer murmured, and then added, "Provided you have the money."

I glanced at her from underneath my helmet. "Thinking back to your wandering days?" She had spent many years in exile among humans—disguised as a poor beggar, I had heard from Thorn.

"Yes," she admitted, and swung her eyes determinedly toward the Boneless King's back. "But one way or another, those days are over. I'll either have a throne, or . . ." She didn't say she would be dead, but I understood.

The street came to a wall of ordinary brick whose gate had a design of oxen. Here lived the ordinary folk, crowded into four and five stories that crowded shoulder-to-shoulder. If the houses had been painted once, the sun had faded their faces so that they were now the original pink of their stones. The windows were shuttered or boarded, and there was no one out. The only sounds were the tramping of our feet and the clopping of hooves from the Boneless King's and Horn's mounts. As we moved through the narrow canyons, the sounds echoed. It felt more like an invasion by an enemy than an army leaving its home.

As we passed through a gate decorated with rats, I said, "I can smell the sea."

As Indigo tried to avoid a pile of garbage, she frowned at it. "Among other things."

We had reached the less desirable houses and shops that formed the final ring at the harbor. Here the buildings were jammed in even tighter—they seemed more like hills with tiny caves than houses, and the sky was a narrow strip like a faded blue ribbon. People openly dumped their garbage in the streets, and sullen faces stared at us from the windows, where, if curtains hung, they were ragged.

Indigo fussily picked her way over the garbage, grimacing in disgust. "How can they live like this?"

"I know this section well." Shimmer plowed heedlessly forward. "They do the best they can, but life here is as hard as it is on the farms."

A twist of the road brought us to the harbor, where I could barely see any water because of all the ships. Round, tubby merchant ships had been commandeered, some as supply ships, some as troop ships. Riding beside them, sleek as greyhounds, were war galleys. And everywhere little rowboats scooted back and forth like water bugs. It was a regular forest of masts, and from every mast hung a pennant with the golden dome and chrysanthemum—the symbol of the kingdom.

A metal net had been hung at the mouth of the harbor, and soldiers stood alertly by catapults or with crossbows as they kept a watch for dragons from the sea. And the wharves themselves swarmed with men loading crates and sacks onto the ships.

"Now, which is the flagship?" I muttered, and then watched the Boneless King riding up to the largest war galley. Next to the galley, soldiers were unloading some crates that we had seen before with the other wagon column. Throwing the reins of his stallion to a soldier and dismounting, the Boneless King strode impatiently up the gangplank while Horn was still struggling to get down from his little donkey.

"I bet Thorn is there," I said, and I began changing myself into a sailor in wide pants and a sleeveless tunic.

The next moment, Shimmer had changed herself

and Indigo into sailors as well. Our disguises let us mingle unnoticed in the crowd bustling around the flagship. Since a dragon couldn't tell a satisfactory lie to save her life, I knew I would have to take the initiative in getting us on board.

Noticing a pile of casks, I squatted down. "Take one of these," I grunted, and hefted a cask to my shoulder. When Shimmer and Indigo had copied me, we moved in a single line toward the flagship, where we joined the soldiers bringing the crates on board. The guardsmen keeping watch at the gangplank didn't challenge us.

Our leathery feet slapped the worn planks as we climbed toward the deck of the ship. Through the oar holes, we could see guardsmen in tunics without armor sitting by the oars. They didn't look any too thrilled about their new duty.

"Careful," a bowlegged sailor was saying at the top of the gangplank. "Careful." But when we reached him, he stopped us. "Whoa, where do you think you're sailing, mates?"

"We've got the water casks," I said quickly. "Or do you plan to drink sunshine the whole voyage?"

"Can't you read?" The sailor pointed at a big warning sign over the hold into which the soldiers were taking the crates. Then he pointed toward another hold. "Water goes over into number-three hold."

I took a quick look into the hold where the crates were being placed, but I didn't see Thorn. "Right." I winked at the others and led them down into the third hold. Once there, we wound our way among coils of heavy rope and even a spare mast until we could dump our water casks in a convenient spot.

Finding a bucket and some mops behind a door, I handed them out. "Your weapons. And try to look bored—as if you belong here." I changed my staff into a mop.

"You needn't give me acting lessons," Shimmer grumbled. "I didn't survive in disguise for a few hundred years without learning something."

Climbing back on deck, I took a quick look around. On the aft deck, high above everyone else, the helmsman stood by the great wheel that controlled the rudder. Next to him was the ship's captain, conversing earnestly with the Boneless King. On his other side was the white dog, Snowgoose, that had now acquired a gold collar studded with jewels. General Winter was there too. He wore elegant white armor with gold-leaf decorations all around—so much gold, in fact, that he looked like a beetle that had rolled in gold dust. He was the general who had given us such a hard time around the Boneless King's empty tomb. The little wizard, Horn, was seated on a coil of rope before a cabin that rose like a small cottage just beneath the aft deck.

Desperately, Horn thumbed through a leather book no bigger than his hand. "Sea cat, sea dog," he was muttering anxiously. "Ah, seasick spells."

"Come on," I whispered. "I think I've found Thorn." I began swabbing the deck with my mop, and

75

Shimmer and Indigo copied my example. Closer and closer, we mopped our way across the deck. I held my breath, glancing up at the Boneless King. He and his dog looked even more dangerous towering above everyone. But neither fear nor common sense had ever stopped me before. I began to mop toward the very front of the cabin.

"Your Highness," the Captain was insisting, "for the safety of the ship, I really must know what's in those crates."

"You'll find out soon enough, Captain Bellows," the Boneless King answered, and added ominously, "So will the dragons."

Trying to looked bored, I knocked at the cabin door. Horn looked up in mid-spell. "You can't go in there," he objected. "That's His Highness' quarters."

I shrugged. "The captain left orders to have it cleaned." I turned so that my staff nearly hit the wizard. "But it's no skin off my nose."

Suddenly, up above, Snowgoose began to growl. "Down, girl," the Boneless King ordered. "What is it?"

Industriously, I ducked my head and began to concentrate on the deck right in front of me, as did Shimmer and Indigo. We could hear the Boneless King turning slowly above us as he inspected the deck and us.

"And that's another thing, Your Highness," Captain Bellows said. "Your dog isn't used to sailing. We can't take your pet along."

"Quiet, girl," the Boneless King ordered Snow-goose. And then to Captain Bellows, he said, "I'll decide who's to come and who's to go. I am not to be trifled with."

Down on the deck, Horn gulped when he heard that. He seemed torn between his fear of offending the King and the need for security. "Did he really say to clean it?" He glanced up to where the Boneless King was still talking.

I nodded up toward the Boneless King. "Go ahead and ask him yourself." As the wizard licked his lips and began to open his mouth, I added hastily, "But I don't think he'll like being bothered about trivial orders. He was very serious about how dirty the cabin was."

"Very," Shimmer agreed.

"Yes, very, very serious." Indigo slashed a finger across her neck. "In fact, that serious."

"Oh, indeed." Horn set his book down on the deck and took a key from around his neck. "I wish he would tell me these things."

The Boneless King was scolding the barking Snow-goose. The noise seemed to make Horn uneasy as he opened the door and motioned us inside. The cabin was small, perhaps barely four meters on each side and only some two meters high. Even so, that was probably spacious by a war galley's standards.

Against one wall was a bunk where uniforms and armor had been heaped. On a table on the opposite wall were rolled-up charts and piles of paper. And almost lost amid all the paper was Thorn.

I recognized the familiar hard lines of Thorn's sides.

"Be quick about it," Horn commanded, and then he slapped the pockets of his robes as if he had forgotten where he had put his book.

Shimmer would have gone right for the cauldron, but we would have been caught a moment later. Instead, I blocked her with my own body. "The job's got to be done right." As I set the bucket down, I leaned close to Shimmer. "Work your way slowly toward the table, and when I distract our friend, you transform Thorn."

Shimmer nodded her head in understanding. As the three of us began to swab the deck, I kept an eye on the wizard, but he was almost in a state of panic at the thought of not being able to cast an antiseasickness spell.

I mopped closer and closer until I was almost ready to trip him, but right at that moment he looked up from his pockets. "Say, how can you wash the deck without water?"

I cursed myself at my own oversight. I suppose Shimmer wasn't the only impatient one. Raising my mop, I nudged Shimmer with the handle. "Stupid, did you forget again? I swear that you'd lose your own head if it weren't screwed on."

Horn leaned forward and squinted first at me and then at Shimmer. "In fact, there's something awfully familiar about you." Before he could turn to shout for help, I had swung my mop into his mouth. As Horn made gagging sounds, Indigo brought her mop handle down on top of his head, crumpling his wizard's cap. Making a funny noise through the mop, the wizard collapsed on the floor.

Instantly, Shimmer sprang to the table and began to work a transformation spell. The next moment there was a thump up above. "Snowgoose, come back here," the Boneless King shouted.

The huge white dog landed with a thud right outside the cabin. Its lip drew back in a snarl, revealing wickedly sharp fangs. Around its neck there was a broken leash, as if it had snapped it to get at us.

I swung my mop toward it, but before I could change the mop back into my staff, Snowgoose was already leaping for my throat.

CHAPTER EIGHT

"You can find somebody else to chew on," I said, and fell over backward. As its jaws snapped on empty air, my feet caught the belly of the beast and sent it flying against the rear wall of the cabin.

Shimmer snatched up Thorn. "I've got him. Let's go."

I could hear feet thumping on the deck above. Thinking of the Boneless King's magic, I shook my head. "We can't fight against both his navy and his magic."

The Boneless King was shouting, "To the cabin! See what's wrong." The planks beneath our feet shook as a herd of soldiers and sailors thundered toward us.

Hurriedly, Indigo slammed the door shut and bolted it.

"We're trapped." I changed the mop back into a staff. "Well, this is one victory that won't come cheap."

Shimmer cradled Thorn against her as she looked accusingly at the stunned dog. "That flea-bitten mutt ruined everything."

"Flea." Indigo snapped her fingers. "That's it." She went over to stand beside the unconscious Snow-goose. "We need to change into fleas."

Shimmer clung stubbornly to Thorn. "Right. I'll change him first."

Already axes were thudding at the door.

"There's no time." Shrinking my staff and tucking it away safely, I stood next to the dog. "You can change either yourselves or Thorn."

Indigo tugged at Shimmer's arm. "It won't do Thorn any good if we get ourselves killed."

I was already changing myself into a flea; and believe me, even as humans both Indigo and Shimmer were an impressive size from a flea's point of view. But the next moment Indigo was shrinking.

"Thunderation." A frustrated Shimmer set Thorn down before she was below table height. "We'll be back," she promised him.

In the meantime, I had hopped onto the dog near the gem-studded collar. When I looked back at my two companions, Indigo was already out of sight and Shimmer was about the size of a mouse.

The door shattered under the force of a half dozen axe blades. The Boneless King, sword in hand, peered through the hole. Fortunately, even at mouse size Shimmer was barely visible, since the Boneless King was looking for normal-sized thieves.

The next instant, Shimmer and Indigo had bounded onto the golden collar beside me.

"I'm not a bad looking flea even if I do say so myself," I said.

"That comes from long intimacy with them, you little fur bag," Shimmer whispered. "Now be quiet."

I made a face at her where she and Indigo were crouched behind an emerald. As I caught sight of my reflection in a gem, I could see that a flea could make a pretty grotesque face. But Shimmer was too busy watching the King.

Cautiously, the Boneless King reached through the hole with his free hand and unbolted the door. "Careful," he said as he jerked the door open. Behind him were a score of guardsmen and sailors.

He stood for a moment inspecting the cabin. He seemed relieved when he saw Thorn. Going over to Horn, he kicked at the little wizard's foot. "Who was in here?"

From behind the King, Captain Bellows took in the disorder. "The wizard must have come in here to steal something. Your dog sensed it, and in the ensuing fight both were knocked out."

The Boneless King stooped abruptly and picked up one of the mops. "If that fool wanted to steal something, why should he bring these along?" He held out the mop handle to a nearby guardsman I recognized as Lieutenant Crusher.

"Your Highness?" the lieutenant asked in astonishment.

"Cut this in half." The Boneless King thrust the mop at the captain. "We have to see if it's a dragon in disguise."

Nodding his head, finally understanding, the lieutenant swung his sword back and neatly decapitated the mop. As the mophead went rolling across the cabin, the Boneless King pointed his boot at the other mop. "Now that one."

"Yes, Your Highness." Picking up the other mop, the lieutenant beheaded it as well.

Exasperated, the Boneless King slashed at the bucket. As it fell apart, the Boneless King nodded to Captain Bellows. "Wake up that fool wizard and see what he can tell us."

A bucket of water was brought up and the contents were thrown over Horn. With a splutter, he sat up. "To arms, to arms," he gasped. "Thieves, robbers, burglars, footpads!"

"Yes, yes, we know all that." The Boneless King sat down at the table, the sword dangling in his hand. "What did they look like?"

Horn began to squeeze the water from his corkscrew-shaped goatee. "Why . . . they . . . they looked like sailors."

The Boneless King stood up. "There was no one in here."

Horn looked around, frightened. "If they're dragons, they could have changed themselves into anything."

"I was afraid of that." The Boneless King picked up Thorn. By the emerald Shimmer began to rise indignantly, but Indigo pulled her back down.

With Thorn tucked safely under his arm, the Boneless King swept his sword about to take in everything in the room. "Destroy every object in this room."

"Everything, Your Highness?" Captain Bellows asked in surprise.

"Cut up the furnishings, hack the walls." The Boneless King nodded toward the charts and papers. "I suppose taking a corner off each sheet of paper should suffice." He tapped his sword against the hanging lantern. "Anything in here could be a dragon in disguise."

Captain Bellows spread out his arms in alarm. "Your Highness, I beg you to reconsider. This is my cabin when it isn't at your disposal."

The Boneless King pressed the point of his sword against the captain's chest. "Would you rather have me dispose of you as well as the contents of your cabin?"

Captain Bellows swallowed and then spun around. "Fool," he shouted at a sailor, "why are you standing there? Destroy the cabin."

The sailors began to smash up the cabin gleefully—and with an enthusiasm that suggested they were settling old scores with their captain. The guardsmen were a bit more methodical though no less destructive. Mattresses were ripped up, the table and chairs were chopped apart, the lantern was smashed and even its support chain was hacked in two.

While all this mayhem was going on, the Boneless King crouched beside Snowgoose and began to pet it. "Wake up now, old girl. Wake up."

Blinking its eyes, Snowgoose started and rolled onto its feet. Suddenly its head shot up and it growled. Instantly the sailors and soldiers began to retreat.

The Boneless King, though, got a grip on its collar, his fingers looking like pink walls. But I couldn't help noticing that his huge fingernails had been chewed to the quick. "What is it, girl?"

Sniffing the air, the dog twisted its head this way and that. Frightened men tried to back out of the crowded cabin. And as I clung desperately to its collar, I began to have more respect for the stick-to-itiveness of fleas.

Snowgoose could smell us since we were practically under its nose, but couldn't see us. And that seemed to drive it crazy. Barking excitedly, the dog tugged its master forward. Sailors and guardsmen pressed against one another, trying to keep out of its way. But heading for the remains of the table, it began growling.

The Boneless King looked doubtfully at the chopped sides and legs but nodded to the lieutenant.

Obediently, the guards officer took another slice at the wood. But as the heavy sword blade thunked into the wood, Snowgoose looked puzzled. Turning to a pile of charts, it began to growl at them. At a nod from the Boneless King, the lieutenant quickly sliced those into ribbons.

Genuinely confused now, Snowgoose began investigating everything. But of course, since we were so close to it, each thing must have smelled like us. Even the spare clothes in the royal trunk were reduced to rags. And when everything had been dutifully slashed and chopped, poor Captain Bellows looked ready to cry.

Out of sheer frustration, Snowgoose began barking at the empty air. By that time the Boneless King himself had lost patience with his pet. "What's gotten into you, girl?"

"Perhaps it's the colic," the little wizard suggested timidly.

"Or," the captain added maliciously, "perhaps she should be left behind."

Snowgoose went into a frenzy of barking, twisting this way and that and jerking the Boneless King around like a puppet. I don't recommend riding a dog when it's going crazy. I felt as if I were caught in a combination of an earthquake and a tornado, but somehow I managed to hold on. Finally, the now thoroughly exasperated King shouted, "Shut up."

When his huge pet refused to obey, the Boneless King nodded to Captain Bellows. "Lock her up in a hold until she quiets down."

Captain Bellows picked out the two nearest sailors—who had also done the most damage to his cabin. "You heard His Highness. Lock her up."

The sailors didn't look too happy about their new duty. Gingerly, they sidled up to the huge white dog and took the collar from the Boneless King. As soon as his hand was free, he straightened up. "I just wish I knew where those spies are hiding."

Surrounded by a mob of guardsmen and sailors, the snapping, barking Snowgoose was led out onto the deck. Instantly, the crowd of spectators scattered to other parts of the ship. With a kerchief taken from his sleeve, Captain Bellows mopped at his forehead, and he nodded to the bowlegged man. "First mate, find new furnishings for His Highness."

"I can take a table from the officers' mess, but I don't know about a mattress. All we've got left are hammocks," the first mate objected.

"Then stuff a sack with some clothes." Captain Bellows jumped back as Snowgoose's jaws nearly took off his thigh. "And see to it that this animal is put some place strong enough to hold her." As he shuffled backward, he added, "And put our biggest locks on the door."

"I know just the place, sir." The first mate was careful to keep far ahead of the men struggling to lead Snowgoose.

He took them down among the rowers, who shrank away from the furious beast. I noticed Slowfoot and Corporal Tubs and others of Lieutenant Crusher's men. Apparently their punishment for letting us escape once was still going on.

Stopping before a door, the first mate unlocked the steel padlock. "This should hold her. The door's solid oak." He opened it to reveal a room full of swords and spears. "Let her chew on a few sword blades. Maybe that'll take some of the ginger out of her."

Shoving and tugging, the men managed to get the dog inside the small room. As soon as they let go, they leapt back to the doorway, barely ahead of its flashing teeth. With a satisfied grin, the first mate slammed the door shut on the dog's face. And as Snowgoose scratched and barked at the door, we could hear the padlock being snapped shut again.

A frantic Snowgoose dug its claws at the door, both forepaws going higher and higher until it was standing only on its hind legs. But we heard the sailors pad away.

Indigo was looking as green as the emerald to which she clung. "I feel sick."

I held on to the gold collar. "So do I," I had to confess. "A flea's life isn't an easy one."

"Come on. You can be sick outside." Shimmer leapt from the collar onto the floor. A moment later Indigo and I jumped after her, landing on our powerful flea legs.

Snowgoose was still standing against the door, so it didn't see us hop under the narrow crack between the door's bottom and the deck. As we paused outside the door, trying to clear our heads, the dog stopped barking since it could no longer smell us as strongly. Instead, it began a puzzled whining.

Shimmer rubbed a leg along her long proboscis. Of all her disguises, this probably came the closest to having a snout of a proper dragonish proportion. "Well, at least that's one enemy out of the way. Feeling better?"

Indigo was sitting on her hind legs. She nodded awkwardly. "I'm ready for another try."

Though fleas are small, they cover a lot of ground quickly. It was rather like flying. A powerful spring would take you into the air, and you'd sail along for a moment, then land, then hop again.

None of the rowers noticed us—either because we were too small or because fleas were too common a sight aboard the ship. But we did recognize Lieutenant Crusher, who had joined his men below.

We had just reached the steps leading to the deck when the great war drums began to beat, the boom reverberating through the ship. Behind us, the rowers began to work at their oars—though Lieutenant Crusher and his men were slightly out of rhythm with the others, as if they needed more practice. As the ship gave a lurch, Shimmer groaned, "The ship is setting sail."

CHAPTER NINE

By the time we had made our way up all the steps and reached the deck, the flagship had swung away from the wharves and into the center of the harbor. The drums changed their pitch, and the oars stopped. We heard the Boneless King speak on the aft deck, his voice carrying across the harbor. "Today we strike a blow for freedom," he intoned. "Today we strike a blow against the tyranny of all dragons." He paused for a cheer, but only a few humans indulged him.

"The war's not popular even with his own navy," Shimmer said with some satisfaction.

The Boneless King went on. "For too long those scaled leeches have sucked us dry—taking our hard-won wealth. Be brave, be steadfast, and all that will be yours."

"Meaning they can loot the palace," Shimmer snorted.

At that, a loud cheer went up, ringing through the harbor and into the city. The Boneless King said more things, and his forces, with the prospect of the dragons' treasure vaults in front of them, now cheered his every sentence.

By the time we reached the deck, the Boneless King had finished, and his flagship was once again rowing through the crowded ships toward the mouth of the harbor. Marines had already cranked up the net, and just outside the mouth an advance force of a dozen war galleys waited.

Behind the flagship the other galleys were following in a line, oars sweeping them along like many-legged water bugs. And beyond them, on the supply and troop ships, I saw thousands of sailors prepared to take their own ships out of the harbor in a flood of wooden ships.

Once the ships were outside the harbor, the oars were shipped so that only the paddles protruded from the holes. Then the crew raised the sails, and the great cloth sheets puffed out like giant pigeon chests. Suddenly it was as if the ship had come to life, sliding calmly across the sea just behind the advance guard, which had also unfurled its sails. Behind us a hundred ships blossomed with sails. It was like watching a field of white flowers suddenly bloom.

It's not every day one gets to see a great fleet set sail, and I might have enjoyed the spectacle if we hadn't had more urgent business.

As water foamed and hissed before the bow, sailors

were replacing what furniture they could in the King's cabin. I overheard the first mate planning to get more furnishings from the other ships at the first opportunity.

The Boneless King had kept hold of Thorn all this time, but now as he climbed down the steps from the aft deck, Horn held out his hands. "Shall we put the cauldron where it's safe, Your Highness?"

The Boneless King scrutinized the wizard. "You were the only other person in the cabin when I entered."

Growing pale, Horn fell to his knees. "Please, Your Highness. I swear I'm your wizard."

"If you're my wizard, cast a spell," the Boneless King ordered.

As Horn frantically began to cast a spell, the sailors stepped back fearfully.

The Boneless King cradled Thorn. "Don't be afraid. He forgets his serious magic when he gets excited."

Sitting up abruptly, the wizard thrust his fingers at the sailors and wriggled his fingertips. Instantly a dozen giant bubbles floated over the deck and began to dance in and out among the masts as if playing tag.

"Drat." Discouraged, Horn set his hands in his lap. He normally provided the entertainment after banquets, but the Boneless King had selected Horn at random to act as a front for his own magic. That way no one would suspect that he was not the Butcher.

Laughing, the sailors lifted the protesting wizard

up again and the first mate tied a line around his ankles.

I looked uncomfortably at Shimmer. "I suppose I should do something."

"Don't worry about him," she explained. "The Boneless King won't let it go that far. He still needs the wizard."

And the sailors had no sooner begun to lower Horn over the side than the King motioned for them to haul him back on deck. "He can't be a dragon. A dragon would never put up with such an indignity."

Disappointed, the sailors dumped the little wizard unceremoniously on the planks and left him there. With a groan he lay there, too miserable even to untie the rope around his feet. "Has anyone seen a small book of spells?" he asked the first mate.

"That's the least of my troubles," the first mate said.

"That's what you think. I never got to cast my spell against seasickness." Groaning, he flopped over on his belly and, his legs still bound, grasped the railing and began to pull himself up.

"No, he's definitely not a dragon." The Boneless King chuckled.

The next moment the lookout on the mast shouted, "Dragon, dragon." He was pointing skyward. "He's flying."

Instantly, guardsmen ran to the racks on the deck and picked up crossbows while sailors sprang to the catapult in the bow.

"Hold your fire," shouted the Boneless King. He whirled around to Captain Bellows. "Signal the other ships not to shoot unless ordered."

Captain Bellows turned to a sailor beside him, who began to beat a quick tattoo on the signal drums. We could hear the message being repeated down the line as the dragon spiraled out of the air, hovering safely out of crossbow range. "Are those idiots going to shoot?"

"Come on down." The Boneless King waved his free hand.

The dragon descended until we could see he was Pomfret. Matching his speed to the motion of the ship, he angled in toward the side. An aerial landing on a ship wasn't all that easy for a big dragon with all the ship's rigging laid out like nets. However, with all the flying skill of his sister, Pomfret gave a quick flap of his wings and landed neatly on the deck.

The Boneless King stepped over Pomfret's tail. "Shrink yourself a bit, will you?"

Drawing himself up, Pomfret panted, "A dragon has to be the proper size."

I rolled my eyes at Shimmer. "It must be in the blood."

"Well, a dragon does have to be the right size." Shimmer sniffed.

I pretended to compare lengths. "Even as a flea, you have to be a little bigger."

"Oh, go bite an old sailor and get poisoned," Shimmer grumbled. As the Boneless King climbed up on the aft deck, we made our way cautiously toward him. "Botheration. With Pomfret around, we can't just grab Thorn and go over the side."

Having shrunk himself, Pomfret slid up the steps to the deck. "The dragon army has assembled," he puffed, "in the Hundred Children. They are waiting some twenty kilometers to the east."

Shimmer's nose quivered in shame and outrage. "Now he's spying for the humans."

Indigo leaned in. "But what's the Hundred Children?"

Just that moment we had to leap for our lives, as a bare foot—looming as large as a mountain—nearly squashed us. Landing near a hatchway, we took refuge in a crack between planks. "On the human charts," Shimmer explained to us, "it's marked as an archipelago, but on the dragon maps it's marked as a range of undersea mountains. When the Weaver was forced to give up the throne of the High King, he fled with his clan west to the Inland Sea, taking the dream pearl with him. But some of the younger dragons bravely formed a rear guard to halt the pursuit. They outfought everyone until they were changed into these peaks. It would take most of the day to go around to either side."

In the meantime, though, Pomfret went on with the dragons' strategy. "They're waiting for you to turn to sail around the Children, and then they plan to take you in the flank."

The Boneless King beamed at the prospect. "Good. Then they're not expecting us to go right into the Children."

95

Dismayed, Shimmer sank down upon her powerful flea legs. "The Children will turn into a trap for the dragon army." Then, more determined than ever, she rose. "We have to get Thorn and escape to warn the dragons."

At another signal of the drums the twelve war galleys ahead of us had formed a "V," and more warships shot past us to join either flank. While they were forming up for a battle, the supply and troop ships were huddling behind the flagship like a flock of sheep. More war galleys ranged themselves on either flank and in the rear, sliding back and forth like eager sheepdogs.

While the ships were maneuvering, the Boneless King was quizzing Pomfret about what he had seen. I gathered that he had disguised himself as a common marine to spy on the defenses. As Shimmer listened to him report calmly, she shook her head angrily. "You'd think he was talking about the weather instead of betraying our whole race."

I glanced at Indigo, and she looked at me as if she were thinking the same thing as I: How could two dragons be brother and sister and be so different? For all Shimmer's flaws, there wasn't a treacherous bone in her body. All of those seemed to have gone to her brother.

With a battle imminent, sailors and marines were coming and going on the steps. I looked at the moving forest of legs and whispered to Shimmer, "It's worth our lives to try to climb the stairs."

"I know." Tensing her powerful legs, Shimmer

leapt up to the railing. The wood, though painted, was old enough to have cracks and holes for a flea, so though a breeze was blowing, we were able to make our way slowly up the railing toward the aft deck.

If we hadn't been in the middle of an invasion, I would have said it was a pleasant day for a sail. Under the sun the blue sea glittered like a golden net over a giant sapphire. And the galleys knifed through the water, sleek and hungry as sharks.

The sunlight reflected so brilliantly from the surface that we didn't notice the glowing lights at first. But they began darting about beneath the blue surface like fireflies beneath a pane of colored glass.

Poised on the railing just above the aft deck, I could see that bricks had been laid out on the aft deck in a square to support a little portable stove—probably for Thorn.

The flagship's drum beat out a command, and sailors, with anxious glances at the sea, began to climb the riggings to lower the sails while the marines took up positions on either side with their crossbows. At the same time, the rowers unshipped their oars, the long shafts sliding through the holes, the paddles poised and waiting to plunge into the water. All over the fleet I could see the other crews working with the same machinelike precision, which spoke of long months of hard drill.

"Now you'll see what you've been carrying," the Boneless King said to Captain Bellows. "Arm the catapult," he commanded.

The first mate led a group of sailors below, and

they returned with small black globes that I recognized. They contained living fire, a secret taken from the tomb of the Boneless King. Once lit, the fire would keep on burning, and water would merely feed the flames until the chemicals exhausted themselves.

I didn't see how they had survived the inferno that Civet had created, but perhaps the Boneless King had been able to use some magic to protect them. Most likely there had been some other cache of them—or some had been buried inside the tomb itself. Whatever their source, the globes were bad news for the dragons.

Suddenly the marines on the port side gave a cry. When we looked in that direction, we saw a strange creature that seemed to be mostly mouth, with rows of murderous, needlelike teeth. It was about the size of an adult human, and the hide of its head—or body; I couldn't say where one ended and the other began— was covered with blue scales. And though it didn't seem to have any eyes, there was a glowing light hanging from a stalk at the end of its nose.

Suddenly, the creature leapt out of the water on huge hindlegs like a frog's. A puny set of forepaws dangled from its chest. Jumping upon the bank of oars, it sprang onto the deck itself and then over the starboard side back into the sea.

On board the flagship there was instant confusion. Oars clashed against one another, while sailors ran back and forth in a panic, their leathery feet slapping loudly against the planks. When another of the creatures hopped up on the bow, it gnashed its teeth. A marine panicked and, without waiting for orders, fired his crossbow. The catapult crew barely had time to duck as the bolt buried itself in the wooden side of the catapult.

Still gnashing its fierce teeth, the creature leapt back into the water again. Like a pond full of frogs, the sea was filled with leaping creatures. The fleet had steeled itself for dragons, not these strange, unnerving monsters.

In a matter of minutes the fleet ceased to be a smoothly operating war machine and became a chaos of panicking humans. Discipline and practice were forgotten. Oars tangled together with loud clacks or were dropped by frightened rowers into the sea. One galley collided with another. Other galleys had gotten their oars intertwined. And all around, the frightful creatures kept hopping about maddeningly.

"Let's get Thorn," Shimmer said.

"That's easier said than done," I said, eyeing the forest of legs that danced back and forth.

But before we could take one hop forward, Pomfret raised himself and called out in a commanding voice, "Stop. Those creatures live on the bottom of the sea. Real ones couldn't stand the light. These here are just an illusion. It's just a spell of the dragon mages."

"Signal the fleet," the Boneless King ordered, but though the drummer signaled to the other ships, their crews were too panicked to pay attention.

Seeing his fleet dissolve around him, he turned and

with his free hand picked up the still-seasick wizard from the stern railing, where he had draped himself. "Dispel the illusion."

The little wizard rolled his eyes miserably. "I'm too sick to work magic. But even if I could, what could I do against the might of all the dragon mages?"

"Have faith in yourself." The Boneless King planted Horn on his feet. And though the little wizard swayed back and forth dangerously, he managed to stay erect while he began to chant in a shaky voice.

Hopping around behind him, we could see the Boneless King's own lips moving as he placed his free hand within the cauldron to make his own magical signs. And one by one, the creatures began to disappear with a pop.

The wizard gazed in amazement at his suddenly rediscovered prowess. "Don't stop now, you fool," the Boneless King snapped.

With confident sweeps of his arms, Horn began chanting. As the creatures continued to vanish from the sea, a sailor threw his cap up into the air. "Three cheers for the wizard."

For a moment I couldn't hear Horn because of the cheering marines and sailors. The cheering spread from the flagship through the rest of the fleet.

As Horn wearily lowered his arms, the Boneless King clapped him on the shoulder. "I knew you could do it."

The wizard gazed down in astonishment at his hands. "I just wish I knew *how*."

With the disappearance of the creatures, order

quickly returned to the fleet. Galleys fell into formation again, and in a moment the fleet began to row forward. I hadn't thought the rowers could make a ship go that fast, but the bows sliced through the water almost as fast as when the ships had been under sail.

"That fool Pomfret." In her frustration, Shimmer indulged in some very imaginative curses gathered over several centuries of exile.

In a few minutes we had covered another kilometer. "The Children," the lookout called from above. Everyone on board strained to catch a glimpse, and I thought I could just make out a few scabs of land on the horizon. But suddenly they were shut out from view by a golden, flickering line. Anxiously, the crew scanned the sea as the fleet swept on.

As we drew closer, we could see magical flames dancing upon the water. They twisted into strange, horrible heads with fanged mouths ready to devour the ships.

Horn rubbed his chin. "In my opinion, this is just another illusion." He turned to Captain Bellows. "Ignore it."

The Boneless King, though, glanced at Pomfret, who shrugged. "It might be, and then again it might not."

At a shout from the lookout we looked up to see the wall of fire begin to advance on the fleet.

"Go on," Horn urged. "The dragons want us to stop."

But the oarsmen could see the flames now through

the oar holes, and the ship drifted to a halt, as did the rest of the fleet—though the supply and troop ships, still using their sails, tried to turn, colliding with some of the escorting galleys.

"Come on," Shimmer whispered. With a leap we landed on the deck, taking refuge once again in a crack between two planks. The sides of the planks loomed over us like the walls of a canyon as we began to make our way toward Thorn.

In the midst of the shouting and confusion, Horn kept shrilling to move on. But we could hear the crackling now and feel the heat rolling toward us. Captain Bellows mopped his face with a kerchief taken from his sleeve. "That's the realest illusion I ever met."

The Boneless King leaned over and whispered into Pomfret's ear. Nodding, the dragon slid his long body down the steps and swept along the deck. Sailors and marines barely had time to jump out of his way as Pomfret snatched up a wooden bucket.

Then, clambering onto a railing, he launched himself into the air and spread his wings to begin gliding toward the wall of fire.

My curiosity got the better of me. I leapt onto Captain Bellows' knee. Another leap took me up to his belt, and a third jump brought me to his shoulder, from where I saw Pomfret gliding low over the surface of the sea past the lead galleys toward the advancing flames themselves. At the last possible moment he banked sharply, releasing the wooden bucket. It splashed in the water, bobbing up and down as the flames roared down upon it. Instantly the wooden bucket started to burn.

"Well." Horn laughed nervously. "Fancy that. It was real."

Captain Bellows glared down at him. "We were meant to assume that they were illusions and burn ourselves up."

"Now, now," the Boneless King chided the captain gently, "don't pick on our marvelous little magician." He put an arm around Horn. "Now that he knows what he's really facing, he'll be able to do something about it."

Horn fingered his collar uncomfortably. "I . . . I will?"

"Certainly." The Boneless King gripped the wizard's shoulder and faced him toward the flames.

All eyes were on the wizard as his hands began to make magical passes and his voice rose and fell in some ancient chant. Only we three kept our eyes on the Boneless King for the real magic. This time, perhaps because he was dealing with real flames, he needed both hands. When he set Thorn down in front of his feet, Shimmer touched her forehead. "Now!"

CHAPTER TEN

I knew Shimmer didn't have time to change Indigo to anything else, so I yelled, "Indigo. Hop on me." Even as I changed myself, I hoped she had climbed onto me somewhere.

It must have been startling for the humans to have a dragon seem to materialize out of nowhere. But there Shimmer was, a kiloton or so of muscle and claw right in their very midst.

Her claws clanged against the cauldron's metal sides as she seized it. "I've got Thorn."

"And I," the Boneless King announced triumphantly, "have you."

And at a quick pass of his hands, two nets appeared, one over Shimmer and one over me. Even as I was trying to change my staff into a weapon, the strands glued themselves around me. As I rolled on the deck, I could hear Shimmer twisting and thumping beside me while humans scattered this way and that to get out of her way.

Then, rearing up, Pomfret threw himself over Shimmer, pinning her to the planks. At the same time sailors surrounded me with cutlasses. Satisfied that we were harmless for now, the Boneless King ordered Horn to begin again.

Distracted by events and with barely enough room to work now that there were two dragons on the aft deck, Horn took longer than last time. His forehead creased anxiously and his voice rasped. Ahead of us the sail of a galley burst into flame. And I was just wondering if the flagship was going to burn too when the flames vanished as suddenly as they had appeared.

This time there weren't any cheers for the wizard, only sighs of relief from the crew. And none was more relieved than Horn. Shaking his fist toward the Hundred Children, he crowed to the dragon mages, "Try to fool me, will you? I've enough magic for anything you try."

Placing his hands on his hips, the Boneless King gazed down at us. "So Snowgoose was right after all. I hoped that I could draw you out. But where's the girl? Or did you lose her, too?"

Shimmer tried to rise, but Pomfret closed a paw about her throat, forcing her to subside to the deck once again. "She's free and she's warned the dragons about your little tricks."

"I think you're bluffing." The Boneless King put his hands on Thorn. "But I am not." When he nodded to Horn, the wizard began to make more motions with his hands, and in a moment the part of the net over Shimmer's forepaws dissolved. Apparently he knew enough magic on his own to make it go away.

Pomfret tightened his claws about his sister's throat so much that she released Thorn and the Boneless King could snatch back our friend. Then, just as a half dozen crossbowmen took Pomfret's place, the lookout shouted, "Dragons!"

By now we could clearly see the Hundred Children. On the surface these legendary, petrified dragons looked like little volcanic scraps of rock, though I knew they were the tops of mountains that might be a kilometer or more in height. Flowing out of a channel were thousands of tiny lights, twinkling and flashing like stars.

"More illusions?" Captain Bellows wondered.

Pomfret shook his head. "No, that's the sunlight shining off steel-tipped claws."

The crew was silent, staring at the spectacle. The advancing dragons began to fill the sea from one end of the horizon to the other. "Ha," Shimmer laughed. "You're not going to trap them in the Children."

"Yes, well, their impetuosity might make things a trifle awkward." The Boneless King straightened anxiously. "Fire the catapults. Drive them back into the channel."

There was a delay while the drummer righted his

drums, which had been knocked over by Shimmer. At his quick signal there was a thud as the catapult arm released and a black globe arched through the air. Almost at the same instant, globes rose from the forward galleys.

While the catapult crew hastily cranked the arm down, the Boneless King looked toward the Children. The globe splashed into the sea just in front of the army. It took a moment before the chemicals burst into flame. A dozen other globes burst ahead of it, and thirteen fiery flowers seemed to float upon the surface like giant lily pads.

But the deadly wonder did not slow the dragon army at all. More and more of them flowed through the channel. "Fire!" the Boneless King ordered again.

Once more the catapults thumped. This time the bombs must have burst among the dragons. Surely they knew by now that the fire was not an illusion but all too real. And yet the threat did not slow them one stroke. Like a sparkling tide, the dragons swept toward the humans.

Captain Bellows clutched the Boneless King's sleeve. "Your Highness, we must retreat."

"Not yet." He held Thorn out to Pomfret. "Fill this with seawater."

Except for us and Pomfret, no one knew what the Boneless King was up to. As Pomfret slipped over the side, he spread his wings and glided gently into the ocean.

At his station on the main deck, a marine watched

the dragon suspiciously, then turned toward the Boneless King and shook his fist. "Turn the fleet around."

Immediately, other marines and sailors took up the cry. And though Captain Bellows didn't join his crew, he didn't interfere either. With a mirthless smile, the Boneless King motioned Horn to cast a spell over the mutineers.

The little wizard, though, had had enough himself and shook his head. "No, Your Highness. This is madness. We must go back."

Believing the King to be without magic, the crew surged toward the Boneless King. But right then Pomfret reappeared by the stern. "You fools," he said, "this cauldron is all we need."

"Hoi!" a dragon called defiantly from the sea. "Do you have enough fire for all of us?"

Pomfret rose higher, hovering in the air. "Ask my Uncle Sambar if he isn't missing one of his treasures."

There was a gasp of dismay from the dragon. "The bowl!" she said, using the ancient dragon name for the cauldron. "You and your sister are worse than krakens."

The sailors already had started a fire in the portable stove on deck. When Pomfret set the cauldron on its top, there was a loud hiss.

"It's true," Shimmer said miserably. "Intentionally or not, I've betrayed my entire race."

And suddenly a flea-sized voice was whispering in my ear. "Nobody's watching you. Can you shrink yourself small enough to get out of the net?" Then Indigo was gone.

With a wriggle of my nose and a muttered spell, the world suddenly expanded to gigantic size and the net fibers seemed as big as cables. On my right a crossbowman shouted and slapped at his neck—Indigo's work, I suspected. Taking advantage of the distraction, I grew to normal size again, staff in hand.

"The Sea! The Sea!" I shouted, using the war cry of Shimmer's clan.

A swing of my staff sent a half dozen marines tumbling to the aft deck, and the next moment Shimmer had sprung up. She had done the same thing as I had. The next moment a new net appeared over me.

I did a back flip out from underneath it as it thudded against the deck. "Over the side," I called. I just hoped that Indigo had gotten onto Shimmer.

Another back flip took me completely over the railing and into the sea. The water was warm but not unpleasant. Saying a quick breathing spell, I squinted when I saw something huge plunge into the water. Trusty staff in hand, I swam toward the white column of bubbles as a dragon with blue spikes emerged, with her little jar of needleweed juice bobbing from a string over her shoulder. Shimmer followed.

That had been good thinking upon Shimmer's part. In her human form, Indigo would have been torn apart by the other dragons. Above us was the long, dark oval hull, its outlines a solid black against the shining, ever-changing surface of the sea.

I was just starting to rise to see if my staff could do some damage when a dozen crossbow bolts splashed into the water. The iron bolts shot downward, ribbons of bubbles trailing from their ends. Shimmer and Indigo shot underneath the hull so that it hid them from the marksmen, and with a quick kick I joined them.

Suddenly there was a crash from above, and a huge green form barreled into the water about twenty meters away. As the bubbles rose like a silvery curtain away from him, Pomfret twisted his head this way and that searching for his sister.

I swung my staff up. "You're getting to be quite a nuisance," I said.

He saluted me with a paw. "I might say the same."

A thump shook the galley above, so I knew the catapult was firing. And I tried to decide if the water really did feel warmer or if it was my imagination. "If the King is using the cauldron, you'll be boiled alive."

"Not before I finish you," Pomfret said.

"Make a hole in the ship," I called to Shimmer and Indigo, and swam toward Pomfret.

CHAPTER ELEVEN

He came plunging down toward me like a green mountain, and he spread his wings in order to appear even larger. One huge paw stretched out, claws sharp and long as steel daggers. "Out of my way," he shouted. I think he expected to swat me aside like a fly, which is a mistake many people make—but only once.

I swung one end of my rod up so that the golden ring clinked against his claws and then brought the other end up and under his chin. His eyes shut and his teeth clacked together satisfyingly.

With a hasty flick of his hind legs, he backed up toward the surface. Opening his eyes, he spat out a small, dark cloud that I realized was blood. "Ack, you made me bide my dongue," he complained.

I couldn't help twirling the staff over my head, so

fast that the golden rings blurred into a golden circle. "Naughty, naughty. Don't you know it's not nice to play so rough?" Behind me, there were thumps as Shimmer and Indigo sought to pierce the heavy planks of the hull.

The next moment there were a half dozen splashes in the sea, and marines, transformed into long-limbed golden alligators, swam toward us. Around their waists were belts to which spherical lanterns were attached.

Gleefully, Pomfret rubbed his chin. "I dhoughd dhe glory would be all mine. But I guess I'll have do share dhe joy of dearing you apard." He pointed a claw at me. "Kill him and dhe dragon widh dhe blue spikes, but leave my sisder do me."

While I had thought I was buying time for Shimmer, Pomfret had actually been buying time for the Boneless King to transform some marines into creatures who could pursue us.

"Dive," Shimmer called. She and Indigo were already streaking downward. Below us loomed the lower slopes of the undersea mountain range that formed the Children. The archipelago on the surface was formed by the highest peaks, but the mountain range actually extended farther to the west than what appeared on the surface. If the sunlight had reached far enough, I might have been able to see the foothills, but as powerful as the sun was, its light had never penetrated that deeply into the sea. The tops of some of the peaks had collapsed, and the flat tops were now being used as sea farms by the dragons.

There was an air of ancient sadness and violence about the mountains as they rose out of the black depths. In the dim light they seemed to shift restlessly, as if the dragons resented their transformations. If we lingered too long, we might become rocks joined to their sides.

Regretfully, I shrank my staff and put it away, because I knew I could swim much faster that way.

Unfortunately, Pomfret was the faster swimmer. He shot past me toward Shimmer, sending me head over tail in his wake.

"You've godden old and slow, Sisder," he taunted.

When I had righted myself, I saw that he had cut off Shimmer and Indigo. And then the next moment it was all I could do to save my own life, as the marines swirled around me with snapping jaws and raking claws. Fortunately for me, they weren't used to their new bodies, and that made them a bit clumsy. Even so, I lost a part of my robe and a patch of fur on my shoulder. Then suddenly they were spinning away like scaly balls as Indigo batted them to the left and the right with her great tail. "I could get to like this body," she observed. She'd had more practice with her new body than the marines had.

Shimmer rose toward us, blood trailing from one wing like long plumes where Pomfret's claws had raked her. "To the mountains below. Maybe we can lose them there."

But down below, Pomfret had swum so that he was

113

between us and the dragon army. Shimmer's blood was rising in ribbons from his claws. "You'll never escape, Sisder."

With a grimace, Shimmer whipped through the water toward the mountains directly below us. I saw that there was also blood on her tail. As Indigo and I swam after her, I expected to have the marines snapping at our heels, but they were content, like Pomfret, to herd us away from the dragon army.

As we neared the undersea farms, I saw why. The coral worms rose like beds of flowers and even like strange trees, but they looked as if they were wilting, and schools of fish with silver sides were moving sluggishly in the increasingly warm water.

Overhead, I saw the dark hulls sweeping overhead, banks of paddles rhythmically appearing as they splashed into the sea and then disappearing as they were raised. They swept toward the dragon army like giant caterpillars. The Boneless King would not have to wait until the sea began to boil away—the dragons were probably strong enough to tolerate even boiling water. However, the life forms upon which the dragons fed were far more delicate. He could destroy those by raising the temperature of the sea just a little.

Shimmer glanced at the undersea farms as we passed, and I saw that she understood the problem. As Pomfret and his marines followed us, she curled around a conical spire and then shot through the hole of a doughnut-shaped rock formation. On the other side she slowed enough for Indigo and me to catch up.

"This is no good." I pointed up at the war galleys overhead. "We'll be trapped here. When they're finished with the dragon army, the marines can come after us. All Pomfret has to do is pin us down."

"Or we could be boiled alive," Indigo muttered.

Shimmer nodded to where the mountains seemed to materialize out of the darkness like strange clouds. "We'll go down there where it's dark and slip around them."

I winced as I swam along and wondered if she was feeling any better. "How long can you keep up this pace with those wounds?" I nodded at her wing.

She kept on swimming determinedly. "Long enough to see Pomfret punished for being a traitor. I could fly if I had to."

Dragons are tough beasts, and I wasn't about to let her best me. Well, Monkey, I said to myself, you've sat in a furnace and had a mountain dumped on top of you. This is nothing.

And I remembered that old saying about a dragon feud lasting until the feuders' bones had turned to dust. "I'd hate to get on your bad list."

"You won't be on any list if you don't hold on to me," she snapped, and held out her good wing to me. Taking hold, I let her tow me down toward the dark with Indigo keeping pace beside us.

"Blast," Shimmer swore. "They sent more marines to swim below us."

Glancing below, I saw a half dozen lights bobbing in the darkness like fireflies. These marines must have been supplied with some form of lanterns, too.

"Sisder," Pomfret's taunting voice floated down to us, "not only have you godden old and slow, you've godden *sdupid*."

It was dim twilight around us—which was as bright as it ever got in this level of the sea. It was all I could do to see the staff I held in my free hand, but Shimmer's large eyes were perfect for this low level of light. "In there." She shot into a cave. I could feel rock grate against my back as she pulled me along. For a moment I thought of the mountain that had once imprisoned me and I almost panicked, but I managed to control myself.

"Yes, it's a tunnel," she called to Indigo, who had followed us. And suddenly she was swinging downward and then twisting immediately to the right. "These mountains are shot full of tubes and tunnels," she explained. "I used to play hide and go seek in this area all the time."

I've never gotten airsick despite all the somersaulting that I've done, but I nearly got seasick with all the twists and turns. And if I hadn't been constructed so sturdily, I probably would have been bruised to a pulp. "N-n-now I know how a rattle feels," I said.

"Low bridge," Shimmer announced as she shot out of the mountain and into the sea.

When my head bumped the tunnel mouth's top, I lost my grip, but I managed to snag hold of her tail as her body undulated by.

116

"There she is," a marine cried. Lanterns danced in the water ahead of us. I had gotten pretty well turned around inside the mountain, but I thought they were still between us and the dragon army.

"Apparently," I observed, "your brother played here as well."

"Wait," Indigo's voice echoed from the tunnel. She very nearly barreled into us, but at the last moment she spread out her wings, which helped drag her to a halt.

"No time for chitchatting." In the dim light cast by the marines' lanterns, I saw Shimmer pour her long body into a chimney-shaped cylinder. Clinging with a paw and both feet now, I let myself be towed along like some toy barge. The problem with holding on to her tail was that she used it sometimes like a rudder and sometimes like a paddle, so I wound up being knocked around even more.

"Which way?" I heard her ask herself—she couldn't have been asking me, because everything looked pitch black.

"Will you wait?" Indigo called in exasperation.

"Don't," I urged. "They're right behind us." Despite Indigo's body, which blocked most of the tunnel behind me, I could see lights bobbing toward us.

Shimmer reached some decision and with a wriggle darted forward again. "The tunnel's too narrow for me to turn around, and my rear isn't the best end for fighting."

When I heard her leathery hide rasp against stones up ahead, I knew I was in for a tight squeeze. Fortunately she tried to hold her tail rigid, but even though I wasn't scraped off, I did lose another patch of fur. "There's a cross tunnel," she said. "Which do you think?"

"Whichever way gets us out," I said.

"Thank you for your help," Shimmer snapped. "Do you see any lights?"

"No," I said. "I think we lost them."

Shimmer slowed. "Good. Because we're lost, too." We must have entered a larger area, because she could turn cautiously. Taking advantage of the pause, I followed her tail up to her spine so that I could crouch on her back.

There was a bumping sound. "You might signal when you're slowing down," Indigo said in an exasperated voice. "But now that you've stopped . . ."

Shimmer ignored her. "This way." With an undulation of her powerful body, she raced forward—she must have seen some opening. I bent low, flattening my cheek against her broad back. A less durable— and perhaps smarter—person might have let go of the dragon.

When we broke out into the open sea in an upper level, there was enough light for me to see.

"Dhere," Pomfret called. "Cadch her." Not more than twenty meters away, the half dozen marines suddenly tore around the side of the mountain. They were so close, I could see that the light came from the small globes belted to their waists.

Their light reflected from Pomfret's glittering scales as he plunged down toward us. With a corkscrew roll

Shimmer shot into yet another cave. "Ow!" she yelped, and halted abruptly.

From up above, Pomfret laughed harshly. "Your memory's gedding bad, Sisder. Dhad's a dead end. You wand dhe cave jusd below."

Battered and bruised, I shoved myself off Shimmer's back and expanded my staff. "Then we have to finish it here."

I felt Shimmer's leathery side brush me as she turned to face the mouth of the cave. "I'm afraid so." She cleared her throat. "You know, you're not so bad for a little fur ball."

"Thanks," I said. "I wouldn't want to get it around, but you're not so bad for an old leather bag."

"Will you two stop making out your wills and listen to me?" Indigo demanded.

"If you hide, you might survive," Shimmer instructed her.

Indigo's groping paw found me as she swam over Shimmer. "But I still have the needleweed juice. You can't help but float when you're wearing it."

"What an interesting notion." I remembered how we had skated on the snow and before that floated on top of a lake. "But what if you're already underwater?"

"What have we got to lose?" she asked.

"What indeed?" Shimmer said, but her voice had lost some of its grimness. "There's a space between the cave mouth and the floor where you could probably hide."

"Right. I see it." As Indigo swam, I felt something

tug at my robe and I heard a ripping sound.

I was going to protest, but by then the approaching marines cast enough light for me to see her crouching on the floor, hidden from the outside by the rock beneath the entrance to the cave. She was carefully wetting a cloth from the small jar she had taken from around her shoulder. I looked down at the new hole in my robe. With a sigh I glanced around and saw that we were in a shallow but high-ceilinged cave.

The next moment the first marine wriggled through the cave mouth. But he moved so fast, he caught Indigo by surprise. With a wink at Shimmer, I bounced toward him, staff in hand. "Don't you know you're supposed to knock before you enter someone's home?"

As I swept up my staff, I saw Indigo smear the rag across the paw of the next marine. Instantly, his paw jerked up and began tugging his leg along with it. Apparently the juice was still powerful despite the seawater diluting it. As he floated there, shouting in surprise, the next two marines piled into him. I just had time to see Indigo wiping juice onto their paws when I had my own marine to deal with.

He lunged at me with jaws snapping. However, a quick flip sent me to the side, and my staff whacked him into Shimmer's outstretched paws. "I hope you always wanted a pet."

And then I was somersaulting over to the cave mouth, where Indigo was shaking the jar against the rag as if she were having trouble getting any more out of it. I just hoped it lasted long enough.

There were already four frightened marines now. Unable to control their floating limbs, they were all tangled up together, and as they whirled around against the high ceiling, their shadows went dancing around the cave crazily like leaves caught in a whirlwind.

But the sixth marine had witnessed what had happened, so he only feinted at the cave mouth. When Indigo reached up, he was ready, catching her wrist in one paw. But before he could open his jaws to bite her, I had looped one ring around his muzzle. "Now, now, don't you boys have any manners? It's not polite to bite someone before you've been properly introduced."

Distracted by me, he had let go of Indigo. She took the opportunity to switch the rag over to her other paw and smear the juice over his leg. The next moment, his leg yanked up in the water and he was being hauled toward the surface, whirling round and round like a top.

By that time Shimmer had knocked out the first marine and was using him as a prod to guide the others out of the cave mouth. It was a comical sight to see them spin one by one up toward the surface.

As their belt lights faded, we could see Pomfret hovering about ten meters away. "Now dhad play dime is over, id's dime to ged serious." And he rang his claws together with a chiming sound that had a rhythmic, drumlike beat.

Indigo shook her jar over the rag. "It's empty," she moaned.

"You can'd fool me." Pomfret wagged a claw back and forth. "I wouldn'd led you ged dhad close do me anyway."

Letting go of the unconscious marine, Shimmer took the rag from Indigo. "Let me try."

"Oh, yes, do." Pomfret clanked his claws together.

Indigo tried to snatch the rag back. "Wait. There may not be enough on it."

However, Shimmer wriggled out of the cave. In the twilight outside, I could just make out Pomfret darting over Shimmer to rake her with his hind claws.

Shimmer, though, gave a twist, just avoiding his outstretched claws, and as she slid underneath, she wiped the rag against Pomfret's leg. Instantly, Pomfret kicked away and hovered. But when nothing happened, Indigo shook her head. "I was afraid so. There wasn't enough juice left on the rag."

"Then it's between you and me," Shimmer said to her brother, and glanced at me. "Take Indigo to the dragon army."

"The mighdy dragon army is in redread," Pomfret laughed. "Uncle Sambar's been given dwendy-four hours do surrender."

Suddenly I had an idea. "There may still be some juice left in the jar."

"Maybe," Indigo said thoughtfully. And before I could take the jar from her, she had pitched it straight at Pomfret. Pomfret tried to dodge, but there was simply too much Pomfret to be gotten out of the way.

The jar smashed against his ribs. It was almost funny to see Pomfret suddenly jerk erect in the water like a marionette whose strings have just been pulled. Pomfret must have understood that something in the jar had caused his buoyancy, because he tried to raise his tail to wipe it off. However, after his tail touched the needleweed juice, it shot straight up as well. And then, kicking and wriggling, he soared toward the surface. "Fools, dhere's nowhere do hide from me," he shrieked down to us as he disappeared.

CHAPTER TWELVE

"Nice throw," I congratulated Indigo.

She smoothed a paw over her blue spikes, obviously pleased. "I used to throw pebbles at the chef."

Lights bobbed in the distance, reflecting from the side of another mountain. Nodding her head down toward them, Shimmer spread her wings. "We'd better get out of here. Hop on, you little fur ball."

As soon as I had shrunk my staff and swum over, Shimmer swam forward, and Indigo followed. As the high peaks of the Children soared above us, Shimmer chuckled. "Pomfret's face was a study, wasn't it?"

Indigo and I both had to laugh despite the looming disaster. "The sea seems to be cooling off," I said. "The Boneless King must have stopped boiling water inside Thorn."

Thinking of what Pomfret had said, Indigo asked, "Then what do you think the dragons will do?"

"They have no choice. They have to surrender," Shimmer said. I could feel her begin to swim upward, and I heard her claws scrape rock as if she were following the steep slope of a mountain.

"Then," Indigo said quietly, "Civet's prophecy was true. Humans and dragons will bow before Thorn."

I could have almost gnashed my teeth in frustration at the thought that Thorn was the slave of the Boneless King. "But not the way anyone thought. Poor Thorn. He must be in agony now."

"Can't he resist the magic?" Indigo asked.

"I'm sure he's trying." Shimmer sighed. "But he'll have no choice. His soul is not the master of the cauldron, it's only the raw energy for the magic built into it."

By that time we had risen once again to the twilight, where the strongest of the sun's rays reached. Stubby bits of coral grew like bushes in this region upon the seamount. But in the twilight, the brightly colored coral looked like shadowy patches.

Indigo swam over a particularly large bush. "Did Civet make any other predictions besides the ones about Thorn and herself?"

I scratched my forehead with a paw. "Civet mentioned something about the Great Void."

I could feel the smooth undulations of Shimmer's powerful muscles beneath me. "Yes, there was something about a great chaos waiting."

"Maybe it's something the Boneless King has planned for us," I had to point out.

"Or maybe it's waiting for him." Shimmer turned purposefully toward the dragon palace. "I am going on to my uncle Sambar to get some help for another try at rescuing Thorn. But you and Indigo are going back to the mainland."

Indigo shot in front of Shimmer, her shoulder demolishing a coral bush. "No!"

Shimmer calmly arched over her. "Don't worry. I'll change you back to human form and cast a breathing spell on you that will last until you reach the top of the Rim." That was the way the dragons talked about the mainland, because from a dragon's perspective that's what it was.

I felt the sea flow over my face. "The dragons blame you for the loss of the cauldron."

"So long as they don't blame my clan," Shimmer said, and she slowed as she tried to change the subject. "I always loved this region of the sea."

The coral grew thicker and brighter where the sunlight could penetrate with full force. Corals grew in all different colors and shapes—some were clusters the shape and colors of plums, others grew in huge globes with wrinkled patterns. They swept up like garlands of flowers around the throat of the mountain. And all kinds of brightly colored fish hovered and darted over the coral.

"They don't seem any the worse for wear because of the heating," I said, paddling up to her.

"It wasn't long enough." Shimmer paused here as if she wanted to catch one last glimpse.

Suddenly a green head was thrust in front of us. "It's certain death to go to the dragon palace," Indigo insisted.

Lowering her head, Shimmer gently butted her out of the way. "Don't worry. Monkey will help you find some nice, quiet corner far away from the Boneless King."

"Yes," I chimed in. "My master says that there isn't one world, but thousands and thousands, each a little different from this one. We'll go to some other world where they've never heard of the Boneless King."

Indigo seized one of Shimmer's legs and tugged her to a halt. "Come with us."

Shimmer corkscrewed her body, gently freeing her leg. "No, I have to go. It's the least I owe my clan in the middle of this catastrophe."

"Pomfret will see to them," Indigo argued.

"Even if I trusted the Boneless King to keep his word to make him King—which I don't—what will happen to my clan in the meantime?" Shimmer began to swim toward her right to circle around the mountain. "The rest of the dragons will be angry. They'll be looking for scapegoats for this defeat."

Indigo, though, was not having any of that. "You mustn't. You can't."

"I'll be all right." Shimmer tried to smile. "I'll suggest to my uncle that he give me one last chance to redeem myself. After all, what's he got to lose? If I bring back Thorn, then he's got what he wants. And if I'm caught, well"—she shrugged—"the Boneless King will inflict a far worse punishment than anything my uncle could come up with."

With an abrupt lunge, though, Indigo bulled into Shimmer, knocking her with a crash into a row of coral. As we lay there dazed, Indigo loomed over us. She sounded as if she felt betrayed. "I thought you were different from the other dragons. I thought you were smart. I thought you weren't stuck-up. But you're just as bad. You're just as full of lies."

Shimmer stiffened with fury, but somehow managed to control herself. "I think it's time for you to turn back into a human."

"Good." Indigo whipped her tail about in such an angry frenzy that she disappeared in a cloud of bubbles. In some ways she was like one of those bombs of living fire—there was so much hostility inside ready to explode. "Then I'll be done with you," she said from within the cloud.

Shimmer sat up, brushing off bits of coral—she had taken most of the blow. Though she appeared calm, she was barely able to control her own temper. "Monkey, I think we've come to a parting of the ways." It was a measure of her anger that she didn't try to hide the transformation spell from me but touched her forehead and worked it openly, along with something I recognized as a simple breathing spell like I used.

When the bubbles dissipated, Indigo was a young girl again. In contrast to the large dragon she had

been, she seemed especially small and fragile, and remembering who she was, Shimmer relented a little.
"Thank you for your help. Monkey will look out for
you now."

"By all the hairs on my tail," I promised solemnly.
"And there's nothing that frightens a monkey more
than the thought of a bald tail."

However, Indigo hunched her shoulders and
wrapped her arms around herself, the action making
her sink slowly. "I don't understand. Just tell me why
you're going."

Puzzled, Shimmer gazed down at her. "I told you
why: It's for my clan."

Indigo balled her hands into fists, and the sudden
motion made her drift backward. "But what have
they done for you?"

"They've given me their trust," Shimmer stated
simply.

For a moment Indigo stared at a patch of red coral
as delicate as peacock feathers. Frustrated, she swiped
at it as if she hated it for being so lovely and so weak.
Instantly, the worms disappeared within the stonelike
tubes of their home. "'Trust' is a word people use
when they want something from you."

Shimmer ducked her head as a little sea hare swam
by, its orange and red sides fluttering like a frilly
fringe in the wind. "I used to think like you."

In pure rage Indigo flung herself away from the
seamount and began driving the anemones into hiding with flailing arms. And then she whirled around.

"What made you grow so dumb?"

Shimmer lashed her tail angrily, rising out of the explosion of silver bubbles. It was well she had changed Indigo back into her human form, or the two of them might have fought it out right there. "Maybe you'll understand one day—but I doubt it." Still hurt, Shimmer turned her back on the child and jerked her head at me. "Take that ungrateful pup away before I do something I'll regret."

"Come along, Indigo." I gave a kick, then drifted toward her.

However, Indigo had been raised undersea and was a far better swimmer than I was. Kicking and twisting, she darted around me. "No, I didn't mean those things I said."

"I heard you the first time," Shimmer said testily. "Dragons and humans should never mix together. It brings only misery and anger."

Lunging forward, Indigo clung to one of the dragon's legs. "Don't send me away."

Surprised, Shimmer slowly began to tilt since she could not swim with that leg. "It's for your own good."

"I don't understand," Indigo insisted. "I just . . . don't understand."

Gently but firmly, Shimmer used her other forepaw to shove Indigo away. "You're the intelligent one, and I'm the fool."

Indigo's head drooped and her shoulders began to shake. If we hadn't been in the middle of the sea, Indigo would have wept tears that we could see. "I . . . I . . ." her voice drifted off in a mumble, and we couldn't hear her.

Shimmer inclined her head. "What did you say?"

Indigo, though, could only hunch her shoulders and sob, absolutely desolate.

After an uncomfortable pause, Shimmer patted her clumsily with one great paw. "It's all right. Think of the good times when you think of me."

Indigo raised a face that was a mask of misery. "I said . . ." she sobbed, "I love you."

Shimmer's paw shot away as if Indigo had suddenly turned into a red-hot coal; the dragon looked. . . well . . . frightened. "Me? With my temper?"

Indigo threw herself at Shimmer's foreleg. "You're the only thing I've ever loved."

Shimmer stared at the child clinging to her and then shook her head ruefully. "You must have led a desperate life if you've picked out someone like me." For once the dragon looked at me for help.

However, I was just as much out of my depth as she was. "I suppose it's possible for someone to fall in love with even an overgrown frog." Swimming over to the girl, I put my arms around the delicate shoulders. "It's hard to lose the only one you've loved. And when you're young, you don't ever think you'll find someone else. But you will."

Shimmer managed to shove Indigo away. "You don't want to love me. Look what love did for poor Thorn."

Indigo made no attempt to change her direction. She just kept floating away. "Who said it was easy loving me either?"

"I should have been firmer with you once we escaped from Egg Mountain. I've already risked your life enough. I can't be selfish anymore." Shimmer cleared her throat and became her old, brusque self. "Well, I hate long good-byes, and this one has taken long enough." And with a kick, she rose in the water.

Suddenly Indigo's head snapped up as a new thought occurred to her, her hair spikes bobbing and waving. "Wait," Indigo called. "How do you know that I'm not part of Civet's vision? Maybe you need me to defeat the Boneless King."

Shimmer bent her neck to look between her legs at me. "And maybe you aren't and I don't."

Indigo pressed her advantage. "Can you be sure? Can you take that risk? The entire world could be lost just because you want to look noble."

I hovered in the water with long, slow sweeps of my arms. "I don't have much business with visions and prophecies, but I think she may have a point. I know you don't want to be selfish to her. Even so, you have to balance her existence against that of the world itself."

Indigo seemed glad of an excuse for staying with Shimmer—even if it meant risking death at the hands of the Boneless King again. Grateful to me, the girl took off my cap and threw it up, though it didn't rise very high in the water. Catching it, she set it on top of my head. "After all, it's my right to choose."

Shimmer looked thoughtful and then shook her head. "You said I was a fool."

Indigo kicked her way toward the dragon. "Don't write your tombstone yet. With the help of a few volunteers, we could get Thorn back."

Shimmer gave her a bemused smile. "Do you really think so?"

Indigo spoke with care, like someone picking her way around dangerous traps. "I really can't say. But maybe it's wise not to give up hope."

Shimmer threw back her head and laughed. "Perhaps not."

Laughing with relief, Indigo held her arms away from her sides. "You ought to change me into a dragon if we're going to the palace. Humans won't exactly be welcome there."

"Yes," Shimmer mused, "but something less conspicuous."

Indigo indicated her blue spikes of hair. "I think a prickly hide suits me."

Shimmer gave a chuckle. "Perhaps it does." Touching her forehead, she changed Indigo back into a dragon—one with blue spikes.

The girl swirled around in the water as if she enjoyed having the body of a dragon once again, and then she nodded to me. "Monkey isn't exactly on the guest list either."

I rejected the idea right away. "Give up my fur for scales? This body is as tough as a dragon's." I did a backward flip and then floated through the water over Shimmer's head. "Besides, if Sambar's guards have two targets to shoot at, it'll give Indigo more of a chance to escape."

Indigo coiled in the water, her forepaw nervously brushing the blue spikes that ran down her tail. "Maybe you ought to give them a smaller target," she suggested to Shimmer.

"A dragon princess—" she began.

Indigo uncoiled with a shower of bubbles. "I know," she sighed. "A dragon princess must be a dragon's size."

CHAPTER THIRTEEN

We swam under the surface in the open sea until the sun began to set. Then, as Shimmer darted forward, her paws left glowing streaks in the water. And looking behind us, I saw how my body left a faint, glowing trail. "What's that?"

"I'd forgotten that it's still the season of fire." Shimmer slowed for a moment and swiped at the water with a paw. A brilliant bar of green light hung in the water. "It's a type of plankton that grows around this time of year. It rises toward the surface at night and gives off a glow when it's excited." The light faded away even as we watched. "But touching it doesn't hurt the plankton."

Indigo wrote her name in the water and watched as it lit up her face with an eerie light. "I'd heard about it, but I never got to leave the palace to see it. How pretty."

"We used to have parties, and there were contests for drawing pictures in the water—both as individuals and in groups." And for a moment Shimmer showed off by waving all her paws and her tail, sketching an elaborate design in the water.

I looked back toward the Children. "This is going to make it pretty hard to sneak up on anyone from under the water."

When Shimmer nodded her head, a sad halo surrounded her. "That's probably why the humans picked this time of year for the invasion."

"Then we'll have to do it by air," I said.

Indigo spread out her wings so that sheets of light went flashing through the sea. "I'd like to try out these things again."

Shimmer craned her head up, and her motion through the water raised ghostly streamers behind her. "I don't want to be a gloomy gus," she said to me, "but what makes you so eternally cheerful?"

I used my tail to draw a glowing mustache across her snout. "We're alive, aren't we? And what were the odds for that?"

"Not very high," Shimmer had to admit. As she raised a leg, the light spread out behind her like a wing. "But I'm not sure that's a consolation. We may have used up most of our luck."

Puckering up, I blew a glowing kiss at her. "We've made our own luck—between your brawn, Indigo's brain and"—I wriggled my eyebrows—"my beauty."

Shimmer dodged the kiss. "It's impossible to hold a serious conversation with you."

"You worry enough for two anyway." I used my tail and feet to draw designs behind me.

We must have swum for another three kilometers before we caught up with the dragon army. After the setting of the sun, the sea seemed as black and vast as the night sky, and the movement of the dragons in the waters filled the ocean with twinkling lights and streaking comets. Units in formation maneuvered through the water like massive constellations.

"It's like a living sky," Indigo murmured.

Even Shimmer was awed. "I've never seen the whole dragon army gathered together." Back on the Boneless King's flagship we had seen only the vanguard.

Of course, our glowing wakes were like huge signs announcing our arrival. Sentries streaked toward us like fiery arrows, and we slowed to wait for them. At about ten meters they fanned out to encircle us, making the sea burn with strange, ghostly shapes. "Halt, who goes there?"

Shimmer coiled up in the water. "Shimmer, Princess of the Inland Sea. And these are my companions—"

A dragon shot forward. "The sister of the arch-traitor." Around his neck was the steel disk with the double concentric circle of a lieutenant. "You've got some nerve coming here without brotection." He must have been a southern dragon, because he pronounced his p's as b's.

I drew myself up with all the dignity I could muster, but on Shimmer's advice I had shrunk my staff. "I beg your pardon?"

However, the scaly twerp ignored me. "Haven't you done enough damage? What brice did the humans bay you? A bond in the Butcher's garden?"

Even I might have flinched with a dozen angry dragons ready to tear me apart. Shimmer, though, held her head up as proudly as ever. "I've come to help you get the cauldron back. Take me to my uncle."

"The general will decide." The lieutenant signed to a dragon who sped off with the message.

But of course as the news spread, the other dragons began to gather until there was a solid sphere of dragons around us. There were so many that their moving bodies caused the sea to glow like a small sun.

"I should have made you and Monkey leave," Shimmer muttered to Indigo.

Indigo did her best to stare back at the other dragons, but she didn't seem nearly so confident now. "It was my choice."

"And mine." I scratched behind my ear so that I could get out my staff. "Are all your family reunions so much fun?"

Word soon came to the lieutenant to escort us to Sambar's palace itself. Luckily for us, discipline was still more important than their hatred of us, so the other dragons reluctantly parted, forming a kind of living tunnel. It seemed to take forever to move through that horde as they glowered at us and clinked their steel-tipped claws together meaningfully. I'd never seen so many angry dragons at one time—and I hope I never do again.

Surrounding the palace was a ring of flat-topped seamounts where the dragons grew delicacies and decorations for the palace itself. Seamounts were undersea volcanos whose tops had collapsed. But I thought it was odd when I saw the light playing on top of each. "It's a little late to be gardening, isn't it?"

The lieutenant glared at me bitterly. "They're not gardens anymore. They're being used as hosbitals for the dragons that the living fire hurt. That was the brice for your selfishness."

I thought of Thorn and Civet. "We've paid our price too."

Apparently word had also reached the seamounts, for as we passed over them, a hundred dragons arched upward, streaking toward us like angry meteors.

Quickly the lieutenant nodded to two of his dragons. "Watch the brisoners and make sure they don't escape."

There was a dragon wearing a disk with the small triangle of a corporal. "Why should we defend them?" He nodded down toward the ascending dragons. "They have the most reason to hate her."

"It doesn't matter," the lieutenant insisted. "We

have our orders." He himself took up a position to defend Shimmer.

Shimmer tilted up her head, the light from the rising dragons illuminating a face filled with sorrow. "Give me to them, but let these two others go." When she nodded her head, it was surrounded by a globe of light. "Whatever happened was all my doing."

Flipping out my staff, I shouted, "Change," and then used it to hold off an advancing soldier. "Ha! Shimmer couldn't have fought a plate of noodles without me and my toy."

But as the lieutenant's dragons moved to intercept the mob, the newcomers halted about some twenty meters away, drifting slowly upward. I could see now that some had terrible burn marks on their hides and some had even lost parts of their paws, tails and limbs.

"Stay back," the lieutenant warned. "We're taking these brisoners to the High King."

A dragon with one wing rose. Burn scars on the side of his face made it hard for him to talk. "Not if we have anything to say about it," he growled.

"Get back," the lieutenant barked as the other dragons floated past us. And then he shouted to his own dragons, "Drive them back. Don't let them surround us."

However, our guards seemed reluctant to strike their injured comrades, and as the dragons moved past us, the glowing light from the plankton lit up their cruel wounds. When we were encircled by an even larger sphere of dragons, a dragon shoved her way forward.

The disk around her throat was partly burned, but I could see the large triangle of a sergeant. "Give us our princess," she said to the lieutenant.

Shimmer leaned her head forward curiously. "Chukar?"

The dragon tried to draw herself up proudly and winced. "Yes, Your Highness."

Shimmer looked at the dragon with one wing. "And Slug?"

The dragon found it easier to nod than to speak.

Shimmer glanced all around as if she hardly dared to hope. "Are you all from the Inland Sea?"

"Yes, Your Highness. The ones who could swim." Sergeant Chukar nodded back toward the seamounts. "The others would have come if they could."

"Now see here." The lieutenant blundered between Shimmer and the other two. "We'll overlook this insubordination, but you must return to your hosbitals."

"Not without our princess," Sergeant Chukar insisted.

Seizing the lieutenant's tail, Shimmer swung him into the paws of some dragons from her clan. "Chukar, what happened?"

"We were put in the vanguard so we could redeem our clan's honor." Chukar laughed harshly. "They would have put us there anyway. We frontier fighters are the only ones who have seen any combat out by the Abyss." The Abyss marked the deep undersea territory of the dragons' enemies, the krakens.

Slug looked contemptuously at our escort. "Not like these fat little parade worms."

It takes a lot to make a dragon apologize, especially a dragon princess. But Shimmer bowed her head now to the invalids. "I'm sorry. I lost the cauldron to Pomfret."

"That traitor," Sergeant Chukar grumbled. "We'll help you get it back."

The lieutenant managed to wriggle free from his captors. "Don't be brebosterous. Some of you can barely swim, let alone fight."

A one-eyed dragon with wounds on a hind leg bumped his chest against the lieutenant, who backed up hastily until he was among his own dragons again. "We'll show you how we can fight, Sonny—unless you scoot back to your camp where it's nice and safe. It wasn't us who held back from the attack. It was the rest of you toy soldiers."

I glanced at Shimmer, but she could see as well as I could that these dragons were in no shape to follow us back into battle with the Boneless King. However, Shimmer was also reluctant to insult them.

So I jumped right in then. "But what about the rest of your clan?" I demanded. "If you mutiny now— even if it is to prove your honor—what will Sambar do to them?"

There were uneasy looks among the dragons at what I had said, and Shimmer was sensitive to their discomfort. "I'll go to my uncle and explain, and then

I'll lead you back to avenge our honor."

"And make a couch out of your brother," Slug said, holding up a claw.

"Upholstery is too good for him," Shimmer grunted.

"All right," Sergeant Chukar declared. "I'll pick out an escort of thirty of the strongest. The others will wait here for word from you." She glanced significantly at the lieutenant. "Just to make sure Her Highness has no accidents along the way."

The lieutenant didn't look any too happy about having guards for his guards, but he didn't have much choice. Even with their injuries, Shimmer's clan could have overwhelmed the lieutenant's squad.

True to her word, Sergeant Chukar selected thirty of the healthiest, and Slug and some of the others objected when they weren't picked. "You aren't in much better shape than me," Slug pointed out to his sergeant.

But Sergeant Chukar jabbed a paw at Slug, forcing him to duck. "I could still box your ears and make you eat your tail. Get back to that hospital."

When the other dragons had reluctantly returned in a shining cloud back to their seamounts, we continued, the dragons of Shimmer's clan intermingling with the lieutenant's squad purposefully so that each of the lieutenant's dragons had two and even three of Shimmer's clan to watch them.

Shimmer, Indigo and I each had our own escort as well, and the sergeant swam along beside her princess. When the lieutenant tried to step up the

143

pace so that he and his squad could outdistance Shimmer's clan, the wily sergeant just signed to the others of her clan, and they began to deliberately bump and knock the lieutenant's squad until our pace was as slow as before.

Shimmer put a paw upon the old sergeant. "The last time I saw you, you were fighting off a horde of krakens."

The sergeant chuckled but winced when she tried to shrug. "We've been fighting off krakens for years. Give us an honest fight and we can more than hold our own. But those devilish bombs"—she shook her head—"are another thing."

"How bad was it after I 'borrowed' the cauldron?" Shimmer wanted to know.

"Bad enough," the sergeant admitted. "His Most Exalted Majesty needed scapegoats, and we were convenient."

The one-eyed dragon nodded his head. "It was double shifts for workers and the most dangerous assignments for the soldiers."

Shimmer sighed. "You needed a home, Wort, and I failed."

"You tried your best," Indigo said, attempting to console her.

Shimmer, though, was past consoling. "It was Thorn who did his best. If I had done my best, my people would have their home, and Thorn would still be alive."

I thought of something my master, the Old Boy,

had once told me. "Just because two goals are good ones," I observed, "doesn't mean that they're automatically compatible. It would be convenient if they were, but often they're not. And so you have to make a choice."

Shimmer considered that for a while. "And feel bad about whatever choice you make."

CHAPTER FOURTEEN

At the center of the ring of seamounts lay the mountains that formed the palace of the High King of all the dragons. Rising all the way from the dark seafloor, the peaks swept upward into the points of a crown, the coral at the top transforming the tips into bits of rainbow colors.

The palace had actually been started in just the upper portion of the mountain by that greatest of High Kings, Sambar VI, the fourth son of Calambac. However, subsequent generations of artisans had been hollowing out the other mountains and decorating the sides so that the mountains seemed more like giant sculptures. I doubt if the oldest dragon could have detailed all the terraces, pavilions and chambers. The very scale of the palace spoke of the ancientness of the dragon kingdom. In some places the artisans had created glowing falls of colored sand that recycled endlessly.

Even at this late hour the palace blazed with light, and dragons streaked back and forth, their wakes shining like fiery peacock tails. As they saw the light marking our approach, the dragons began to gather, servants and nobles, generals and privates, all swirling together to form an angry wall.

With a kick, a tense Indigo shrank against Shimmer. "I never thought I'd see this place again."

But Shimmer's clan swarmed closer round us. "Make way," Sergeant Chukar barked before the lieutenant could say anything. "Make way for Her Highness, the Princess of the Inland Sea." Normally used for giving orders on a parade ground, her voice carried commandingly through the water.

Their wounds made Shimmer's clan seem all the more fearsome, and the mob parted—though that didn't stop some hecklers on the fringe who shouted insults.

Shimmer ignored them as we dove past. Instead, she made a point of twisting her head to look at me. "Since my uncle the King of the Golden Sea may also be here, it might be wise to keep a low profile. He might not understand that you've merely been 'borrowing' his magical staff until he needed it again."

At the same time, Indigo was glancing behind her at her blue spikes and trying to make them stand up straighter on her undulating back. "I won't have the cook laughing at me."

We landed on a great terrace whose green marble was carved with all the creatures who had ever brought tribute—from flying elephants that I recognized from that crypt under the lake to phoenixes and fox people. There were even humans with spiked hair who I thought might be Indigo's folk.

Within the palace, there was lively music. "It sounds almost like a party," I murmured to Shimmer.

"It'd be like my uncle to have one last fling," Shimmer said. The hallway to the throne room was decorated with the likenesses of dragons of the past. Shimmer's great-grandfather the Weaver was there, looking wise and noble. And there was Baldy, who by hook or by crook had gotten the cauldron for the dragons in the first place. They were all there, larger than life and staring down at us as we swam by, as if they were taking our measure and finding us wanting.

Their stern faces seemed to contrast sharply with the music and the laughter from within the throne room. The throne room had been hollowed out of the center of the mountain and rose for a half kilometer to the rounded mountaintop. Against the black ceiling worms glowed like stars, and more lamps filled with glowing worms had been brought inside the throne room. Through the star-shaped windows I could only occasionally see the flash of a dragon passing by.

The throne room was so immense, in fact, that there were entertainments going on in different parts.

In one section was a team of acrobatic swimmers whose bodies undulated like ribbons; in another were jugglers whose arms seemed to juggle in slow motion; and in a third were clowns. All the court dragons had decked themselves out in their finest jewelry and covered their claws and even limned their scales with bright paint. It should have been an impressive sight, but almost everyone was laughing a little too hard or singing a little too loud—as if they were doing their best to convince themselves that they were having a good time.

I have to admit, though, that their idea of a banquet left me a little queasy. All the bowls were covered with lids, but enough were being raised at any one time for me to get an idea of what they were eating.

"There isn't one entree that isn't alive and wriggling," I muttered to the still tense Indigo. In fact, a horde of servants was kept busy catching the various delicacies that escaped whenever a lid was opened.

Shimmer, though, overheard me. "My uncle fancies himself a gourmet." From her tone, I gathered that she didn't exactly approve either. "It's a shame, in a way. He ruled rather well during the first years of his reign, but the temptations were too much. And he's just simply gotten greedy."

In the center of the throne room was a series of platforms rising like the layers of a giant cake. On the lowest level were the dragon mages, officers and court officials wearing plaques of brass. Above them was a level of silver, where the nobility dined. Higher still was the royal family, dressed in gold chains and plaques. And on the highest level, some twenty meters above the common folk, was a jade dais on which lay the ponderous bulk of Sambar the XII, High King of all the dragons.

Shimmer's uncle had gone in for the full show—perhaps since this might very well be his last night as His Most Exalted Majesty. The rainbow pearl rested on his forehead, and around his neck was the jade cloud-shaped plaque of the first High King, Calambac. In one paw he held the mirror of truth. He just seemed to be making himself comfortable.

A dragon butler stamped his foot loudly and roared out in a voice that cut across the music, "His Most Exalted Majesty, Sambar the Strong. All bow."

The throne room fell silent and all the dragons bowed low to the High King above them. Only Shimmer's resentful clan hesitated until Shimmer herself bowed to her uncle. "Let us bow to the office," she whispered, "and to the great dragons of the past."

However, Sambar wasn't standing on formality. "Traitor!" he thundered across the throne room when he saw us. The rainbow pearl in his forehead flashed angry colors across the domed ceiling, and the plaque bounced on his fat chest. "How could you take the bowl and give it to our enemies?"

"I took the cauldron only to restore my people's home," Shimmer said, holding up her head high. "But my brother treacherously took it from me. I've come to help you get it back. If I were a true traitor, I would have stayed where it was safe rather than risk my life."

"Then you're a reckless fool," Sambar snapped, "which makes you almost as bad as a traitor."

Shimmer's voice shook with indignation. "If you had treated my clan as you should have, I would never have had to take the bowl."

It was Sambar's turn to be indignant. "We gave them homes."

"In the forges and the mines, in the outposts on very edge of the Abyss," Shimmer countered, "where your own people were afraid to go because it was so dangerous."

An outraged Sambar reared up so fast that he floated off the dais. "Beggars cannot dictate how they are to live."

"They are not beggars now," Shimmer said, and lifted the flap of flesh on her forehead that hid the dream pearl. There was a gasp as a soft, iridescent light spread through the throne room. "We have this."

Instantly, her clan began to protest. "No, Your Highness, that is yours," Sergeant Chukar scolded her. "You went into exile to keep that pearl."

"And so it's mine to do with as I choose," Shimmer said gently to the sergeant, and faced Sambar again.

Despite himself, Sambar roared with laughter. "You realize that our time to grant such things is short—thanks to you and your brother." He subsided to a chuckle as he settled back on his dais. "But since the next ruler is likely to be your brother,

151

he might let these particular decisions stand. What are your requests?"

"I ask that you take this temporarily in place of the bowl," Shimmer said, "so that no blame may be attached to my people and they may be treated fairly and honestly from now on."

Sambar played with the plaque around his neck. "Hmm," he said thoughtfully. "And what is your second request?"

"That you give me a company of your best troops to reinforce my own guard." Shimmer nodded to her clan. "So I may regain the bowl and redeem my pearl." I suppose she planned to designate her clan as a reserve to keep them safe while she led the other dragons against the Boneless King.

There was a ripple of laughter at the thought of her old, injured dragons being a guard. However, Sambar himself merely spread his paws over his wide belly. "If the Butcher kills you, what entertainment is there for us? Whereas an execution would provide some solace in our remaining hours."

"You'll take the princess over our dead bodies," Wort shouted.

Sambar's paw threw the nearest bowl. The lid flew up in the water, releasing orange-fringed worms that darted in all directions. "That, my dear fellow, can be arranged also."

The imperial guards closed around us, their gold-tipped claws replaced with very businesslike steel ones, and I was just reaching for my staff when I heard a commotion from the terrace behind us.

A young dragon, gashed along one side, stumbled past the butler. Turning, Shimmer recognized him. "Thrush, what are you doing here?"

"Your Highness." He winced as if in great pain. "I bring terrible news. There is an army of krakens rising from the Abyss. The Spine is overrun, and the forges and forts are all lost." The Spine was a chain of undersea mountains and volcanos where the dragons used volcanic heat to forge steel.

Sambar must have stripped the forts of troops for his war with the humans. Whether the krakens were allies of the humans or just simply taking advantage of the situation I didn't know.

Sambar sagged upon his dais. And Shimmer and her escorting kin looked worried. "Most of her clan had to live on the frontier that the krakens have just overrun," Indigo explained to me.

With a kick, Shimmer rose above the other dragons so she could reach and grasp Thrush. "Our clan. What's happened to them?"

"We fled here along with everyone else who lived between the Abyss and the palace," Thrush gasped. "We couldn't think of anywhere else safe."

Shimmer caught the dragon before he could fall. "But safe for how long?" she said sadly. "I've failed them as I've failed poor Thorn. His sacrifice was wasted." There was a terrible, hollow ache in her voice.

I understood how she felt. "So this is the end," I

said. "The dragons can't fight two enemies at once."

"Not entirely," she said, rousing herself. "I don't choose to live like my brother—a slave of the Butcher. I would rather go out to meet my enemies." She looked at her clan. "Will anyone come with me?"

Her clan, with one voice, shouted their agreement. Sambar uncoiled himself from the dais and held a paw to Shimmer. He might have been fat and spoiled now, but for a moment I could glimpse the younger dragon who had earned the nickname of "the Strong." "We're of the same blood, you and I," Sambar declared. "I'll fight beside you." He gazed around his throne room. "Who else will go with us?" He drifted up from the dais.

There was a little cough from the hallway and an elderly dragon swam into the room. "I will," she said. "I once cut quite a figure in the tournaments long ago."

"That's Lady Francolin," Indigo whispered to me. "She's Thrush's grandmother and heads one of the branches of Shimmer's clan." She added, "She used to be Shimmer's history tutor."

But there was very little of the tutor in her now. She had a dozen small wounds, and in one paw she held a bone from some giant fish as if she had been using it as a club. Pausing before Shimmer, she bowed low. "My branch of the clan is at your disposal."

Shimmer made her straighten up. "No, it's I who should bow to you for what you've endured, and because I've failed you."

"My branch of the clan will also follow you, Your

Highness." An elderly dragon entered with a lance that I recognized as a long miner's drill. "As a child I drummed for your grandfather."

Shimmer was openly weeping as she passed Thrush down to Sergeant Chukar. "Lady Francolin," she said, and to the new dragon, taking his paw: "Bulbul. Thank Heaven you're safe." Then she caught sight of the miner's drill. "How many of our clan are here?"

Lady Francolin brandished her makeshift club. "We had to improvise weapons, but we gave the krakens too much of a fight for their taste. We managed to evacuate the other dragons who lived between us and the palace and escort them here."

Suddenly Shimmer seized a steel bowl and overturned it, dumping out orange frilled sea hares that fluttered lazily in the water. Holding out the bowl to Bulbul, Shimmer asked, "Will you drum for me as you did for my grandfather?"

"As you wish, Your Highness." Shortening his grip on the drill, Bulbul began to beat the bowl against it. And the beat was a rhythm that was like the beat of my own blood.

Lady Francolin smiled proudly. "The world hasn't heard that sound in ages."

Floating above his dais, Sambar smiled sadly down at Shimmer. "Perhaps," he called loudly over the drumbeat, "it's been too long since that sound was heard. For that, you have our apologies, Your Highness." It was the first time he had addressed Shimmer by her proper title. Sliding off his throne, he asked,

"So how do you choose to die? Shall it be against the Boneless King or the krakens?"

Shimmer gave a deep, heartfelt bow to her uncle. "I have more scores to settle with the Butcher than with the krakens. But it is he who must die."

Sambar lashed his tail more cheerfully. "If you could work that magic, you would rank right up there with the Weaver."

Shimmer lifted a paw and pointed toward one of the windows. "There," she cried. "There is your miracle."

I turned my head at the same time as all the grand dragons in the throne room and looked in the direction she was pointing. There, summoned by the ancient drumbeat, were dragons of the clan of the Lost Sea pressing their faces against the panes of crystal. In fact there were dragons at every window of the throne room as they sought to catch a glimpse of their princess.

Then, from the lowest platform, a general raised her voice. "That's ridiculous. You can't lead amateurs against professionals."

Shimmer whirled around. "They'll be fighting for a home and a chance to leave the misery you've forced them into."

Sambar suddenly looped through the water over everyone's head. "Princess Shimmer, if you can hold off the human fleet even for a while, we might have a chance."

"And if we do?" she asked with new hope.

"Assuming that we can then defeat the humans, you can have whatever you need to renew your kingdom." Sambar chuckled. "Assuming that we can also recover Baldy's bowl."

Indigo leaned in close to me and whispered, "That seems like an awful lot of ifs to me."

I could only nod my head.

CHAPTER FIFTEEN

Shimmer was busy with the last-minute plans. We were in Sambar's own private chambers—though they were more like a series of caves and grottoes. Through some trick of air pressure there were pockets of air in various caves, and some magic helped renew the air—which had allowed Sambar to install a huge human bed with silk covers and a canopy in one room. A real waterfall spilled down into the pool that filled the lower half of the chamber. In other rooms there grew a giant form of sea lettuce—a kind of kelp that clings to rocks—but this type was so huge that it was like cushions.

As Sambar replaced the gold tips on his claws with steel, Shimmer finally broke the news that we were facing not the Butcher but the Boneless King in the Butcher's body.

"I thought the Masters dealt with him long ago?" Sambar demanded.

"Ah, well," Shimmer said in embarrassment, "we accidentally helped him get away."

"My, my, you have been busy." Sambar frowned at his claws. "But since none of us are likely to live, I suppose it doesn't matter." He threw one of the steel tips at a wall and the servants ducked. He glowered at it as it embedded itself in the wall. "These things don't fit anymore."

The armorer cringed apologetically. "It has been a long time since His Most Exalted Majesty wore them."

Sambar gazed down at his fat paw and then at his large stomach. "I suppose I have let myself get a little out of shape."

The armorer bowed. "I've sent to the armory for a sampling of sizes—if you wouldn't be insulted to wear a common soldier's."

"So long as it does the job on kraken hides." Sambar clicked his claws meaningfully.

I sat upon a rock in the middle of the pool beside Indigo. "I don't suppose it crossed your mind to shrink down," I said to Sambar.

The King looked as if he would have liked to throw a steel tip if he'd had any more. "A dragon High King must—"

I waved my paws hurriedly in the air. "Yes, yes, I know. Never mind."

Shimmer shot a warning glance at me not to annoy

her uncle anymore. "If you don't mind, I'd like to keep the dream pearl a bit longer," she said. "I have plans for it."

Sambar laughed. "Do you need anything else? My crown? My throne?"

Shimmer bowed again. "Some of your mages would help too."

"If it truly is the Boneless King, then you'll need all the magical help you can get," Sambar said. A servant entered, and Sambar arched his brow. "Yes?"

The servant bowed. "The King of the Golden Sea wishes to pay his respects and to inquire if the Great Sage Equal to Heaven is in your company."

"Make him wait a moment and then bring him in." As the servant left, Sambar turned to me. "I gather that you're not ready to return your staff?"

I put my paw nervously to my ear. "It would be useful in the coming battle."

With a smile Sambar pointed toward a circular door to the side. "Take the back door, then. I'll tell him that he just missed you."

I rose hastily and bowed to the High King. "I'm sorry for anything wicked I've ever said about you."

"No, you're not, and the next time I see you, I'll expect you to return his property." He dismissed us with a wave of his paw, and when we left him, he was still trying to pull on his old steel tips.

As we swam along the corridors, Indigo kept close to Shimmer. "You're up to something."

Shimmer nodded absently, her mind occupied with

dozens of details. "Frankly, I don't think the mages are any match for the Boneless King, but he'll be expecting something." She touched the pearl still in her forehead. "So he might overlook the real deception." Shimmer slowed and glanced at Indigo. "But there's no reason for you to go."

There was an awkward silence. "For years when I was slaving away in the kitchen, I kept myself alive in this place by dreaming about going home," Indigo said slowly.

Shimmer stopped kicking and just drifted along. "And now you're invited into the High King's private chambers."

Indigo shrugged as if such things didn't matter to her. "What was important was going home and finding my own clan."

Shimmer found a space between the blue spikes along her back and gave her a pat. "And then you found them gone."

"All I have is you now," Indigo said.

Shimmer batted away a stray sea hare with her paw. "I swear to you that if we survive, you'll always have a place with me."

Indigo corkscrewed through the water. "Try getting rid of me." And then she halted, but the corridor was too narrow for her to turn around in. "I think I can help add to the distraction if I can raid the kitchen. Some of your uncle's snacks would terrify any humans—especially if they were told that the creatures were poisonous."

"But the sailors would know poisonous sea snakes," Shimmer objected.

"They know the ones on the surface, but your uncle has a lot of strange things from the bottom of the sea." She was already turning into a corridor that angled down.

"And some of those things look pretty strange," Shimmer agreed. "I suppose if we shouted down that they were poisonous, the humans would believe us." She gestured with a claw at me. "Better go with Indigo. She may need your arts of persuasion. I'll send help down when I can."

That was easy for Shimmer to say. I didn't know the palace the way the former servant did, and I wound up getting lost. But when I heard banging and crashing like a hundred cymbals, I figured that Indigo had to be at the center of it.

The kitchen was a huge cavern with a section where another air pocket had been created with magic so that they could have fires. Within the watery area Indigo was in the middle of a tumble of pots with a huge, froglike creature pinned under her paws. I figured that he must have been one of her worst tormentors during her service there. "I've got a good mind to bite your head off, but that wouldn't begin to settle my score against you," she was saying to him.

We should have known that she wouldn't need any help. Hastily I swam up and gave her tail a slight tug. "Besides, it might ruin your appetite for dinner." I had taken the precaution to get out my staff on the way here. I looked at the rest of the kitchen workers, who were cowering in a corner. "I take it that the rest of you are going to cooperate. Our personal friend . . ." I paused and whispered to Indigo, "What's the name of that old pill of a grand mage?"

Indigo grinned as she realized what I was up to. "Storax," she whispered back.

I flicked a paw. "The Grand Mage, Storax, has personally promised to pay for anything used, and he says anyone who opposes us will be changed into a guppy."

Indigo leered wickedly at the chef. "And you'd make an awfully ugly guppy."

Letting the froglike creature rise, Indigo rattled off a quick series of commands. "But those are the rarest and costliest items in our larder," he objected.

Indigo lashed her tail, denting several giant vats. "Spoiling my appetite just might be worthwhile after all," she said, and clacked her fangs together. "Or maybe I'll wait until you're a guppy."

Terrified, he darted out of the kitchen, and the other servants weren't much slower. Indigo did a back flip over a pile of tureens. "The longer I stay in this body, the more I like it."

Before I could answer, Lady Francolin's grandson Thrush swam in. Bandaged and probably salved, he seemed stronger. "Her Highness said we were to follow your orders." There were about two dozen dragons, either young or elderly, with wounds that would keep them from the real fighting. From their sullen expressions, I guessed that they knew it and resented it.

"We'll need containers about this big." Indigo held her paws about two thirds of a meter apart. "Then we'll need to fill them with the animals that the servants will bring, and then we'll have to seal them somehow."

The dragons, though, did not move. "This isn't make-work, is it?" Thrush asked suspiciously.

"No. It's to make a sort of bomb for the human ships," Indigo said, and explained her plan.

Thrush and the others cheered up visibly at the idea and began to sort through the kitchen for containers the right size. As Indigo and I searched for something to seal the lids with, Thrush swam in with an armload of pots and dropped them with a loud clatter. Still floating upside down, he nodded at Indigo's spikes. "What sort of a dragon are you anyway?"

"I'm no dragon." Indigo shrugged. "I'm not anything." I could understand her not wanting to admit that she was human in this place.

A dragon's sense of territory is almost as strong as his pride. "Well, where do you come from then?"

I could see Indigo remembering the forest known as the Green Darkness and the disappointments she had met there. "No place," she finally said.

Thrush scratched his jowl. "No family. No home. Do you at least have a name?"

Indigo cocked her head suspiciously to the side.

164

"Indigo. Why?"

"Well, I think the clan has plenty of room for a clever person like yourself." And he winked at her.

"That's true," an elderly dragon grunted. She was carrying a huge vat into which she had piled a lot of smaller pots and jars. "We've lost enough of our own, heaven knows. And there'll certainly be enough work for all."

"Thank you." Indigo smiled sourly. "But it's a poor joke."

The elderly dragon was offended. "It's no joke, girl. Don't judge us by these Deep dragons. Oh, I'll admit we had our airs at one time, but we've had most of them beaten out of us over the centuries."

"Nowadays we judge creatures by what they can do"—Thrush spun upright—"and not by their pedigrees. So it's a lot harder to impress us."

The elderly dragon nodded her head. "But so far, dearie, you're doing just fine." With a pat to Indigo's foreleg, she churned away.

Indigo was speechless for a moment. "Thank you" was all she managed to say again—but this time I think she meant it.

"Don't thank me. I've just invited you to a life of long hours, low pay and short rations." Thrush ambled off in another direction. "I thought I saw some parchment and some membranes for cooking— though cooking *what* I can't imagine. Still, we might be able to seal up some things with them."

Looking very thoughtful, Indigo spiraled down

onto a table. "Strange, isn't it?" she said to me. "I mean, to start hoping when anyone with any sense knows that it's hopeless."

With a kick, I drifted up next to her. "Well, I could say things like, 'There's always hope.' But you'd just laugh at me."

Indigo glanced at me sardonically. "Very loudly, too."

"I thought so." Taking off my cap, I showed her the gold circlet on my skull. "Do you know the story behind this?"

When Indigo shook her head, her blue spikes rattled. "No."

I scratched my scalp in the center of the circlet. "Well, through a series of 'misunderstandings,' I was imprisoned under a mountain."

I couldn't fool Indigo though. "You mean you were caught for your crimes and punished."

"I prefer it my way," I said, and tapped the circlet. "And the Old Boy put this thing on my head to keep me from escaping. It shrank painfully when I didn't obey." I tugged at it. "I still can't get it off."

Curious, Indigo tried to shove it from my head and couldn't. "It's like it's glued into your skull."

I sighed. "I'll probably die wearing it. But the worst was being under the mountain."

Indigo looked around at the stone walls. "We're in a mountain now. How do you stand it?"

"Because I know I'll get out eventually." I circled

around her head leisurely. "I didn't know how, but someday I knew I'd get free. Just like a little seed under a stone. Somehow it finds a way to grow around that great weight. And sure enough, the Old Boy came back. 'I'm sorry, but you made me do it. Do you mind?' he asks. Of course, I can't answer because I've got a mountain on top of me. So he up and frees me. Never used the circlet, either."

Indigo blew out a stream of bubbles and watched them rise. "What about Civet and Thorn? They didn't have a way out."

"They did, if you think about it," I said. "But some choices are harder than others." At that moment the kitchen servants returned with the froglike creature. "Ah, your former comrades have returned. Who is that fellow, anyway?" I nodded to the froglike creature. "He looks properly cowed."

"He's the chef," Indigo explained. "He used to beat me the most. I still have a lot to pay him back for."

"Good," I approved. "I've sampled his cooking for the prisoners. While you're at it, give him a lick for me."

Shimmer's clan was properly disgusted by the "delicacies" that the court chose to eat. The chef, however, was distraught at seeing both his larder and his kitchen utensils disappear. To add insult to injury, Indigo had the chef himself help fill his precious pots. But even with all the utensils, we actually came up short.

"That fleet was pretty big," Indigo said, looking wistfully toward the huge vats into which the various snakes, worms and other things had been put temporarily. "I hate to leave those behind."

While the chef was on the verge of a breakdown, I looked around the kitchen, but everything of the proper size had already been used. "If Shimmer and the mages weren't so busy, we could ask them to make more jars."

"I wanted to do this on my own," Indigo said. Suddenly she spied a cabinet. "What's in there?"

"Just some old junk," the chef said, but I saw him glance uneasily toward it.

Indigo had seen that look as well. "Let's see that old junk," she ordered Thrush.

"No," the chef protested. But Thrush lunged toward the cabinet. With one pull of his powerful paw, he broke the lock and opened the doors. There, sitting in row upon row, were jars of blue-and-white porcelain.

Indigo frowned. "I know those jars. You beat me because you said I'd broken them. And when I said I hadn't, you beat me even more. But you stole them yourself. What were you going to do? Sell them?"

"I didn't know about these others," the chef insisted as he spread out his arms. "Then I was wrong. Rejoice. His Most Exalted Majesty's antiques have been found."

"Correction," Indigo said. "My antiques. I've paid for them with my bruises."

The chef made sad croaking noises as we filled the antique jars with the last of his delicacies. As the dragons led the servants off, Indigo hovered above the chef. "I had intended to knock you into next week," she said.

The miserable chef didn't even bother to raise his head. "Go ahead. You couldn't do anything worse than what you've done already."

Indigo held her claws right in front of his face so that he shrank back. "You're wrong. I could do far worse to you. And I will—if I hear any tales about you abusing any of the servants."

As we followed the others out of the kitchen, Indigo gave a smug wriggle from the tip of her snout to the tip of her tail. "I do *like* this body."

When we got outside, we found Shimmer surrounded by a hundred of the swimming wounded, all veterans like Sergeant Chukar. They were formed up in a big sphere so all could hear her, but we could see her in the center. "I'm going to leave the miners and the smiths in their original crews. They're used to working together. We'll see if they can fight together. The old are going to be one of my reserves. The young will form our scouts, but they aren't to go into battle themselves."

"They're our future," Sergeant Chukar agreed.

"Keep that in mind. We don't have time to drill, so I'm going to assign each of you to a group of civilians. You have your instructions, but I suspect you'll also have to improvise."

The sergeant grinned, and I saw several missing fangs. "You get used to improvising on the border."

"Then Heaven protect us all," Shimmer said. When she raised her paw, they swirled away to their various groups. Despite all her worries, she laughed when she saw us assigning the jars out among the young dragons. "Look at all those jars. Sambar is going to be on a diet."

"It might be a good thing," Sambar boomed. "I could barely fit into my armor." He drifted down from some upper palace terrace. Around him was a glittering array of generals with gold plaques and helmets. And following them was an escort of guards in shiny helmets with plumelike worms. Their gold-tipped claws had been replaced with practical steel, but they still wore the decorative plaques and chains in a magnificent show. As a group they made quite a contrast to Shimmer's shabby clan.

Sambar held up a paw to show the scarred steel tips on his claws. "These are from the armory. Some common soldier used them before this. So does that make me look even less like a king and more like a worm?"

If it were possible for a dragon to blush, I think Shimmer would have. "How did you know our nickname for you?"

Sambar chuckled. "I haven't been the High King this long without keeping my ears open. I know what you and your brother used to call me—and what you used to say."

"You look every meter the King right now," Shimmer said.

Sambar looked at the clan as it massed in groups that the veterans were trying to range into a ragged cubic formation. "Well, at the very least people will say that we knew how to die well."

"Let's save the noble speeches for when we feast in my banquet hall," Shimmer said, and held out a paw.

Sambar clasped it. "Done."

Letting go of the High King's paw, Shimmer rose with a kick toward her ragtag army. When she raised her paw, Bulbul began to beat an old drum. The sound boomed through the mountains and out across the seamounts. And cluster after cluster of her clan began to swim westward toward the Boneless King and their freedom.

CHAPTER SIXTEEN

With one mind, Shimmer's clan rose toward the surface. They had been kept deep under the sea all this time, so in a way it was like a small homecoming for them to see the sky once again. As for the young ones, you couldn't keep them still. Some of them had never been away from the forges, so they had only heard of flying. Now they could spread their wings and soar among the stars. And so for a moment the old veterans were helpless to keep order.

The Grand Mage, Storax, left the other mages and swam over to us, shaking his head. "And you want to take these children against the human fleet?"

The sea was still phosphorescent, so circles of light rippled outward when Shimmer ducked as a whooping youngster swept overhead. "Chukar," she shouted up to the sergeant, who herself was gliding overhead, "keep them in some order."

The one-winged Slug floated over to Shimmer. Pitching his voice low, he gently reminded her, "It won't hurt to let them have their moment of fun. This might be the only chance some of them will ever have to fly." Slug looked up wistfully, as if he wished he could be up there as well.

Shimmer cleared her throat. "Yes, of course."

The Grand Mage mumbled something about dragons being better behaved in his day, but he didn't complain anymore. However, I couldn't help thinking that it would be both tragic and ironic if a second group of children met their deaths in the Hundred Children.

Watching dragons, young and old, looping and coiling overhead, Indigo tentatively spread her wings. "I wonder . . ."

"Go on." Shimmer jerked her head skyward. "Try your wings again."

Rather self-consciously, Indigo spread her wings out fully. "Here goes nothing." With an awkward flap of her wings, she clumsily rose skyward, nearly knocking a fat little sea gull from the air.

"Watch it. Coming through. Excuse me," the sea gull puffed.

Slug immediately reached a paw up and snagged it neatly by its throat. "What are you doing here?"

The sea gull beat its wings feebly at the dragon's claws. "I'm on the Exalted's business, you fool. Let go." Twisting its beak, it appealed to Storax.

"It's me, Bombax."

Storax leaned forward to squint. "You were supposed to be back hours ago."

The sea gull sagged in Slug's grasp. "I got lost."

"You know this sea gull?" Slug demanded.

Storax's smile was a thin line. "Unfortunately. Change yourself back—if you remember how." And then the Grand Mage turned apologetically to Shimmer. "We sent a spy to see what the humans were up to, Your Highness."

"Let him go," Shimmer ordered.

When Slug had obediently set the sea gull down on the surface, it muttered something about "goons from the sticks." And then with a muttered spell, there was a little dragon floating in front of us. He seemed to be mostly smile and was more like a plump alligator than a dragon.

"Give your report to Her Highness," the Grand Mage ordered the little dragon.

Bombax hesitated and then shrugged. "As you wish, Master." I nearly fell from my seat in the sky when Bombax popped his left eyeball from his head. "It's only glass," he said, winking his good eye at me.

"Humph. Quit showing off," Storax ordered brusquely.

"As you wish, Master." Bombax threw the eyeball up into the air, where it hovered; and suddenly it was as if there were a round window in the air and we could see the glowing sea beneath us with whitecaps that burned like fire. I realized we were getting a gull's-eye view, so to speak.

Shimmer realized it too. "Slug, find Bulbul and Lady Francolin." She looked up into the sky as the sergeant was beginning to restore order. "Chukar, get down here. I want you to see this."

Leaving it to the other old soldiers to restore order, Sergeant Chukar descended from the night sky. She was moving stiffly, as if her wounds were still bothering her. A moment later Lady Francolin and Bulbul came sliding over the waves. They were panting as if they had been up in the sky flying with the youngsters as well. With them came Indigo and Thrush. Lady Francolin was eyeing Indigo's blue spikes rather dubiously.

"Watch this," Shimmer ordered.

Before us in the glass eye were the dark, shadowy shapes of the Children. Bombax's claws wriggled, and we seemed to zoom in on the Children. Long-legged golden alligators splashed in the water. "Those are transformed human marines," Shimmer explained.

They didn't seem to be suffering any ill effects from the sea. I supposed the chemicals in the living fire had burned out.

"The news gets worse," Bombax said. The galleys seemed to have withdrawn from the channel for the moment, and in their place were the round, tubby merchant ships that floated high up now as if they had been emptied of their loads. And all around their sides, like little four-legged bugs, scooted rowboats. Troops carried timber and supplies onto the various islands. And on the islands themselves had sprung up forests of wooden toadstools.

I leaned forward. "What are those?"

"Here." Bombax's claws fussed at the air and we zoomed in.

"Forts," Chukar grunted. "Prefabricated forts."

They were simple structures as such things went—like boxes some fifty meters on a side, with walls about three meters high. In the walls facing the dragon palace and the heart of the dragon kingdom were squarish openings through which catapults could shoot. There were some dozen or so forts planted on the islands facing the dragon palace. I couldn't help wondering if all the wood came from Indigo's forest, the Green Darkness.

Bulbul shook his head. "We can sink wooden ships, but how can we sink mountains?"

Finally I realized the full scope of the Butcher's plan—it had to be the Butcher, because the Boneless King would not have had time to make such preparations—and I had to nod my head in appreciation. "The humans have built a citadel right in the heart of the kingdom."

Chukar rubbed her chin thoughtfully. "He'll probably have the merchant ships withdraw and keep the galleys in the channel, where the forts can protect them. And the galleys can go out raiding when they need to."

I shook my head. This was going to be an even harder nut to crack. "Except now the humans have

Th— I mean the cauldron. They can sit tight and boil away the whole sea if they want."

"Where's the King?" Shimmer sounded worried.

"I think this must be his headquarters," Bombax added. "They seemed to be taking extra care with it."

Though the walls were prefabricated wood, the base was of stone. A wizard oversaw a squad of winged guardsmen who were plastering the sides. As quickly as they covered a section, the wizard dried it.

I pointed at a flag flying proudly over the fort. "See that standard? It has the golden dome and chrysanthemum of the King. He must be there."

Over the fort itself hung a net of ropes with thorns woven into them like a giant spider's web. That would keep any dragons from landing within the fort. Inside the fort itself, we could see, a dozen wizards worked on the wire framework of a giant bird.

"It's a flame bird," Shimmer said. "We've already run into one of those."

I studied it. "That's to force you dragons from the skies and into the range of the firebombs."

Off to the side was a pile of firewood over which a small crane had been mounted. The crane was away from the fire for the moment, but hanging from it was Thorn.

Facing eastward toward the dragon palace were a couple of catapults. The Boneless King, looking very satisfied with himself, stood upon a parapet with Snowgoose sitting on one side and the puppet wizard standing on the other. Pomfret sat on his haunches on the floor, his long neck letting him look out over the fort.

Suddenly Pomfret spun around as if sniffing the air, and then he seemed to point straight up at us. "At that point I thought I'd leave." Bombax made a pass with his claws, and the view disappeared. He plucked the floating eyeball neatly from the air and popped it back into its socket.

Overhead the old soldiers were slowly restoring order, but it was silent in Shimmer's little circle. She bobbed up and down among the waves for a moment and then looked around. "What do you think?"

As the only real professional, Chukar spoke first. "The defenses would take a terrible toll of real troops."

"You can't go to war with these babies." I nodded up at the giddy youngsters who were clustering in the sky like flocks of excited sparrows.

Shimmer shook her head grimly. "I have no choice."

"As Sergeant Chukar said, the young dragons are the future of the clan. But I am old, Your Highness, and I don't have many years left." Bulbul sounded apologetic. "Let me lead a company of the elderly. Perhaps they'll use up their firebombs on us."

Storax snapped, "It's all academic anyway while they have the cauldron."

I tipped my hat forward. "That's only because you don't know how to . . . um . . . 'borrow' something. Leave the cauldron to me."

"There's still the forts and the fleet," Lady Francolin said.

"They'll exact their price, that's true." Shimmer sighed. "But perhaps that's the price of freedom."

"Only if you pay it." Indigo glanced left and right. "Don't you see their mistake?"

"Their preparations looked pretty thorough." Chukar frowned.

Spreading her wings, Indigo flew high into the air to do a creditable back flip and then splashed back into the water, sending waves of bright fire spreading over the surface. "But their catapults aim only eastward."

Chukar splashed the glowing water joyfully. "They expect a frontal assault."

Shimmer patted Indigo. "You may have just saved the clan." As Indigo basked in her praise, Shimmer turned to the others. "I don't think we'll oblige them, will we? We'll swim around the Children and come at them from behind."

Chukar considered that. "It'll be a hard swim."

"It's for our freedom," Lady Francolin insisted. "We'll make it."

"And it could be risky if they discover us," Chukar pointed out. "We'll be coming between the mainland and the Children. They could send galleys against us with firebombs."

"Not if we provide them with a distraction." Shimmer pointed meaningfully at the dream pearl. "They expect us to come at them from the east. Let's oblige them—with an illusion."

"It would have to be on a large scale and projected to a great distance," Storax warned. "It could be dangerous to the one who casts such an illusion."

Lady Francolin, who in her better days had tutored Shimmer in history, corrected him. "Be careful what you call illusion. The pearl is the most ancient of the clan's treasures, given to us by Calambac, the first High King of the dragons. It is said that its magic is intertwined with the creation of the world, for Calambac went to the few First Ones remaining in this world."

"Who were a tricky lot," Storax observed.

"And this bit of magic was more whimsical than most," Lady Francolin explained. "There is a story, recorded in the oral tradition but not in the histories, that it was paid for in the oddest fashion. Calambac ordered all the dragons to bring every bit of gold— necklaces, plates, cups, nuggets—everything. And out of love for Calambac the dragons brought their treasure to the beach even though they were convinced they were about to lose it all. In fact, they say there was so much gold on the beach that it shone as bright as the sun.

"Then Calambac flew into the air and commanded them to clink the gold together. Although they were puzzled, all the assembled dragons obeyed—again out of love for the High King. And the sound, it was said, could be heard on the other side of the world.

"As the noise swelled around him, Calambac held

out his paw." Lady Francolin held out her own paw in illustration. "And the dream pearl appeared there. The sound of gold clinking was the payment. Sound for illusion."

"A very pretty story." Storax sniffed. "But I'm sure the First Ones demanded more tangible payment." With a well-practiced flick of his wrist, Storax produced a glowing globe of light in his upturned paw. "This comes from a transformation of water."

"My mother once said that for dreams one pays with shadows." Shimmer smiled sadly as she remembered, but recovered quickly. "But in any event I am willing to take the risk. I can't ask my people to do more than I am willing to. I'll send the illusion and then perhaps"—she bowed to Storax—"you'll indulge us with one of your fog banks."

In the past few moments Shimmer and her clan seemed to have risen in the Grand Mage's esteem. "It will be a fog to remember, Your Highness."

Thrush turned to Lady Francolin. "Grandmother, don't you think we owe a word of thanks to her?" He waved a paw at Indigo.

Lady Francolin inclined her head to Indigo. "You'll always be welcome in our home."

Thrush said, "If any of us live," but with the confidence of youth, he didn't sound as if he thought he would die.

Indigo tried hard not to seem pleased. "Don't jinx us."

"And if you don't like their hospitality," Bulbul

promised, "you'll always be welcome in my branch of the clan." He held up his claws. "Or they'll answer to me."

For once Indigo seemed to be at a loss for words, so Shimmer spoke up for her. "I think," she said, "that our young friend might have her own plans."

"Oh, I don't know," Indigo said slowly. "I could do a lot worse."

"What about the Green Darkness?" Shimmer asked.

"That's what I mean by worse," Indigo said.

"But you hate—" I caught myself before I said the word "dragons."

However, Indigo understood me. "This clan is different. They've been treated with the same etiquette book as I have."

"That we have," Shimmer agreed. "But no longer. Bulbul, beat the drum. Gather the clan. We'll make our plans as we move south."

CHAPTER SEVENTEEN

Considering the riot of flying dragons, Shimmer's clan got on the move rather quickly. Submerging beneath the water, they moved far underneath the luminescent plankton that might betray their route.

A worried Indigo swung over to me. "Shimmer won't tell me about the danger in using the dream pearl." And a friendly Thrush followed in her wake.

I glanced at Shimmer and the Grand Mage, who were intently refining the illusion with Lady Francolin, Bulbul and Sergeant Chukar. "I doubt if you're going to get a square answer out of any of them. But that Bombax seemed a decent sort."

"He went with the vanguard to show them what they would be up against," Thrush offered.

So together we darted through the water toward the vanguard. We passed over companies of miners trying to learn the manual of arms from the one-winged Slug as they swam, their long lancelike drills bobbing as they moved. The dragons from the undersea forges, their fore and hind legs bulging with muscles, also tried to learn how to maneuver. Even the reserves of the elderly—who would be commanded by Bulbul and Lady Francolin—were trying to swim in a tight formation.

As we neared the front, we could see young dragons, barely into their whiskers, floating just above the darkness as they acted as sentries. They were looking very determined and very scared. And as soon as one of them spotted me, he called for me to halt.

Panting, I trod water. "Glad to." The dragons were already setting a hard enough pace, and swimming up to the front like this had taken everything I had.

In the distance I could see Wort. He paddled over toward us stiffly, as if his wounds were bothering him. "All right. Close up with the others."

Two young dragons darted to either side of us so that we couldn't escape. As Wort wriggled over toward us, I grinned. "Very efficient."

Despite his stern expression, Wort seemed worried. "Hope you don't mind, sir. We're trying to drill as we march."

Now that the sentries were closer, they looked even younger. Staring at the young dragon on my right, I asked him, "How old are you?"

The young dragon glanced at Wort as if I had just asked for top secret information. "Go ahead," Wort said.

"Twenty, sir," the young dragon said. In dragon

years, that was barely being hatched from the egg. It was like going to war with infants.

I glanced at the old veteran, who gave a slight shake of his head as if he didn't like it any more than I did. "We'd like to speak to Bombax if you can spare him."

"That one?" Wort winked his one good eye. "Yes, he's through scaring the youngsters. Bring the apprentice mage here," he instructed one of our guards.

Full of the importance of her message, the little dragon went streaking off into the darkness. She returned a moment later with the pudgy Bombax.

With a salute to me, Wort shepherded his two charges away. I couldn't help studying the apprentice. "Most of the dragons I see are puffed up as big as whales. I don't often meet one your size—at least in the open."

Bombax waved a paw at his body. "My story is a sad one. I've tried every sort of spell, tonic and pill to grow bigger, but this is as large as I can get."

I had to scratch my head at that. "But I thought dragons could grow any size."

"My whole family runs small," he sighed.

I compared lengths to him. "Personally, I think you're just the right size. It's all the others who are bloated too big."

"What about the dream pearl?" Indigo rolled around us in her impatience.

"Pardon?" Bombax spun around to face her.

"What danger is it to the princess?" Thrush inquired.

185

Bombax nodded as he understood. "It gives power and it takes power. For a short time and on a small scale, the user would feel a minor discomfort."

"But to create the illusion of an army?" Indigo demanded.

Bombax was grave. "It could exhaust the user to the point of death."

Alarmed, Indigo stopped dead in the water. "Shimmer."

"As she says, she's only running the same risk as the rest of us," Thrush said.

"She's already risked enough," Indigo snapped. Swirling around abruptly, she darted back toward the princess.

Thrush looked at me, puzzled. "She acts as if she's the only one who loves the princess. But we all do."

Remembering the scene on the seamount, I said, "But you haven't centered your whole world around her." With a flip, I turned around and began to churn after Indigo. After a moment Thrush joined me.

After another five kilometers we turned west, entering the stormy region to the south of the Children. Deep under the sea it was still as calm as ever, but the scouts reported that the seas were choppy overhead. Making good time, we turned north to come around from behind the Children.

I hitched a ride with Indigo, who with her dragon eyes could see in the darkness. All around me I could feel the little currents created by hundreds of bodies swimming along and hear the clink of their claws or the rattle of their wings as they used those to help speed themselves along. In the distance came the sound of drilling as the veterans desperately tried to prepare their charges for the coming battle.

When it was time, we all gathered upon the top of a mountain some three hundred meters below the surface. Too far below the surface for the sunlight to penetrate, the barren mountain stood like a brooding symbol of ancient treachery.

Besides the mages I heard Lady Francolin and Bulbul, both as representatives of their branches of the clan. Indigo was there, of course, as was Thrush.

"Your Highness"—the Grand Mage coughed politely—"I feel I must warn you that there is some danger."

Shimmer had coiled herself about thirty meters away so she could concentrate. "Fiddlesticks," she sniffed. "My mother used to put on all sorts of wonderful pageants and things."

"She also died young," Lady Francolin reminded her.

"Some people use magic," Storax said solemnly, "and other people are used by it."

"Let me take a turn too." Indigo's tail made anxious swipes in the sea.

"That's right," I chimed in. "Don't hog all the glory."

"I've lost one friend already. I won't let that happen again." And saying that, Shimmer nodded to the Grand Mage, who nodded in turn to Bombax. Almost immediately, the little dragon cast a spell and a globe as big as me appeared. Under the globe's light, the barren mountaintop was illuminated. Overhead the waiting clan poised like a cloud of green daggers.

Shimmer looked at me and then at Indigo. "Civet knew when it was her time and so did Thorn. Now it's mine." She raised the fold of flesh upon her forehead.

Immediately, bright sheets of colored light spilled over the rocks, etching each of them with sharp edges. And when she eased the pearl from under the fold and onto her paws, the pearl began to grow brighter, flashing a glittering rainbow light all around the mountaintop.

As the pearl rested upon her paws, its iridescent sides seemed to flicker like hungry flames. "Your shadow!" Indigo gasped, and she drifted forward, but Thrush and I caught her.

Though our shadows were sharp, black silhouettes upon the rock, Shimmer's had become fluid, spreading and contracting like thick syrup.

Storax darted nervously back and forth over Shimmer's shadow as he studied it anxiously. "Your Highness, you may pay with more than a shadow. Some of your soul passes into the illusion too. And the greater the illusion, the more the pearl demands."

"That was the fate of your mother, poor creature." Lady Francolin clasped Bulbul's paw.

"She would do the same as I am," Shimmer insisted.

Sheets of colored light began to pour from the pearl as if someone were unrolling bolts of bright-colored silk. They rippled outward like veils behind a dancer.

I could still make out Indigo's features and those of the surrounding dragons; however, Shimmer herself began to blur.

When she gave a cry, Indigo called, "Let go of the pearl."

It was like watching a chalk drawing slowly dissolve in the rain, and from somewhere within that wavering outline, Shimmer said, "It's all right. I was just caught by surprise. It's never acted this way before—like a doorway opening."

"Or a hungry mouth," Storax said authoritatively.

"I'm fine," Shimmer insisted. "I've just never asked it to do so much before."

And as her own image began to fade, the pearl itself appeared as a small, shining globe. Indigo clutched at my arm. "The pearl! I can see Shimmer."

Fascinated, I nodded my head, because I too could see the pictures appear on the pearl. Though it was small, every detail was distinct enough to make out. We were all there on the surface of a moonlit sea, moving westward toward the Children.

Shimmer was in jewels and gold, and the dream pearl shone from her forehead. Indigo, still a dragon, swam in armor of blue lacquer edged with rubies, and there was a helmet of blue spikes.

Despite everything the artist in me couldn't help murmuring appreciatively, "A nice touch. I didn't know the old gal had in it her."

"And there you are." Indigo pointed excitedly.

To my relief, I saw that I was in a clean robe and tiger skin, my staff whirling over my head so the gold rings formed a blurred circle.

Sergeant Chukar slid easily over the billowing waves, but now, hanging from a necklace across her chest were the golden concentric rings of a general. "Thank you for the promotion," she said, chuckling.

Two elegant dragons followed, heads raised haughtily, their scales edged in gold. "Oh, Bulbul." Lady Francolin clung to the other dragon. "We're young again."

"And you're as beautiful as I remember," Bulbul murmured.

"But is this what she's imagining, or are we seeing what's happening?" Indigo asked.

On the pearl could be made out black smudges on the twilit horizon—they must have been the Hundred Children. "It's what's happening, I think."

"Now for the real test," the shadowy real Shimmer announced, and raised her other paw to the pearl.

And we saw within the pearl a vast, glittering army of dragons, forming ranks upon the sea behind the image of Shimmer. And even more fell into lines up in the sky. However, the more illusions she brought to life, the less real Shimmer herself became. Though it was easy enough to see the pearl and its images, Shimmer was even more blurred.

"That's enough illusions, Your Highness," Lady

Francolin begged.

It took Shimmer several tries before she could speak. "No . . . must make them . . . think the whole army . . . is in front." Shimmer's voice shook with the strain. She could be hard on everyone else at times, but no harder than she was on herself.

"Stop it!" Indigo shot past us and between the surprised mages. She swirled around her friend in a frantic circle.

Shimmer turned to her because she was the closest. "Help me," Shimmer pleaded hoarsely. "Can't hold . . . up . . . pearl."

"No, I won't help kill you." Indigo kept her paws resolutely at her sides. "You've got no right to ask me to do that."

I started forward immediately, as did Sergeant Chukar and Lady Francolin, but the Grand Mage stopped us. "We don't dare distract Her Highness."

"If she drops the pearl," I argued, "she'll break the illusion." And with the shattering of the illusion, all our plans would be ruined and perhaps the clan with them. However, we stayed where we were.

And somehow Shimmer managed to hold on to the pearl. "The clan," Shimmer groaned. "Must protect them." But as the pearl blazed even brighter, Shimmer's shadow seemed to flow like water into the pearl itself.

"Look at her shadow," Indigo gasped, horrified.

"It's her soul," Storax intoned softly.

Indigo whirled around, pleading tearfully with the

rest of us. "Make her stop." But, when we were silent, Indigo turned back toward Shimmer—who now seemed to be more pearl than dragon. "If no one else will, then I'll do it."

Lady Francolin shook her head. "It was her choice. She is doing what she must—as soon all of us will."

"Help . . . Indigo." The pain was etched in Shimmer's voice. "Can't hold . . . much longer."

Poor Indigo. Shimmer was, after all, the only creature she had ever really loved. Lips quivering, Indigo waved for me to come over. "Monkey, you do it."

I darted under Storax. Too late his paws closed over the spot where I had been. However, as I started to swim toward them, a ghostly Shimmer begged, "Help me now. If you love me, help me."

Indigo wagged her head sorrowfully. "I can't."

"Hurry," Shimmer moaned in a voice that was barely a whisper, and started to drop the pearl.

I was still just a little too far away. "Indigo," I called desperately, "remember what Shimmer said back in the throne room about the pearl. Her life is her own to keep or surrender."

The last thing Indigo would have done was to help kill Shimmer. Yet she also knew how much Shimmer wanted to save her clan. It was only a moment of hesitation, but it seemed to take an eternity. In that moment, Indigo made her decision—not for what she wanted but for what she knew Shimmer wanted.

Raising her paw, Indigo found the outline of Shimmer's forepaws to help maintain that critical illusion.

In that instant she crossed some line in her own mind from being the smartest of people to being one of the most foolish—and perhaps one of the noblest. "This is wrong—all wrong," she murmured over and over.

Swimming up beside them, I held up my paws. "Let me take over."

"No," Indigo said quietly, "she asked me." Even so, she began to sob as Shimmer's outline blurred even more. "But I feel like I'm stabbing her right in the heart."

I hovered nearby, ready to take over. "It would have hurt her worse if you had let her fail."

Face to face with Shimmer's pain, she winced as if she shared the agony of her friend. "That's what I keep telling myself."

From the Children a black object rose into the moonlight and landed in the sea well in front of the illusions. I figured it was one of the catapults, but Shimmer had wisely stopped out of range. Even as I watched, fire rose from the sea, blossoming like a strange, terrible flower.

Shimmer writhed now as if she were lying on a bed of coals, and she was gasping irregularly. "We've got their attention." I nodded to the Grand Mage. "Raise your fog so we can stop the illusion."

Storax passed the order on to the other mages, concentrating instead upon the princess. Within the pearl, the great gray fog bank rose around the make-believe army.

"Let go," I said to Indigo.

Relieved, Indigo released Shimmer's paws, and they fell away from the pearl. But the jewel merely floated there; and though Shimmer's great body sagged, the pearl seemed to hold it suspended in the water.

"We must break the spell." Storax joined Indigo and me as we tried to pull her away, but tug and shove as hard as we could, we could not budge her.

"It's as if she's glued there," Storax admitted.

"It's out of control." Bravely, Indigo tried to grasp the pearl herself, but an invisible hand tossed her down onto the mountaintop.

I helped her up. "It's one soul at a time, I guess."

"Or maybe it's saving us for dessert." She closed her claws into a fist. "We'll have to destroy it somehow."

I stopped her. "Let it be on my head. Sambar's already mad enough at me anyway." Taking my staff from behind my ear, I shouted, "Change!" As the rod stretched itself out, I twirled it for what might be the final time.

"Hurry." Indigo had put a paw to her mouth as Shimmer began to twist and churn.

Swinging my staff above my head, I brought it down with all my strength upon the pearl. The golden ring, though, just seemed to bounce off the round sides, and my own arms ached as if I had just tried to knock down a mountain. And then the shining globe broke like glass. As it shattered into a thousand pieces, there was a faint musical sound that I couldn't place at first—until I realized that it was a metallic clinking, ringing sound coming from over a great distance of time and space. As the fragments of the pearl simply vanished, the sound rose higher and higher in pitch until it had become a merry tinkling—almost like laughter.

Shimmer collapsed.

CHAPTER EIGHTEEN

Indigo curled next to Shimmer. Taking one limp ankle, she looked up at us. "She's still alive."

Storax had taken another ankle. "But barely."

I shrank my staff and stored it away. "You take care of her. I have a few favors to pay back."

"Remember," Indigo called to me, "once you find Thorn, you only need to hold the fleet."

Lady Francolin and Bulbul swam away at the same time as I did, and we three stopped at the companies of elderly dragons who were to form the reserve. "We heard the princess was dead," one dragon said.

"No, just unconscious," Lady Francolin said.

As I sped through the ranks of miners with their drills, I found that the rumor had also spread among them that the princess was dead. They were mourning Shimmer and vowing vengeance.

Slug was still in charge of them, and I paused long enough to tell him that she was still alive. "Then where is she?" Slug demanded, rattling a lancelike drill at me.

"Back on a mountaintop," I said. "She's resting."

"She's near death," Slug announced to the others.

If I'd had the time, I might have argued some sense into them, but I didn't, so I went on. The companies of smiths had already worked themselves into a frenzy of grief—I didn't even bother trying to correct them.

In front of them was a company of the few remaining healthy warriors, who had transformed themselves into long-legged, golden alligators. Instead of sharing the others' nervous anticipation, they were almost fatalistically grim.

Near the surface I found the companies of youngsters, each with several pots from Sambar's larder. They were sobbing openly over Shimmer. I slowed long enough to call over to Sergeant Chukar, "She's not dead. She's resting. Spread the word."

"I'll do what I can." The sergeant looked around ruefully. "But I'll have my hands full here trying to hold the children back."

"Give me until sunrise, just like we planned," I insisted, and swam on beyond the clan.

They had stopped about a kilometer from the sad, haunted mountains of the Children. When I was within a hundred meters, I saw the great wooden ovals overhead. The plankton had begun to settle lower, but there was still enough to make faint phosphorescent rings around the hulls. Old Gruesome had believed Shimmer's deception and sent the nonwarships to what he thought was the rear.

Changing myself into a rather handsome fish, I wriggled among them. Within the channel were the long, slender ovals that marked the hulls of the war galleys, ready to dash out in pursuit when the dragons had smashed themselves against the forts. The ships were arranged in a formation of two columns.

As I neared the mouth of the channel, I saw the alligator marines waiting on ledges or crouched in holes, waiting to defend the channel. I was sure they were scattered around the Children, ready to warn of an undersea assault.

Suddenly one golden-scaled head swung toward me, and a pair of yellowish eyes regarded me. I found myself wishing that I was in a shape that could use a staff. Fortunately, he didn't seem to find the idea of raw fish appetizing. When he had pulled back into his hole, I risked raising my head out of the water.

In the dying moonlight, I could make out the fort with the flag. As I peered out, I saw a soldier, leaning forward to counterbalance the weight of his new wings, coming down to the channel with a bucket in his hand. From within the fort smoke rose, as if the Boneless King were preparing to boil water in Thorn.

With a lash of my tail I shot across the channel to the spot where the soldier was heading. Ahead of me I could see the bucket in the water held by what seemed like disembodied hands.

Beating my fins and wriggling my tail, I managed to get up a dragonlike speed. Just as the bucket started to lift out of the water, I leapt. And as I slipped into the bucket, I muttered a spell.

"What?" the guardsman said from up above me, and peered into the bucket. But by then I had changed into water myself. "I'll be glad when we're away from here." He shivered. "This is the queerest campaign."

I rode the bucket right inside the fort. While the wizards put the finishing touches upon the wire frame of the flame bird, the Boneless King, Pomfret, Snowgoose, and the King's puppet wizard were supervising the fire. Thorn hung on the little crane off to one side.

The Boneless King turned to the admiral next to him. "Signal the guard in the sea to come out."

"But it isn't sunrise yet, Your Highness," Pomfret protested.

Ignoring Pomfret, the Boneless King simply gave the admiral a look. Nervously, he pivoted and nodded to a drummer, who began beating against a drum that hung on the wall. The vibrations passed through the fort and into the rock itself. Outside, there were loud splashing sounds as the alligator guardsmen rose from the water.

One of the sentries on the wall called out, "They're signaling that they're all clear."

The Boneless King held out his hand. "Then let's

give those lizards another taste of what it's like to be lobsters boiling in the pot."

The guardsman passed the bucket to the Boneless King, who poured me into Thorn. I felt Thorn tingle all around me in welcome as the Boneless King raised a boot and swung Thorn over the fire with his foot.

"Change!" I shouted, returning to my regular shape. As the startled King stared at me, I grinned. "Strange weather we're having, aren't we?" And with my paw on his face, I shoved him onto his backside. The next moment I had my staff out from behind my ear. "Change!" I yelled.

With my trusty weapon in one paw I picked up Thorn in the other. It took a tap here and there to teach Pomfret and the guard some manners. "Sorry we can't stay, but we just remembered we have to be at a barbecue." And I leapt upward, somersaulting toward the net.

"Stop him," the Boneless King bellowed.

I swung my staff at the net, but much to my consternation my staff merely bounced off the ropes. The homemade net was a little too loose to snap easily. For a moment I wasn't sure what to do, because though I could shrink myself small enough to slide through the spaces between the ropes, there wasn't enough room for Thorn.

Right then, beneath me, there came a loud flapping noise, and I looked down to see guardsmen rising unsteadily toward me with swords. Apparently, they had not had much time to practice with their new wings. In fact, they reminded me so much of a flock of drunken pigeons that I had to laugh despite everything. But their swords were no joke. I ducked and dodged vicious cuts, skittering like a fly on a window. Fortunately the only damage they did was to the net.

As the net sagged downward, I slipped through the hole and hovered above them. "Thank you, gentlemen."

Even as I took a mock bow, the wizards below were crying out, "'Ware, above!"

When I saw the guardsmen dropping to the ground, I decided to start somersaulting away. But before I could, there was the stink of sulfur and a strange wind sucking me into the fort, where the wire frame now blazed.

As I righted myself, fire clothed the frame like red and yellow feathers, and the bird's head blinked its eyes and swung up to glare at me. As I desperately climbed out of the fort again, the flame bird rose after me.

I had the presence of mind to move toward the fog bank as if toward the dragon army. Behind me the flame bird burst through the net, and the fire spread from the burning edges rapidly across the entire net. "Quick, get another net up," the Boneless King was shouting at his men.

I had been planning to head for the water anyway because the Boneless King had a neat little spell that could take away the power of flight—at least as long as he could see you. When I plunged into the sea, I felt a blast of heat as if from an open furnace door, and there was a little nip at my tail.

As I floated just beneath the surface, the flame bird looked like a glowing ball disappearing into the sky. Since I was sure I would be safe for a moment, I checked behind me and saw that the tip of my magnificent tail was singed. What the snout is to a dragon, the tail is to a monkey. "That overdone chicken needs a lesson," I muttered to myself. Besides, I didn't want that overgrown firefly roaring unannounced right into the middle of Shimmer's clan.

At that moment my obnoxious friend Pomfret plunged into the water after me. Well, they say that if you can't beat them, join them. I swam back to the island while the flame bird circled overhead, red light reflecting over the water. Shrinking my staff, I tucked it away while Pomfret churned toward me like an angry whale.

"Finders keepers," I said, and with a silent apology to Thorn, I let him go.

"You stupid ape!" Pomfret dove with outstretched paws to intercept Thorn.

While my chum was occupied, I gave a shiver and muttered a spell. And in the next instant, I had joined the ranks of the green and scaly. I just hoped no one reputable saw me, or I would never live it down.

And then the next moment, I had popped to the surface, waving a paw. "Help, help! This monkey is too fierce for me."

The Boneless King waved to me angrily from the parapet. "Then get back here, Pomfret."

Spreading my wings, I began to flap back toward

the island. Guardsmen were busy restringing the net from both above and below. Stretching out my long neck through one of the openings for the catapult, I said to the Boneless King, "He was changing his shape as I was leaving."

The Boneless King leaned through the opening to stare. "What was it?"

I hung my head sheepishly. "I don't know. I was too busy retreating."

"You mean running away." The King snorted in disgust. "Well, he'll still have the cauldron."

Horns blew and drums beat in a regular din from within the fort. Soon company after company of alligator guardsmen swam out of the channel to pursue, and even a squadron of galleys rowed out in pursuit. And overhead, the flame bird kept patrolling. Every now and then as it passed overhead, I could feel a hot breeze blow down over us.

Pomfret suddenly surfaced, holding Thorn triumphantly over his head. "I've got the cauldron."

I jabbed a claw at him excitedly. "That's him. That's Monkey. The nerve of him! He's taken my shape to try to fool you."

Pomfret bobbed up and down in the water as he squinted at me. "Is that . . . me?"

"Kill him," the Boneless King ordered.

Marines on the galleys began to shoot their crossbows, and bolts began to splash all around the indignant dragon. Outraged, he shook Thorn at them. "*I'm* Pomfret, you idiots. *He's* Monkey. He's taken my shape."

I settled back against the wall to enjoy the spectacle. "Oh, come now. You don't expect to fool clever
fellows like these with a story like that. If I'm Monkey,
why am I sitting here and why are you out there with
the cauldron?"

Pomfret had as much of a sense of humor as his sister—that is, none at all. "Because you threw it away."
Almost the moment he said it, he knew how silly he
sounded.

The Boneless King was pounding his fists on the
wall. "I don't care how you do it: Just bring me the
cauldron."

As the fleet bore down upon him, Pomfret lost
his nerve. "Wait, wait, I can explain." Spreading his
wings, he flapped into the air.

The wizards pointed at Pomfret, and the flame bird
swooped down at him. As the flame bird and the fleet
converged upon him, Pomfret realized his mistake.
He tried to duck under but surfaced almost immediately as golden alligators surrounded him.

Spreading my wings, I bowed to the King. "Your
Highness, if you'll tell the wizards to pull out the
flame bird, I think that fool will be ready to surrender
himself and the cauldron."

"Once the flame bird is out, it's done. And we have
no more," the chief wizard informed the King.

"While I would gladly see the end of a brave and
clever opponent like Monkey, the flame bird could
also burn up the cauldron," I pointed out.

"Then you'd better—" Suddenly the Boneless King
stared at me over the parapet. "What's that singe

mark on your tail? You didn't have it before you left the fort."

Drat! I hadn't had time to check my disguise before I'd left the sea. "I must've gotten this in the fight."

"How?" the King demanded suspiciously.

"Uh . . . let me show you." With a flap of my wings, I rose into the air straight for Pomfret.

With the flame bird sweeping down on him and twin attacks from the surface and from below, Pomfret took to the air. "Wait, wait. I can explain," he cried again.

To tell the truth, he wasn't a bad flier. In fact, he was almost as good as his sister. Darting and twisting to avoid the crossbow bolts and bombs, he raced right over the squadron of galleys.

However, his momentum carried him straight over the channel, where the rest of the fleet still waited. And then it worked out better than I could have hoped, for the flame bird, still pursuing Pomfret, tried to skim right through the midst of the ships.

One fiery wing caught on a mast of the lead ship and there was a screeching of metal as the wing tore from the body, setting the head of the column of ships on fire. Still flapping one wing, the flame bird went tumbling over and over and smashed into another galley. Fortunately for the humans, it was close to shore, so its crew could leap onto the land or even use makeshift plank bridges before the flames engulfed the ship.

At the same time the galleys at the rear of the channel began to unship their oars and try to back up.

There was already the crunch of sterns hitting beaked prows and the clattering of oars getting tangled up with one another until most of the war fleet was hopelessly jammed in the channel.

Then the firebombs on board the burning galleys began to explode, spewing sheets of flame onto neighboring ships and into the channel, where the streamers drifted like deadly snakes toward the other ships.

We were out of sight of the Boneless King, so I felt it was safe to slow down. Pomfret was hovering in a daze and gazing down at the disaster he had created.

I think the sailors were just as unnerved as the dragons by a chemical fire they didn't know how to extinguish. "The flames are spreading," a captain shouted from one of the galleys. "Abandon ship." Gongs and drums began to beat on the other warships.

Instantly crews throughout the channel began to jump onto the surrounding island. Others swung from the mast ropes. The amphibious guardsmen had panicked at the alarm as well and were joining the ones on the shore.

Because they were in two columns, every ship was within easy reach of shore, so the galleys were empty in no time at all. By then the ships surrounding the original victims had begun to burn fiercely. As their load of firebombs went off, living fire spread down the channel.

Well, you know what they say: If you can't join

them, beat them. Changing myself back into a handsome, furry shape, I soared up and took my staff from behind my ear. Changing it to weapon size, I tumbled down through the air. "You know," I said, laughing, to Pomfret, "If I were you, I wouldn't expect a birthday gift from the King."

"You! You're the cause of it all." As the renegade dragon swung his head up to glare at me, I brought my staff down with a clunk on his thick dragon skull. His eyes rolled a moment and then his wings stopped. Leaning over, I stretched out a paw and snagged Thorn just before Pomfret fell unconscious out of the sky.

He made a rather big splash in a patch of clear water in the rear of the fleet where the ships had not yet caught fire. I dove after him. I would have preferred flying to swimming, but I didn't want anyone to see the direction in which I was heading.

I didn't see Pomfret, but it was pretty dark in the channel. Up above, the ships were so jammed together that it looked like market day in the city. And I could see the brilliant light from the spreading flames behind me. All in all, it hadn't been a bad night's work.

"Now," I said to Thorn, "to bring you back to some old friends. You're just the medicine one of them needs."

And in my paw I thought I felt an answering tingle.

CHAPTER NINETEEN

Beyond the channel, the rising sun was just beginning to fill the upper waters with a ruddy light. I would have estimated the rear third of the war galleys had managed to back out of the channel among the merchant ships.

Even as I emerged, I saw the dragons, disguised as long-legged alligators, rising like shadows. "The Sea!" I whispered the clan's war cry.

"The Sea!" Slug whispered back to me. He eyed the cauldron and raised a triumphant fist.

"Careful, the channel's on fire," I warned with a wink that let him know I had had something to do with it.

"Tell the others to be careful." Slug flashed a toothy smile.

As the others surged by, they nodded approvingly when they saw I had Thorn. If all went well, they would mix with the transformed humans, infiltrate the forts and disable what bombs they could. Now that things were so confused behind me, I had more faith in the success of their mission.

I found Sergeant Chukar waiting with her young, excited charges. Beneath them were the miners and smiths. I darted over to her. "Most of the ships in the channel are already disabled." I nodded behind me. "The others are in confusion." I added, "I wouldn't bother with the merchant ships. You'll need something to ship the prisoners back in."

"Think so?" Sergeant Chukar gave some quick orders to a young dragon, who swam off smartly.

"How's the princess?" I asked, cradling Thorn.

"Still no better," Sergeant Chukar said, "but still no worse."

"She's too tough to die," I assured the Sergeant, hoping that it was true.

Wort led the miners and smiths surging past like a dark, menacing river beneath us. "So are we," the sergeant said. She dropped below to give some last-minute orders to the warriors leading those companies; then she quickly rose to keep order among her young charges.

I should have gone on, but I couldn't help lingering long enough to watch the companies split into teams, each team heading for the dark oval of a war galley. Heads bent, necks stretched in streamlined profile, they kicked their legs and wriggled their tails as they built up a reckless speed.

The miners led the charge, long iron drill-bit lances thudding into the war galleys' hulls. Though the galleys' hulls were of stout oak timbers, oak was nothing to muscles used to drilling through hard rock at the crushing pressures on the seafloor. The points bit deep into the wood, and the partners came up with heavy hammers to pound the drills all the way through.

At the same time the smiths, with their heavy hammers, swept past to pound at the weakened hulls. Others turned sharply, swimming in straight lines parallel to the banks of oars that rested in the water. They stretched out their hammers like children drawing sticks across fences. However, these were no human children but dragons used to pounding steel over volcanic fires. The paddles snapped like matchsticks as the dragons swept by.

Galleys were already beginning to take on water as I turned. "I'll be back as soon as I can."

Below, I found the elderly dragons as impatient as the children, and Bulbul was almost sulking. "I didn't get a chance to beat the drum," he said.

"It was an oversight," I assured him.

I left all of them a good deal cheered that I had regained Thorn. Indigo and the mages were still on the mountaintop, their watchful faces illuminated by the light of several globes.

"How is she?" I asked.

The Grand Mage, Storax, might be pompous and

patronizing at times, but he was a conscientious doctor. He was checking Shimmer's pulse. When he was finished, he barely glanced at me. "Her heartbeat has steadied. It's almost normal now."

Indigo gave a joyful cry when she saw Thorn in my paws. "You got him."

I set it down beside the unconscious Shimmer. "This should cheer her up when she wakes."

Indigo fretfully caressed Shimmer's forehead. "She might even forgive a few of your crimes."

"It'd be a shame if she did. We wouldn't know what to talk about." With a kick, I sprang up from the seamount. "I'll be back."

By the time I returned to the battle, the sea overhead was filled with the churning legs of the marines, rowers and sailors; and the galleys were sinking slowly into the dark depths, trailing long chains of silver bubbles. What few galleys remained were being destroyed by swarms of gleeful miners and smiths. Deciding to lend a hand, I swam up and began tapping at the hull of a galley with my staff. But I didn't have nearly the muscle or the mass of the dragon miners, so I barely stove in a plank.

Hearing the noise, Slug swam around beneath the hull and saw me. He saluted me with his drill. "Begging your pardon, sir, but the ship's already sinking." He nodded to the other side, where the hole must be.

"I . . . uh . . . knew that," I said, pretending to tap on the hull. "I was just curious about the wood. It's oak, I think."

"I wouldn't know, sir," Slug said politely. "I've

never even seen a tree."

There was a splash overhead, and a captain, still in armor, began to sink through the water. Slug neatly snagged the struggling human by an ankle and held him upside down until he could free himself from his armor. Then with a playful poke with his drill, Slug sent the captain back to the surface. "You might tell the sergeant that this job is just about finished."

As I swam back through the water, I could dimly hear the crews of the merchant ships desperately shouting that they wanted to surrender. I couldn't say that I blamed them. The thought of treading water in a sea of angry dragons would panic me, too.

I found the unflappable sergeant sending a message to Lady Francolin's company. "Ask her ladyship if she would please take the surrender of the transports and round up the crews from the sea."

Bulbul had joined the sergeant by then. "Now?"

"No, not yet." Chukar was glad when she saw me. "Sir, if you wouldn't mind reporting to me about the progress of the saboteurs?"

I tipped my cap to the sergeant. "Glad to help."

Rising from the water, I flew over the channel filled with burning ships. It looked like a candlelit blue rug. I was glad to note that all the crews seemed to have made it to shore, where they were still milling around on the barren volcanic rock and looking very lost. Some of the officers were trying to organize those with weapons into some kind of unit. But almost all of them looked as if they wished they were back home.

I was just in time to see the first dragon saboteur slip out of the catapult port in one wall. He hadn't bothered to transform himself back into a dragon but had simply grown wings upon his back. In his paws he had one of the firebombs. Crouching upon the parapet, he threw it behind him and soared into the air.

Flames instantly sprang up behind him. "The Sea! The Sea!" he shouted, as he rose into the air out of crossbow range. As smoke rose in a column, other dragons sprang into action. Another column of smoke serpentined upward in answer, then a third and a fourth. Soon, all told, there were six forts burning by the time the dragons gathered in the sky.

Of course the remaining six forts were thrown into chaos. The transformed guardsmen immediately were suspected of being dragons, and if their hides hadn't been so tough, they might easily have been killed before they could provide their credentials. As it was, I was sure they would have bruises the next day.

Somersaulting as fast as I could, I dove into the sea. "The humans look a bit peckish. I think it's time to serve their dinner," I said to the sergeant.

"Now?" Bulbul asked, as impatient as the children around him.

"Not yet, sir." The sergeant held up a claw while she looked at the twitching youngsters. "Now remember, you're to charge when you hear the drum and return when you hear the drumbeat a second time."

Bulbul nudged Sergeant Chukar. "Now?"

213

The sergeant nodded her head. "If you please, sir."

With a twirl of his drumstick, Bulbul began to beat the big drum. It was hide stretched over a hoop that he held in his other paw. Chukar and her youngsters exploded from the sea in white columns of spray. "The Sea! The Sea!" In their paws they held the vases with various living delicacies from Sambar's larder.

As the excited youngsters swept by, I was tumbled this way and that until I snagged the tail of the exuberant Thrush and held on for dear life as we whipped upward into the sky. Once in the air I was able to catch up with the leading youngsters, who for all their energy still flew raggedly.

Then, with a backbone-cracking set of somersaults, I pulled ahead of the racing dragons. Somehow I managed to find the wind to shout as I somersaulted over the line of forts, "Vipers, poisonous serpents. Beware."

In the air the saboteurs, who had changed themselves back into dragon shapes, began to take up the cry. Water still dripping from their legs and their wings, the youngsters swept low over the forts. The antique vases went right through the spaces between the nets, and the larger jars broke on the ropes, showering everyone beneath with snakes, eels, worms and other repulsive creatures from Sambar's gourmet diet.

The results were quite satisfying. The remaining garrisons, still fighting among themselves, were caught by surprise. I couldn't resist taking a peek into the main fort, and though I didn't see any sign of the Boneless King, I did see General Winter still decked out in his splendid armor as he harangued his troops to quit fighting and form ranks, saying that the creatures were harmless and that this was all just a ruse of the dragons.

"Over here," I called, and pointed toward the general. "Here."

Chukar herself swept in with a squad of youngsters. Before any humans could shoot a crossbow bolt, jars rained down upon General Winter. Because he was in full armor, I don't think he was hurt, but the jars smashing against him made a frightful noise—enough bongs and clongs to make a miniature thunderstorm.

I don't know how these particular tidbits should have been served, but they looked like bright orange-and-purple feathered boas wreathing the general. They began to ooze and crawl all over him. It's one thing to suspect some frilly worm is harmless; it's quite another to have it crawling under your armor. He stood there for a moment, stiff as a statue, and then as one frilly worm raised its head curiously to stare at the general's face—or perhaps it was the worm's other end—he began to scream, high and shrill as a teakettle.

I grinned over at Sergeant Chukar. "Ah, a gourmet." And I began shouting down, "I hope you like being poisoned," twitching and making graphic faces and sounds as if I were dying of poison.

As various horrible little monsters rained down on them, the garrison broke, elbowing and jostling one another to exit through the door or over the walls as if the last one out were going to be the Old Dragon. In the meantime the general stood there, quivering and screaming, "Save me! Save me!"

Having paid him back for past wrongs, I ripped the banner from the fort and then perched on top of the flagpole.

The saboteurs dropped down to join us and to help guide the youngsters' air raids. "The Sea! The Sea!" the dragons began shouting triumphantly.

The capture of the King's headquarters was the last straw for the remaining forts, already demoralized by the loss of their fleet. As all the horrors of Sambar's larder twitched around them, they also began abandoning the stronghold. Even the one squadron of galleys that had been maneuvered in front of the Children had run up a white flag.

Bulbul had somehow managed to keep pace with the sergeant. Watching the whooping youngsters cavorting in the air, the sergeant turned to Bulbul. "If you please, sir."

At Bulbul's signal, Chukar and the veterans began rounding up the youngsters and herding them back into the sea before they could receive serious injury. As it was, I saw some dragons flying awkwardly because of wounds in their wings, and others were holding their paws as if they had taken crossbow bolts.

I didn't go with them but stayed to watch the fun. No one shot at me as I sat in the air—who cares about a small monkey when there's a host of dragons about to trample you, or is it a flock of dragons? Outside the fort, officers ran back and forth, trying to form the confused troops and galley crews into squares out in the open on the islands. In the middle of them, I saw, were Lieutenant Crusher, Tubs and Slowfoot, who had found arms again. However, as soldiers tried to rally, the dragons returned.

Chukar and her veterans led the miners and smiths. And not too far behind them, Bulbul was beating his drum as if he were two hundred years younger. They skimmed in low over the islands, filling the air with the roar of their wings. The sound was so loud that it felt almost tangible—as if the sound could sweep away the waiting humans.

"Steady, steady," Lieutenant Crusher was saying. "Shoot when I order."

Right then Slowfoot pointed a shaking finger at the miners' drills cradled in the dragons' claws. "They've got lances. They'll skewer us like so many cherries."

At that moment Sergeant Chukar called ahead in a voice that had been developed on many a parade ground. "Surrender, and you'll be returned to the mainland."

Sitting crosslegged in the air, I urged, "Go on. You'll find the dragons kinder to you than you would have been to them."

"The Sea! The Sea!" the dragons began to cry until

217

it was a regular avalanche of sound. They were so loud that I barely heard the clang of Slowfoot throwing down his sword.

"Pick that up," Lieutenant Crusher ordered.

"What are we doing here?" Slowfoot argued. "The sea belongs to the dragons, not to us."

"Tubs, arrest that idiot," Lieutenant Crusher ordered.

Corporal Tubs hesitated, glancing up at the onrushing wave of dragons, and then he threw down his sword as well. "Our fleet's destroyed. Our forts are gone. And where are all our super weapons now?" All around them the demoralized humans began dropping swords, spears and crossbows.

"The Sea! The Sea!" The dragons swept in so low that the soldiers threw themselves flat upon the barren rocks. Wave after wave of dragons rumbled over them, creating a huge wind in their wake. When they had passed, the humans rose shakily to their knees.

As the dragons looped and began to return, Sergeant Chukar called again, "Do you surrender?"

Lieutenant Crusher stood there for a moment and then flung his own sword down.

Hovering over the Children, the dragons repeated Sergeant Chukar's demands. Here and there a defiant crossbow twanged, but it was easy to knock some sense into a human soldier. And from all over the Children came the clanging of weapons falling on the volcanic rock.

I supposed once the minstrels got through with the battle of the Hundred Children, it would be called a great and relatively bloodless victory, and perhaps Sergeant Chukar and I would even have time to enjoy it then. But right at that moment, we had thousands of humans pleading to surrender. Distracted by all the little details of our sudden victory, I felt less like a victorious warrior and more like a fussy shopkeeper stocking the shelves—only instead of eggs and boxes, I was placing marines and galley crews upon the islands.

Finally, though, I somersaulted over to Sergeant Chukar and did a pawstand in front of her snout. "Smile, sergeant. You've won. And with hardly shedding a drop of blood on either side."

Sergeants, though, are born without smiles. "Have you seen Pomfret?"

"No. Have you see the Boneless King?" I eyed the nearest group of prisoners, who were all sitting obediently on the rocks under the watchful eye of an elderly, almost toothless dragon. "They could be in disguise."

"Or they could have fled." Sergeant Chukar beckoned impatiently to Slug—who, though he couldn't fly, must have swum to the battlefield. "Take care of the prisoners."

And then motioning to Bulbul, Sergeant Chukar sprang into the air again. With her rose about two dozen of her healthy veterans.

"Don't leave me out of the fun," I shouted after her, and leapt skyward. It was all I could do to keep up with them as the dragons began to search the islands above, at and below sea level. (By that time the fires were out in the channel.) While this was going on, I skimmed quickly over the prisoners for some sign of Pomfret, the Boneless King, Snowgoose or Horn.

When Sergeant Chukar finally joined me, she grumbled, "If they've escaped, we've won only a battle and not the war."

"Don't worry," I tried to reassure the sergeant. "Without the cauldron, they've lost their last major weapon."

I never met an old soldier who wasn't a pessimist. The sergeant grunted and looked eastward, but the fog bank hid everything from view. The magical mist hung, still and unmoving as a painting. "Let's just hope that Sambar does his part."

I slapped her on the back—a gesture that hurt my paw and that she didn't even feel through her tough hide. "Don't worry," I said, rubbing my paw. "I think today even you could tackle a horde of krakens."

Rising in the air, I somersaulted over the channel, where the Boneless King's mighty army now squatted under the watchful eyes of dragons while the forts finished burning. The other forts were being demolished by the smiths with mighty blows of their hammers. Beyond the Children Lady Francolin was keeping a watchful eye upon the transport ships.

With a nod to her I dove into the water and returned to the seamount, still lit by the globe. Shimmer was just beginning to sit up groggily. "What happened?"

I plopped down beside her, relieved to see that she

was all right. She was cranky and fussy, but she kind of grew on you. "You've just won a great victory. And if you could do that while you were asleep, imagine what you could do when you were awake."

Shimmer reached over and grasped my arm. "But where's Thorn?"

"I brought him here." I began to look around the seamount for the cauldron. "Where is he, anyway?"

Indigo looked up in shock. "But you were just here." She glanced over her shoulder for confirmation, and Storax nodded.

"You said you needed the bowl," the Grand Mage said, still insisting on using the old word for the cauldron.

"But I just got here." My stomach began to tighten. "I bet anything that was Pomfret."

Indigo's voice got husky as she realized what had happened. "When he swam off, he said something funny—something about turnabout being fair play." She brought her paws up to her face. "I thought he was you. What have I done?"

"What I did before, I can do again." I twirled my staff grimly. "Which way did he go?"

Shimmer shoved herself up from the seamount. "I'm going with you."

"Your Highness," the Grand Mage protested, "you must rest."

"Not until we have Thorn back." Shimmer rose unsteadily in the water, and a worried Indigo rose beside her.

"I'll show you the way he went," she said.

As I followed them upward with the other dragons, it crossed my mind that perhaps the sergeant was right: If the Boneless King had Thorn, then we had won only a single battle in a long war.

CHAPTER TWENTY

Pomfret had left in the direction of the northern part of the Hundred Children—probably where he had taken the Boneless King and his party during the confusion. Deciding that flying would be faster than swimming, I soared up out of the water into the sky and began somersaulting as fast as I could—so fast, in fact, that I nearly became sick.

Suddenly the water exploded beneath me, and Shimmer and Indigo leapt out of the water. Shimmer looked in the direction of the smoke still rising from the galleys and the forts. There were no more signs of battle, only dragons flying unconcernedly over the area, intent upon their various missions. "So we won?"

"With hardly any casualties to either side," I said.

The beating of her wings seemed a little off, as if she were still feeling the effects of the dream pearl—or of the wounds Pomfret had inflicted. "If we can't get Thorn back, that could change," she grunted. A moment later a worried group of mages joined us.

The little scraps of volcanic rock were barren. And as we flew on, there was still no sign of life. After sweeping over the area, I sat down in the air for a moment. "If I were the King and I had the cauldron, I wouldn't try to hide here. I'd go back to the Ramsgate, where it's safe," Shimmer said.

"Your Highness, you must leave that to someone else," Storax protested. "Rest now."

"If we don't catch them, we'll have to do everything over again, and maybe we won't be so lucky next time." Shimmer turned to Bombax. "Tell Sergeant Chukar to search this section square centimeter by centimeter. They could be any size or shape."

She tried to detail Storax and another dragon to keep watch until Sergeant Chukar could come with help, but Storax insisted, "I must keep an eye upon you." For a pompous old windbag, he could be conscientious too.

Shimmer eyed Storax's wings. "I doubt if you've done much flying."

The learned dragon was puffing with exertion already. "True, but I doubt if you're in any shape to fly, Your Highness."

"We'll see." Shimmer hovered as she looked

around her. "I won't stop for anyone who can't keep up."

Ordering another mage to take Storax's place, Shimmer oriented herself by the sun. Then, banking sharply, she began to fly with rapid beats of her wings toward the capital. Indigo was close on her heels, and the mages began to straggle along behind her.

Somersaulting over the grim dragons, I caught up with Shimmer. "He's right, you know. You're not in any shape to chase them."

"You're fast enough in a sprint, but it takes real wings to carry you in a long race." She thrust out her chin in a brave show of determination.

"It's not going to help any of us if you fly yourself to death," I snapped. I suspect that Storax had been worried about just that but had been too afraid to say it.

"We're not going to catch Pomfret by debating the state of my health." With a sudden flap of her wings, she shot away from me.

"Your Highness! You must rest!" Storax scolded, and flew after her.

For a moment, with all the dragons zooming past me, I felt like an ant caught in a storm of green hail. By the time I had righted myself, the dragons were already dots in the sky. But I knew those lumbering green wagons couldn't keep up that kind of pace. To tell the truth, I didn't like the aspersions they had cast on my own flying.

I glanced down apologetically at my staff. "Sorry,

friend, but I've got some serious flying to do, and I have to concentrate." I shrank it and tucked it away. Then, leaping through the air, I began to somersault after the dragons. About a kilometer on I saw the first dropouts. Storax and another dragon were floating about the ocean, puffing like the Smith's bellows.

I began to gain steadily on them over the next few kilometers. One by one, I could see the mages below me, resting on the waves like fat green gumdrops. By the time I caught up with the vanguard, it was only Indigo and Shimmer—the latter was favoring her injured wing, flying on guts and determination alone. But I didn't think it would be long before she was floating on the sea herself—unless she had a little incentive. And a dragon's most vulnerable spot is her pride.

"Who's going to burn out now?" I asked, cartwheeling over their heads.

Forgetting her own exhaustion, Shimmer rolled her eyes up to glare at me. "First one to catch Pomfret gains the other as a servant for a day."

I buffed my nails against my ragged robe. "Then I should start planning out my menu." I flapped the tattered hem at her. "And when you're finished with the cooking, you can sew up my robe."

It was like waving a flag at a bull. Shimmer forgot about her pain. Instead she gained energy, beating her wings now as steadily as a machine.

Indigo put a hand up to shade her eyes. "Pomfret may have had a head start on us, but he probably picked up the King and the dog and maybe Horn too.

With that load, he's got to slow down."

"What's that?" Shimmer demanded, and pointed.

I didn't have her sharp eyes, but when I stared in that direction, I thought I saw the little dot in the distance. "With a little luck, you'll be holding a family reunion soon."

However, we were able to pick up the pace only a little. By the time the dot had grown to the size of a human thumbnail, we could see the mainland on the horizon.

The three of us were panting now. "I think . . ." Shimmer said, "that I'll . . . make you wear . . . funny hats . . . when you serve me."

She was using her own strategy on me. "When you're my servant, I think I'll make you lose those ugly scales and take on some handsome fur."

"Me? An ape? Never," she declared, and her wings beat faster than ever. And again I was somersaulting through the air with the ocean a blur below me.

Beneath us the wind had picked up enough for the whitecaps to begin to appear—as if the sea were a herd of dark horses with white, tossing manes.

In that final dash we saw that it was indeed Pomfret with three passengers on his back. At the same time, though, we could see the rosy spires of the city and the golden dome of the palace winking in the sun.

"What's that over the city?" Indigo pointed at a streamer of smoke rising like a question mark over Ramsgate. Ahead of us Pomfret straightened out his neck and began beating his wings faster.

"We have . . . to catch him . . . before he reaches . . . the city," Shimmer puffed.

Despite Pomfret's best efforts, we seemed to be edging closer. But it was debatable whether we would catch him before he actually reached the garrison. I thought again of the catapults and crossbows.

"Maybe we should turn back," I said.

"Never," Shimmer insisted.

By the time we could make out the harbor, we were only some thirty meters from Pomfret. The Boneless King was riding first with Thorn. Clinging by its teeth to the Boneless King's cape was Snowgoose, and a very frightened wizard clung desperately to the dog.

Perhaps one of them might have noticed us closing on them, but their attention was all for Ramsgate, where more smoke had risen from within the circles of the red-colored buildings.

I slipped in closer to Shimmer. "I'd say . . ." I whispered, "that the contest . . . was a tie. I'll go for Pomfret's head . . . and make him stop. . . . That should give you . . . a chance to go . . . for Thorn."

Shimmer didn't answer. She merely nodded her head.

I didn't exactly relish a battle over the city, but I didn't see that we had any choice. Holding my head and neck straight, I began to somersault for all I was worth. But by now my arms and legs felt like lead.

Think about Thorn, I told myself. Think about what he went through in the forge. Think about him now— the slave of that evil creature.

And somehow, as heavy as my limbs felt, I put on a

sudden burst of speed that made me dart ahead. However, just as I was drawing close to Pomfret and getting ready to distract him, volleys of arrows and bolts rose from the walls around the harbor.

At first I thought the missiles were meant for us. Then I realized that they were being shot at Pomfret.

Frantically the dragon dodged, almost tossing off his passengers. "I'm with the King, you idiots," he shouted.

A second volley answered him from the harbor walls, and he banked sharply. No one paid any attention as I crossed over the harbor. Beneath me was a mob of guardsmen and city folk all mixed together, standing around the warehouses, taking the weapons that were being passed out of an armory. Next to it the government customs building—where the taxes on freight were collected—was on fire. On the ground lay a few guardsmen, who must have stayed loyal to their King.

I thought over what we had heard on the way down from the mountains—which seemed like an eternity ago. "The revolt," I called to Shimmer. "It's finally broken out."

Instinctively, Pomfret soared skyward, and he could easily have flown out of range of the arrows and crossbow bolts, but the Boneless King shouted at him angrily, "Down, you fool. They have to hear me."

"They're too busy shooting to listen," Pomfret objected.

"Not for long," the Boneless King snapped. "Down!"

Reluctantly, Pomfret spiraled down toward the harbor. "I am your King," the Boneless King announced. "How dare you revolt? Put down your arms or suffer the consequences."

Pomfret flew in a desperate loop away from another volley. "Have you got any other ideas?"

"Punish them," the Boneless King commanded Horn—still keeping up the pretense that the little wizard was the one working the magic.

The wizard, though, was looking almost as green as a dragon and could only groan, "Let me off at the nearest rooftop."

As Pomfret dodged around in desperation, the Boneless King had to concentrate on holding on rather than on working magic.

Shimmer was hovering at the mouth of the harbor. Nobody bothered shooting at her; they were concentrating on the Boneless King.

"If they hit the Boneless King," Shimmer said, "he might drop Thorn."

I took out my staff and had it lengthen into a proper weapon. "You can't go into that mess as a dragon. You might as well hang a target around your neck. But an ape shape would be nice. Everyone loves us cute, furry creatures."

Shimmer whipped her tail impatiently. "Over my dead body." And she shot forward.

As the first volley of arrows and bolts came toward us, I barely tumbled out of the way. "I think that could easily be arranged."

CHAPTER TWENTY-ONE

I tried not to get too close to Shimmer, since she naturally attracted arrows. "Maybe you should change Indigo back into her human shape," I suggested. "Then I can take her on my back."

"No," Indigo insisted, sticking close to Shimmer. "And we don't have time to argue about that."

"All right." I pointed to Shimmer and Indigo. "You two fly over the city and keep him from getting above the streets. I'll follow him. Given a choice, they'd rather shoot him than me."

"You leave him for me to deal with, though." With a sharp flap of her wings, Shimmer shot upward into the sky. Indigo followed her a little more awkwardly. I figured it was better for her to be in the open sky out of range of the crossbow bolts, since she wouldn't be able to dodge as well as Shimmer.

Tugging my cap more firmly down on my head, I began to somersault forward. "Hey, tall, green and gruesome. Who said you could impersonate an ape? It's an insult to all monkeydom."

Startled, Pomfret craned his long neck around to look at me. And that was very nearly his undoing. A crossbow bolt bounced off one hard claw.

Quickly he tried to rise into the sky. "Down," the Boneless King ordered.

"I'm not going to let myself get turned into a pincushion just because you can't handle your own people." Determined, Pomfret tried to rise, but with a sudden flap of her wings, Shimmer swooped down from overhead with outstretched claws.

"Our clan sends their regards, Brother." Her claws clicked together where Pomfret's head had been.

Desperate, Pomfret darted further into the city. "Keep him from getting above the city," I called to Shimmer and Indigo.

With a nod, Shimmer flapped her wings and soared higher, keeping well out of crossbow range for Indigo's sake. Ahead of me the streets were like odd canyons with sides that were perpendicular and pockmarked with windows.

The rebels had commandeered wagons from the wharfs and piled in—I should say that I saw as many guardsmen as city folk; apparently the guard had also mutinied. As a result, they rattled along beneath us, shooting volleys up at Pomfret.

Somehow word of the King's return had spread

ahead of us—perhaps someone with a telescope had seen the battle around the harbor, or perhaps the rebels had set up some kind of rooftop ambush already. In any event, the rebels were crawling over the rooftops like ants on the edges of boxlike cakes. Except these ants had long-range stings.

Some had real weapons; others had hunting bows or antique crossbows. Still others had brought up an assortment of pots and crockery, which poured down on Pomfret in a porcelain snowstorm.

Between the two groups Pomfret kept dodging, weaving back and forth below roof level, looking like a drunken green wagon; and the Boneless King was still kept so busy trying to keep hold that he didn't have time to work any magic.

I could see beneath me bodies on the pavement, as if there had been battles between a few loyal guardsmen and the rebels. Here and there a government building burned while people tried to form bucket brigades.

Unfortunately, the rebels' volleys didn't discriminate between Pomfret and me. Once the arrows missed the dragon, they sometimes came toward me. With a leap, I bounced off a wall on my left, cartwheeled over a dozen whistling arrows and bounded off a tiled roof on my right.

"Take this," a woman shouted from an open window. Just on general principles she assumed any flying creature was an enemy. She threw the first thing in her hand, a tub of soapy suds, all over me. Coughing and spluttering and wiping the soap from my eyes, I blundered on after Pomfret.

Even at that, I was having an easier time than Pomfret. He and his passengers were covered with everything from soap to soup, and the King's armor was dented from various household utensils.

I had thought the Boneless King would work his way gradually out of the city so he could escape into the open country and perhaps to whatever secrets were buried in his tomb. However, he kept moving deeper toward Ramsgate's center and his palace.

And then below us the wagons piled straight into a vegetable cart. Cabbages and fruit went flying into the air, wooden boards splintered and people went flying—though the peddler's stock was ruined, no one seemed hurt.

We burst out of the narrow city canyons over the ring of villas and mansions, and I felt almost as if I had emerged out of a cave. I was afraid that they might get away, but Pomfret had no sooner shown his snout above a garden wall than a shower of arrows flew up at him. There were guards on the estates, and it didn't matter to them whether they were sympathetic to the revolution or simply doing their job.

When Pomfret tried to get out of range, Shimmer and Indigo swooped down at him. "The Sea! The Sea!"

A back full of passengers hampered Pomfret's ability to fight with Shimmer, so he dove back down again. Missiles whistled by him as he shot low over a pond, knocking a statue over into the goldfish. A squad of gardeners flung themselves into a bed of lilies as Pomfret zoomed past them. I tried to close up with him—a tricky proposition since I didn't want to get so near that I was within the pincushion zone.

If I ever survived, I promised myself, I would take a more leisurely flight over that part of Ramsgate. There were a lot of houses pretty as cakes with icing. And they sat in terraced gardens with miniature ponds and mountains and even forests of dwarf trees no bigger than mice. Once we flushed a flock of peacocks, who fled screeching with their tails widespread behind them.

Overhead, I was glad to see, Shimmer had the good sense to rise back out of range—perhaps it was concern for her companion that made her be so prudent.

Then, from the top of the hill where the palace grounds sprawled, came a rhythmic booming sound that echoed through the entire city. Wondering what it was, I risked rising higher in the air and saw the mob at the palace gates. The sound was being made by a battering ram, hammering at the cast-bronze gates to the cheers of the crowd. The walls themselves were strangely deserted, as if all the guards had abandoned the palace.

Suddenly a crossbow bolt whizzed by my head and reminded me not to play tourist. Swerving, I followed Pomfret under a high, arching bridge, skimming low over a pond of lotus flowers. Terrified frogs went hopping, and frantic ducks went flapping.

Finally, with a sudden burst of energy, Pomfret zoomed above the pond and over a brick wall. I followed him onto the palace grounds in time to see the last of the court officials led by the lord chancellor. They were armed with ornamental swords, but with them were servants armed with clubs, kitchen cleavers and whatever else they could grab. However, the only one who looked resolute was the lord chancellor. At first I thought they might be preparing to resist the mob of rebels, and I was sure that the Boneless King would head for them. However, he had Pomfret glide once around the golden dome and then glide to the front lawn, near the giant pit where the statues were buried.

The exhausted Pomfret bounced once off the lawn and then plowed straight through a field of begonias. When he came to a halt, he lay there gasping with the exertion, and with enough scrapes and nicks now to match his sister's hide.

Hastily, Snowgoose sprang to the ground to stand tense and growling, waiting to defend its master. Horn slid off Pomfret's back in a dazed huddle. Only the Boneless King seemed none the worse for wear. Thorn held under one arm, he swung a leg from Pomfret and jumped down.

"I'll take that," I said, leaping toward them. Snowgoose sprang toward me, snarling and snapping, but I had purposefully hovered just out of reach of those snapping jaws.

Seizing Horn's collar, the Boneless King hauled the wizard to his feet. "Destroy that pest," he commanded.

Horn tried to stay up on his wobbly legs but plumped back down in the dirt. "In a moment."

"The Sea! The Sea!" Shimmer and Indigo cried. Seeing the dragon shadows spreading suddenly across the ground, the Boneless King threw himself at the dirt. Too late, Shimmer's claws closed over where he had been. With a frustrated shout Shimmer let her momentum carry her past the spot. Indigo, who did not have Shimmer's experience, went straight into the earth, plowing her own furrow.

The Boneless King landed with a grunt, and Thorn went bouncing out of his arms. As Snowgoose and I both raced for Thorn, Shimmer banked sharply in the air and darted back, claws outstretched and teeth open. Hurriedly, the Boneless King tried to get to his knees, but Shimmer would have had him for sure if Pomfret hadn't suddenly lunged upward. Brother and sister went over in kilotons of angry, wrestling dragons.

Their bodies lithe as snakes, they coiled and uncoiled, each trying to crush the other while their claws fought to grip and their jaws snapped at one another's throats.

By that time Indigo had scrambled to all fours. Throwing herself forward over the newly dug pit, she threw her paws around Thorn. Snarling, Snowgoose sprang into the air, but I managed to loop a golden ring around its muzzle. With a yank, I pulled the animal up short.

Then, springing, I was between the beast and Indigo. "Why don't you be a good doggy and play fetch with someone else," I said warily.

The Boneless King looked toward the lord chancellor and his defenders. "Seize them," he ordered.

Lord Tower, though, stood defiantly at the mouth of the palace. "Where is the fleet? Where is the army?"

I noticed that he pointedly did not say "Your Highness."

The Boneless King also noted the lapse in etiquette. "They're coming," he lied. "But these dragon spies ambushed me."

Lord Tower, though, was no fool. "You've lost, and now our kingdom lies helpless before the dragons. Even if they do not invade, your capital is in revolt."

The Boneless King squeezed his fingers into a fist. "I'll crush them all just like this."

"The kingdom has had enough of your butchery," Lord Tower declared, "and so have we." And suddenly I realized that the lord chancellor had armed himself and the servants not against the rebels but against the King himself. "As lord chancellor, I name myself regent until the true heir can be located, or another found to take his place."

At that moment there was a thunderous groan as the gates tilted in on their hinges. The rebels stood outside for a moment as if stunned by the noise.

Snowgoose immediately freed itself from the ring at the end of my staff and had bounded over to the side of the Boneless King, while, cut and bleeding,

Pomfret cautiously slithered away from Shimmer toward his master.

Hastily, the Boneless King yanked Horn back to his feet again. "Destroy them," he ordered, and whispered something in the little wizard's ear.

Horn, though, drew back horrified from the Boneless King. "That's the old magic. I wouldn't even if I knew how."

The Boneless King seized Horn by the collar and lifted him into the air, shaking him like a dog shaking a rat. "Yes, you can."

"Let me go." Horn kicked and squirmed. "I can't do any magic except bubbles. I don't know how I cast any of those other spells."

The Boneless King disgustedly let the wizard collapse in a heap once again. "It was time to end this little farce anyway. I'll rule in my own name from now on. The Butcher is dead. Long live the Boneless King."

"You see?" Shimmer slithered over beside Pomfret. "I told you the truth."

Startled, Pomfret turned his head around to look at the Boneless King. However, by now, the Boneless King had the measure of the dragon. "The Butcher was a miser. I will give you not only an undersea kingdom but the mirror and half the dragon treasury."

Pomfret crouched there as if he were weighing something on a balance—perhaps it was his soul. Then he turned toward Indigo. "I'll take that."

"He's the enemy of all living things," Shimmer

protested, and tried to snap at the King. "You can't trust him."

Pomfret shielded his master. "Our mistake was in not throwing in with the strongest. Everything will be all right if the cauldron is in my safekeeping." Without looking over his shoulder, he asked the Boneless King, "True?"

"Of course," the Boneless King agreed quickly. I was sure he had some trick up his sleeve for Pomfret, but Pomfret was too desperate to think straight. Then, with a quick pass of his hands and a muttered phrase, the Boneless King smiled at us. "There, you pests won't be escaping into the air."

Indigo tried to leap into the air and landed on her paws. The Boneless King had taken away our power of flight as he had once before, and the spell would last as long as he could see us.

I glanced at Shimmer, and she nodded her head in grim, silent understanding. Our only chance lay in battling the King.

I raised my staff toward the rebels still outside the gates. "Come on," I shouted as loudly as I could. "What are you waiting for? A personal invitation?"

I wasn't sure how much they had overheard or understood, and I was even less sure how much they believed. But they surged now onto the palace grounds, men and women, tailors and guardsmen, even a few children. However, few of them had any real weapons—most of them had brooms, shears or kitchen knives, or even just pots and pans.

Raising his sword over his head, the lord chancellor commanded his own little army, "Forward."

"Fools. You've condemned yourselves." The Boneless King's armor clinked loudly as he spread out his arms. "Awaken!" he shouted.

All around us the newly packed dirt in the giant pit began to tremble. At first I thought it was dozens of gray worms wriggling out of the soil, twisting and turning. Then I realized that they were fingers. And the fingers were attached to hands. And the hands were fastened to arms. Like giant stone flowers growing from the soil, they rose stiffly, and the pit was transformed into a meadow of hundreds of strange blossoms.

Both groups of rebels had come to a halt at the weird spectacle. Suddenly a head in an antique helmet followed its outstretched arms out of the dirt, popping out of the dirt like a mole. The unblinking eyes glared at me; a scowl was fixed upon its rigid face.

"The statues are alive," Lord Tower gasped.

The Boneless King pointed at us and then swept his arm around in a circle to indicate all the other rebels, both common and noble. "Kill them. Don't leave one of them alive."

Next to me Indigo gave a cry. I turned around to see that another statue head had emerged and the arms had seized her ankle. Even as we watched, more hands rose to claim her other legs.

Shimmer tried to move to her defense, but more

statues had grasped her ankles in an unshakable grip. Raising my staff over my head, I too tried to run over to Indigo before a pair of stony hands clamped themselves about my ankles and I fell face forward in the dirt. As I rolled over onto my back, a stony arm wrapped itself about my chest.

As more heads sprouted from the dirt, the Boneless King turned to Pomfret. "Get the cauldron." And Pomfret rose into the air. In vain Shimmer whipped her tail and twisted her head this way and that, trying to defend Indigo. Ripping Thorn from Indigo's grasp, Pomfret hovered in the air. He could have broken Shimmer's back and was obviously considering the notion.

"Well?" the Boneless King called, and held out his hand impatiently.

Pomfret, though, hesitated—could it be he still had some scruples? At any rate, he flew back toward the Boneless King. "Let these . . . toys do the dirty work."

"A conscience will be a luxury," Shimmer warned him desperately. But then stone hands, clutching at her throat, choked off any more words.

Hugged against the hard chest of one monster, I was having all I could do to fight off a stone warrior who had risen waist high from the dirt. He struck at me with fists of stone, swinging far faster than I would have thought possible—as if the sun were putting life into him. I parried one punch with one end of my staff and hurriedly blocked his second fist with my staff's other end.

And suddenly I found myself rising in the air with my feet over my head. The statue that held my ankles had managed to rise up to its knees and was holding me upside down in its fist.

In the rest of the field, statues were kicking themselves out of the dirt like swimmers rising out of the sea. The horrified rebels had begun to back up toward the gates. Like the dead leaving their graves, the statues began to move stiffly forward.

Even fully armored and armed soldiers would have been slaughtered by the statues, and most of the rebels had only their improvised weapons. "Go on," I called to them. "Run. Hide."

As the Boneless King took Thorn from Pomfret, he laughed harshly. "By all means, try to run and hide," he taunted. The Boneless King gestured, and a half dozen soldiers left the pit and formed an escort around him. "My statues will never tire. They'll hunt you all down."

With Thorn clasped in his arms, he whirled around and headed for the palace, Pomfret floating overhead, Snowgoose trotting at his side. Horn tried to slink off, but Snowgoose had seized his robe and tugged him along. As the statues marched stiffly toward the palace, the lord chancellor and his own little army fled inside.

The worst thing about dying this way was having to listen to the Boneless King's triumphant laughter.

CHAPTER TWENTY-TWO

Desperately, I fought to stay alive. But with one statue holding me and another trying to bash in my head, it was really only a matter of time. Though I didn't dare look, I could hear the screams of the rebels and the heavy tramp of the statues' feet. Against those tireless, indestructible warriors the city was doomed. My arms were already beginning to grow numb from blocking the blows. The only thing that could stand up against a stone warrior was another stone warrior.

Suddenly that gave me an idea. Twisting my tail around me, I shifted my right paw to the middle of the staff to parry the statue's blows. It was an awkward arrangement, but I had no choice. Using my free paw, I yanked out a handful of hairs. Spitting on them, I shouted, "Change!"

A dozen miniature monkeys leapt through the air

to perch upon my captor's head and shoulders, where they began to taunt my attacker in little squeaking voices.

"Ha! Better duck, ugly. Here come the pigeons."

"Your mother is a paperweight."

And so on. Not very imaginative insults, but then when you are dealing with a stone statue, you needn't try very hard.

And the next moment my captor was rocking back and forth as my attacker switched from me to the little monkeys—perhaps somewhere in his rocky brain he thought the little monkeys would be easier prey. Of course, the little monkeys scampered nimbly out of the way of the blows, continuing to insult my attacker. Suddenly, with one great blow, he shattered my captor's head.

A ribbon of blue mist rose from the statue, and the next moment the lifeless hands dumped me unceremoniously onto the ground. Scrambling to my feet, I swung my staff with all my might at the other statue's knees. With a crack, the statue broke, toppling over with a thud, just like a tree. For a moment, its arms flopped in the air like an overturned beetle, and then it laboriously began to roll itself on its stomach so it could crawl toward me.

Stripping more hairs from my tail, I sent a host of little monkeys to help Shimmer and Indigo. Then, with several hard blows, I disposed of the other statue. Again blue mist escaped into the air.

As far as I was concerned, that was something for

mages and wizards to debate. My problem right now was survival. The Boneless King had disappeared inside the palace with his dog, Horn and Pomfret. There wasn't any sign of Lord Tower, so I supposed he was trying to hide inside.

The other group of rebels was by the gate—a true mob now, fighting and elbowing one another as they tried to flee. But there were so many in back still coming that the ones in front couldn't escape. Toward them a hundred statues moved in a steady, menacing rhythm.

Plucking tail hairs by the pawful, I sent a horde of monkeys scampering toward the statues, and it quickly became quite a comical spectacle. There were the stone statues, stamping along like machines of death, and the next moment the little monkeys settled around them like a cloud of mosquitos. The statues halted abruptly, and then one statue raised a fist and smashed his neighbor. In no time, each statue was bashing another over the head with a crack like breaking pottery. It was as hilarious as one of those puppet shows where the puppets would as soon hit one another as speak. My children cleverly led the survivors, arms flailing at their tormentors, toward one another. And those poor souls, released as misty blue streamers, were free to soar skyward.

Suddenly the sky above us began to glow red as a sunset, red as a magical mountain. It was the Smith and the Snail Woman. I used my dusty staff to scratch my head, unsure whether it was a good thing to have them find us. After all, we hadn't exactly parted on the best of terms. In fact, the small-minded might say that we had demolished their home in making our escape.

Shimmer and Indigo had been surrounded by some twenty or so statues, but those stone warriors were now busy swatting at my children—and hitting one another instead, with heavy clunks and clanks. Though Shimmer and Indigo were both free, their sides were heaving and they were rubbing their bruised throats as they sought to recover.

Now that the Boneless King could not see us, his flightless spell was broken. Cartwheeling through the air, I hurried over to Shimmer. Already stone arms, legs and heads littered the dirt around her. With my staff I smashed a few more statues that were too close to her head.

She glanced at me uncomfortably and then croaked like a frog. Embarrassed, she swallowed and managed to whisper a hoarse "Thank you."

"Here you are with little chance to answer back, and I'm too out of breath to insult you." Feeling like a lumberjack, I set to work to clear some statues who were too near Indigo—catching one statue with a swing and then another statue with my backhand.

However, I should have known that it wouldn't take a dragon long to get her voice back. "It'll take you forever your way." Having recovered her strength, Shimmer rose and, with a mighty sweep of her tail, bowled over a half dozen statues. Then, dancing a little two-step, she stomped them into rubble.

As blue vapor rose all around her, I leaned on my staff. "I could get you a nice job tearing down houses."

"Can't you get me something judging works of art?" Squinting with one eye to aim better, she reared up and pivoted on her hind legs so that her tail neatly decapitated a standing statue. And its soul too, finally released, streamed into the air.

"We've got some company, you know." Craning my head back, I pointed up toward the red glowing light, where I thought I saw the silhouette of a giant mountain floating in the sky.

"The question is," Shimmer said as she brushed dust from her shoulders, "are they coming to help us or punish us?"

"They ought to be too busy to worry about us." I nodded toward the stone statues in the garden, who were slapping one another like clumsy clowns. While the king's magical warriors had been destroying one another, the rebels had finally managed to escape. Outside the gates, the streets were deserted except for a litter of lost hats, clubs, knives and assorted kitchen utensils.

Overhead, the mountain had barely materialized when the Snail Woman's chariot rolled out of the cave, pulled by a dozen mechanical cranes. She guided the chariot smoothly with her folded-up fan— when open, the fan could generate wind storms. More cranes flew as an escort on either side, and in their bills were small buckets.

The sun reflected in rainbow colors from the silvery shell upon her back. And next to her was her husband, the Smith, a thin, bony man with a huge steel bucket in one hand and his tongs in the other.

As they swept in closer, I saw that the chariot had been patched hastily from the demolishing I had given it. I should say that they didn't look any too happy to see us.

"What are the buckets for?" I called up to them nervously. "Are you going fishing?"

As the rattling chariot rolled to a halt beside us, the railing on the side of the chariot came off in the Smith's hand. Apparently not all the repairs were finished. "My dear, I believe this is yours." He handed it to the Snail Woman, who stowed it thriftily in the bottom of her chariot for later mending.

When she straightened up, she stared at me hard. "I might have known you'd be right in the middle of trouble. Where is the cauldron?"

There never was a dragon who could think and lie at the same time, so I spoke up before Shimmer could. "Um, out here somewhere." I nodded toward the warring statues. "Did you contact my master?" I was hoping that I might get him to intercede for us.

The Smith bent and selected a hammer from the floor of the chariot while the Snail Woman shoved her sleeves back and got ready to use her fan. "No, we couldn't find him, nor the others."

"Not even the Lord of Flowers?" I wondered.

"He wouldn't come. He always was contrary." The Smith held out the bucket to me. "Now empty this bucket on the statues and then get out of the way." He snipped his tongs at my nose. "But don't go far. We intend to have a good talk with you. Careful. The bucket's hot."

I bowed several times in the air as I glanced into the bucket. It was full of fire-rats. "Stone statues won't burn."

"No, but stone will crack when it's heated and then cooled quickly." Holding her arms up, the Snail Woman let her husband fold her sleeves more neatly.

"Wait a moment then." I called my children back to me, quickly restoring them to my tail. One by one the statues turned and began to stalk back toward us.

Curious fire-rats peered over the sides of the bucket, which was heavier than it looked. Looking up, I could see that the pairs of fire-rats peeped out from the smaller buckets that the circling escort of cranes still held. "It's nice to be fighting on the same side," I said hopefully. "And it's even nicer to forget old wrongs."

"We'll see," the Smith grumbled as he stepped down.

His wife jumped down after him. "Now scoot." She swatted me across the rump with her folded fan.

I leapt into the air, and when the Smith pointed his tongs, the cranes smoothly formed a V shape behind me.

As the cranes dropped their rats among the statues,

I could feel a breeze stir behind me as the Snail Woman loosened up her arm for a real storm. Picking out a spot the cranes had missed, I gently shook out a half dozen fire-rats, which landed on their paws like cats. Scampering about, I left fire-rats in the other spots the cranes had neglected.

The stone warriors stamped awkwardly, but the fire-rats were too nimble. Glowing like little fireballs, they began to climb up legs or coil around shoulders like red, furry collars. But when stony hands reached for them, the playful creatures scampered away. Even before I returned with the empty bucket, the statues were beginning to redden with heat.

As I joined Shimmer, she whispered to me, "Why did you lie about Thorn?"

"You want to get him back, don't you?" I muttered from the side of my mouth.

"But she promised to give him back once the war was over," Shimmer pointed out.

"Do you want to wait on their schedule and their convenience?" I mumbled back. I had thought we would be able to sneak into the palace while they were occupied. But I hadn't reckoned on the cranes.

A mean one clanked its beak at me as I turned.

"Don't get any ideas," the Smith said without looking around.

"I wouldn't think of it," I said, setting the bucket down—though to Shimmer, I said, "If it worked once, why not a second time?"

Plucking out a couple of pawfuls of hair, I sent my

children scampering into the air. The metal cranes were just as clumsy as the stone warriors as they clanked their beaks and stamped their feet.

"Stop that," the Snail Woman ordered.

"You'd better mind the moving pottery," I called to her.

She turned back to the statues. Though they were struggling with the fire-rats and turning even redder themselves, they were still trying to advance with single-minded purpose.

"You dratted monkey, we'll get you for this," the Smith swore.

"If you can catch me," I said with a tip of my cap.

Slipping between the struggling cranes, I cartwheeled into the palace. The entrance was so huge that Shimmer and Indigo could both follow me.

In the course of my adventures, I have seen—and been kicked out of—many palaces. And surely there are more costly palaces and more magical palaces, but there were none quite as imaginative as the Dome.

The entrance lobby was about a hundred meters long and fifty meters wide, and in its very center was a miniature relief map of the kingdom, with golden replicas of the cities, and fields of jade and forests of coral. Even the rivers were marked with silver fluid that flowed through the costly landscape.

Overhead, the golden ceiling was filled with all sorts of wonderful creatures who inhabit the sky— phoenixes and star maidens and magical trees. And the green marble floor had been carved with all the dragons and other, stranger, creatures that the wandering Prince Diamond had seen during his exile when his brother, the King, had been afraid Diamond would seize the throne.

"That"—Shimmer sniffed—"will have to change. I won't have dragons being walked on all the time."

The walls were jet black, with niches in which busts sat. Carved out of solid blocks of jade and decorated with stones, they gazed down at the miniature kingdom. Shimmer studied them curiously. "They were ordered carved by a grateful Weaver," she whispered, "when good King Emerald took the exiled dragons in and got the other kings to cede the Inland Sea to my clan. After that my clan would carve a new bust for each monarch when he assumed the throne."

"But," I said, glancing around suspiciously, "could the King be using them now to work some kind of magical trap? You watch the left side," I instructed Shimmer and Indigo. "I'll take the right."

"All right," Shimmer said, and with a nod to Indigo she moved off. I paid special attention to the busts to see if they had been enchanted like the stone warriors. I passed by solemn faces with real gold crowns decorated with jewels.

However, as I passed one king, something about his features made me stop. "Humph," I said.

"What's wrong?" a worried Indigo asked.

I pondered the bust. I had seen the wide forehead, the narrow nose, the widespread, sleepy eyes before. "Nothing's wrong." I scratched my head. "It's just that something seems familiar about"—I read the little golden plaque beneath the bust—"King Emerald III."

"He probably sentenced you to his dungeons at some time." Shimmer finished circling her side and came over to inspect the rest of my side.

When Indigo came up to me, she halted and her head shot back. "Thorn," she gasped.

Rubbing my chin, I studied the bust. Now that she had mentioned it, the bust did look a little like Thorn—if he had been able to grow older. "I thought that Thorn looked familiar when I first saw him. I must've seen some monument of King Emerald III before that." I shook my head. "But he was just an innkeeper's servant."

"He'd been left at the inn." Shimmer's head bobbed up and down and from side to side as she studied the bust from every angle. "They say the prince and the queen disappeared a short time after the prince's father died."

Indigo pressed a paw against her mouth. "So Thorn is the missing prince."

Shimmer's head drooped. "Much good it does him."

Indigo slowly sat down on her haunches. "So his sacrifice was even greater than anyone knew."

Her head still lowered, Shimmer looked up at the statue. "And yet I think he would have done the same thing even if he had known his true origins."

I thought of that brave, clever boy who had deliberately sacrificed himself to repair the cauldron. He had felt so lost, and all the time he had been the heir to the kingdom. As I sensed the enormity of his loss, I could feel a pesky tear teasing the corner of my eye.

Shimmer's shoulders rose and fell, and teardrops openly rolled down from her eyes and splashed on the floor. "He was already noble even if he didn't have a title."

I could see Shimmer getting ready to throw one of those grand, sentimental fits that dragons love so much. Well, I felt as bad as she did, but we had business to do. Rubbing the tears from my own eyes, I hipped her. "All the more reason to rescue Thorn. And once we're done with the Boneless King, we'll see what we can do for him."

Shimmer sat there for a moment and then raised her head suddenly as if she had just gotten an idea. "Yes," she murmured. "Yes, we will."

I draped a paw around her neck and gave her a squeeze, and the dragon was feeling so sad that she didn't scold me for being so familiar. "And then," I promised, "we can have a proper cry for everyone."

"We may not have to with Thorn." Shimmer shoved me away. "Whatever else happens to us, we must free Thorn. I won't have him be a slave to that evil creature."

I thought of the previous soul that had been released from the cauldron. "You mean break it?" I asked.

"Even if we die trying." And Shimmer got that determined look that I had come to know so well.

"I never thought I'd say it, but you're right," I admitted.

And suddenly the huge golden doors at the end of the lobby slowly were opened as if by invisible hands.

"This is for Thorn," Indigo said. And together we marched forward.

CHAPTER TWENTY-THREE

The throne room was just beneath the golden dome. Designs had been cut into its golden surface so that their shining outlines would fall upon the green marble floor. A huge disk of crystal beneath the dome prevented rain from falling inside. I don't know how they got rid of the water. Both the disk and dome were supported on slender, fluted white columns. The walls of the room were of turquoise and lit cunningly with lamps, so they seemed to spread out like the sky. Some two hundred meters in diameter, it seemed even larger.

At first I thought there were hundreds of people within the throne room, but when they didn't move, I realized that they were bronze statues—lords and ladies and generals, all of them with fists upraised toward the end of the throne room as if paying silent honor.

"The King has a curious sense of decor," I whispered to Shimmer.

"Do you think they're his creatures like the stone warriors?" Indigo suggested.

"I'll take them all on," Shimmer growled, and nodded to the end of the room.

There, rising from the floor, was a dais covered with designs in mother-of-pearl that rose in a series of steps to a throne of gold and silver. Behind the throne was a huge rayed disk like the sun.

To one side of the dais Snowgoose crouched, ready to defend its master. Pomfret lay on the other side of the throne, lost in what he saw in the bronze mirror he clutched in both forepaws. Horn sat miserably on the steps. The Boneless King himself sat upon the throne with Thorn on his lap.

When I thought of the cruel irony, I felt myself grow even angrier. But Shimmer spoke up before I could. "The King is mine."

This wasn't the time to argue—as much as I would have liked to. "All right. I'll take Pomfret and Horn."

"And I'll take Snowgoose," Indigo said.

"Surrender," the Boneless King called.

"Never." With a flap of her wings, Shimmer flew over the heads of the statues. As she darted forward, she gave the war cry of her clan: "The Sea! The Sea!"

Indigo launched herself into the air at about the same time, and raising my staff, I leapt after her. As I passed over the statues, I noticed that their faces all wore expressions of rage. They weren't saluting the throne at all but cursing it. When I saw Lord Tower, I realized that the Boneless King had put down his palace revolt by transforming them all.

As I flew past the last statues, Pomfret set the mirror down and rose, muttering a hasty spell. Suddenly huge blue bubbles floated before me in the shapes of stars, cones and cylinders.

Expecting some horrible trap, I tried to halt, but my momentum carried me right through them—none the worse except for a thin coat of a wet, soapy film.

Immediately, Pomfret squatted down on all fours, covering his eyes. "No, no!" he moaned. "I was only following orders."

The next moment he had changed into his true form: the bubble wizard, Horn. Too late, I tried to turn in midair as I heard a snarling in my ear. Twisting my head, I saw Snowgoose leaping through the air. The dog had been disguised as Horn. The next moment, Snowgoose had smashed into me, carrying me to the floor. With one hand, it knocked the staff from my paw.

Upon the dais the throne crashed backward, and I saw that Shimmer had also run into trouble. From the corner of my eye, I saw that Pomfret and not the Boneless King now wrestled with Shimmer. On the other side, the Boneless King, having dropped his disguise as Snowgoose, was lowering his arms smugly, as if he had just worked a spell. On the steps Indigo crouched, changed into several meters of undulating bronze, one paw raised to strike.

And then I had all I could do to keep Snowgoose from trying to rip my throat out. Grasping its muzzle in my paws, I barely held it off; and, still locked together, we rolled across the floor of the throne room.

Upon the dais, the two dragons had stopped battling. I understood why when the Boneless King suddenly appeared by my side and clicked an iron collar around my neck. Instantly, I felt it constrict. Unable to breathe, I lay there, helpless, as a growling Snowgoose opened its jaws even wider.

However, the Boneless King had other plans for me and grabbed hold of its collar. "Heel! Heel!" he was shouting as he hauled his dog away from me. When Snowgoose stood quivering angrily at his side, the Boneless King gazed down at me. "We don't want your punishment to end so quickly."

As the collar loosened enough for me to wheeze, I sat up. On the dais, Pomfret was picking up the false cauldron that had fallen from his lap when he had been disguised as the King. We had thought it was Thorn, but it was really a mirror. Thorn had been disguised as the mirror instead, and now lay revealed on the dais as the true cauldron. Shimmer lay thrashing upon the steps, clasping at the iron collar strangling her.

Still holding Snowgoose by the collar, the Boneless King went up the left side of the dais, away from the wriggling dragon. "Really, you three amaze me.

You've escaped not once but twice from the prison that held me all those centuries. And"—he rounded on his heel and studied both Shimmer and me—"that presents me with quite a problem. The only way to keep you from spoiling my plans any further is to kill you. But death is too kind a reward for all the inconvenience you've caused me.

"I don't dare send you to any place on this world, because there is nothing that seems proof against your lockpicking. I'd send you into exile on some pesthole of a world, but some do-gooder might rescue you. What would you do if you were me?" He crooked his finger, and Shimmer's collar loosened enough for her to lie, draped over the steps, her sides heaving up and down.

"How about if we wash the palace floors?" I suggested. "That should take a long time."

"I should have known I couldn't hold a serious conversation with you about your execution." The Boneless King sighed and pointed at me. Instantly, the collar tightened so that I could barely breathe, let alone speak.

As I sat down upon the lower step, gasping for air, he rubbed his chin. "Hmm, time, yes, that may be just the ticket."

Horn had dared to sit up again. "Time?"

The Boneless King began to chuckle. "It's a complicated spell for just one person, but it can be done. I'll send them back before there was time—back to when nothing had form or shape. I dare anyone to find them in that. And not even I could escape from there."

The little wizard gave a shiver. "Even you couldn't be that cruel."

The Boneless King smiled as mirthlessly as a skull. "This era lacks such imagination. But I'll fix that."

I could hear through the open doors the sound of distant hammers thumping away and stone shattering like glass. If we could only delay the Boneless King long enough, the Snail Woman and the Smith could come to help us.

However, the King could hear the same sounds too and also know what I was thinking. "I wouldn't hope for any rescue from the likes of those two dreary people. They'll fall into my trap as easily as you did. Perhaps I'll send them to join you."

And with that dark promise he set Thorn down. Then, flinging up his arms, he began a complicated spell. "Come, Chaos."

Clutching the mirror, Pomfret crept over to his sister as if he were determined to have the last word. "Why did you have to interfere?" he whispered. "You've only delayed our clan's homecoming. When I'm King, I'll see that our home's restored and our people returned to their full glory."

I couldn't talk at all, so I could only guess at the effort it took Shimmer. "You're . . . a fool. He's . . . our enemy."

If the Boneless King heard the dragons, he ignored them, for the spell he was working would have been ambitious for a whole college of wizards.

"But I've seen it here. This is the World Mirror created by the Serpent Lady herself just like the dragons' mirror of truth." Pomfret held up the mirror to which he was so addicted. About a meter in length, it was shaped like a fish. The frame itself was all of scales, and the bronze mirror was a smoothly polished oval in the middle. For a moment we could see the reflection of the throne room, and the next moment it washed away, to be replaced by a sparkling sea in which dragons swam majestically. Leading them was Pomfret with a crown upon his head and wearing all sorts of jewelry while his court gazed up at him adoringly. Then I understood the hold that the mirror had on him and why he would beg to look at it as he had back by the Boneless King's old tomb.

Horn glanced nervously at the Boneless King and then crept on all fours over to Pomfret. "I beg your pardon, sir, but I was there when we found it in the Nameless One's tomb. This mirror makes no predictions. It merely reflects the many worlds of which ours is only one possibility. In some the Butcher never rose to power; in others the dragons are conquered."

"I know that," Pomfret snapped. "But the scene here will be repeated in our world."

"Look . . . in the mirror," Shimmer rasped. "See . . . what kind . . . of worlds . . . he . . . will make." She nodded to the Boneless King.

Behind the dais a small hole had appeared like a window. The hole opened upon a strange scene where black bolts of lightning flashed across orange skies, and the orange skies fused into the sides of a giant mountain. Ever changing, it was like nothing and like everything, and I remembered Civet's prediction: Chaos waits. With a growl, Snowgoose prowled at the top of the dais, guarding its master.

"No," Pomfret insisted, "he promised."

The hole had grown larger upon the dais. "What are . . . you afraid of?" Shimmer raised a paw weakly and pointed at the mirror. "Look!"

"There's no need. I've looked in it plenty. It will be a golden age." Pomfret made a halfhearted attempt to stop Snowgoose from attacking his sister, but the dog eluded his groping paw.

"You want . . . to ally yourself with the strong" was all Shimmer had time to say before Snowgoose pounced. The dragon tried to resist, but she was really almost helpless as the dog tried to bite through her armorlike hide.

"You've allied yourself with the weak. Look at what it's gotten you." As Pomfret cradled the mirror against his chest, the hole behind him grew larger. The air carried a strange series of smells: first a scent sweeter than any flowers, then a stench like rotting garbage—and on to other odors. The air seemed charged with an energy that made every hair of my fur bristle.

With a sudden lunge Shimmer knocked Snowgoose down the steps. "What's to make . . . the strong . . . keep their oaths?"

Snowgoose had seized one of Shimmer's hindlegs

264

and was trying to haul the dragon away from the steps. Feebly, Shimmer tried to bat the dog away with her tail, but the exertion was too much for her. I tried to rise, but I didn't have the breath. The best I could do was to crawl on all fours toward the dog.

A tentacle coiled through the hole and groped along the dais. With a cry Horn cringed as the tentacle slithered wetly along, changing from blue to green to black. But just as it touched him, the tentacle dissipated like mist.

I flung myself at Snowgoose, almost blacking out as I clung to the dog. It rounded on me savagely, but that gave Shimmer enough time to stretch out and clasp the mirror. As she collapsed, she pulled the mirror down so Pomfret had to look at the surface. "Look!"

Pomfret stared down at the surface. "All the seas are dry," he said grimly. "Everything's a wasteland." He shook his head stubbornly. "But that's only one possibility."

Snowgoose tried to leave me, but I grabbed hold of its collar and held on for dear life. Shimmer could only lie helplessly upon the steps. "Keep . . . looking," she panted.

Almost desperately, Pomfret grasped the mirror in his paws. "It is the same. Wait. There's another one. No, there's nothing alive." The former King of the inland dragons began to skip from one view to the next. However, it was always with the same result: a wasteland.

As Pomfret gazed into his mirror, the Boneless King kept enlarging the hole until a wind ripped around the throne room. As it swept over me, it felt boiling hot at first and then freezing cold.

The hole now stood some three meters in diameter beginning from the dais—though its outline shrank and dilated slightly like a pulsing, living thing. Through it we could see shapes seething and changing constantly with the colors and the light. Purple trees grew upside down from a pink sky, changing into black flowers and the flowers into feathery tongues of giant yellow worms lumbering over a shaking, exploding desert. It was as if the world couldn't make up its mind what to be yet. Looking at the scene for even a moment gave me a headache, and anyone looking at it for long would surely go mad.

"Bones," Pomfret muttered dazedly, "all I see are dragon bones in every one of them."

"There is . . . no reality . . . that won't be bleak . . . with the Boneless King." Shimmer bravely fought to raise her head. "You were . . . a dragon once. Be a dragon . . . again."

"What did they ever do for you but cast you out?" a voice boomed from the dais. I looked up to see the Boneless King standing there with his fists on his hips. Apparently, he was finished with the spell. For the sake of my own sanity, I tried hard not to look at the scene behind him.

Pomfret seemed to wake from a dream and turned to look up at the King. "The mirror doesn't lie."

"Bah." The Boneless King contemptuously kicked the mirror from Pomfret's claws and sent it clanging down the steps. "You have no more imagination than the rest. Together we can create a world unique throughout the universe."

Pomfret took a deep breath and then let it out slowly. "I will not be lied to."

"Beggars are to be crushed like insects." The Boneless King raised his hand, and another huge iron collar appeared in his fingers. Too late the horrified Pomfret tried to dodge, for the Boneless King easily snapped it around the dragon's throat.

Instantly it tightened so that the former King of the Inland Sea collapsed upon the steps, gasping. The Boneless King stared down at him, satisfied with his handiwork. "Fool, you would have made it easier to carry out my plans, but they will still go forward."

This time when he raised his hand, a tentacle slithered through the hole and into the throne room. Changing color continually, it slid across the dais until the Boneless King pointed at Shimmer. Immediately, the tentacle began to creep toward the dragon princess.

Gasping for breath, Shimmer roused and tried to raise herself so she could escape. However, with a cruel smile, the Boneless King pointed his finger at her collar. It tightened and Shimmer grasped at it for a moment. And yet the collar did not tighten enough to knock her out or make it impossible to move. She could still crawl—though she had such trouble breathing that she could only back slowly down the steps, watching helplessly as the tentacle wriggled toward her.

As Shimmer struggled desperately to escape, the Boneless King began to laugh—a harsh sound, a humorless sound, a sound of pure hatred for all life and things living. The laughter seemed to well up from some black, poisonous pit inside him, as if cruelty were now the only true pleasure for him.

At the first sounds of laughter Pomfret had jerked as if he had been lashed. Chest billowing in and out as he fought to breathe, Pomfret fought to rise from the steps. When he looked down at his sister, I saw tears falling from his eyes.

At this crucial moment, he proved to be of the same tough stock as Shimmer. Somehow he found the last dregs of energy and decency inside himself. Raising one foreleg, he threw himself forward against the Boneless King. He did not have much strength, but his mass carried him into the King, and his outspread foreleg closed around the King's waist.

"No, no, you can have anything," the Boneless King screamed. Frantically he punched at the dragon's leg, but Pomfret clasped the struggling King against his chest. With one final lurch, Pomfret threw himself toward the hole above the dais. And the dragon's momentum carried both into the time before time.

With a heartrending howl, Snowgoose seized Pomfret's tail to try to stop him. Pomfret, though, was already falling into that maddening chaos beyond. When the dragon's tail whipped into the air, the dog rose with it. Then, with a snap, both the tail and the dog disappeared through the hole as well.

For a moment we saw the three of them, dragon, human and dog. And it was hard to say if they were climbing, falling, swimming or suffocating within that bewildering landscape. As the hole closed, the Boneless King uttered one last cry—the memory of its pure hatred will stay with me forever.

CHAPTER TWENTY-FOUR

With the passing of the Boneless King, his spells were broken. The iron collar around my neck dissolved and I could breathe once again. Shimmer, her collar gone, was able to sit up. She looked toward the top of the dais where her brother had disappeared and began to weep openly. "Pomfret died far better than he lived."

As she mourned her brother, I put away my staff and slowly mounted the dais. Horn slid away on his backside. "I was only following orders," he protested again.

I waved my paw at him wearily. "It's all right. I just wanted my friend." When I picked up Thorn, I felt him tingle against my palms.

Down on the floor Indigo and the other statues slowly came to life—the bronze melting away to reveal flesh and cloth. When she was back to her scaly form, she plopped down. "It's hard work being a statue." She scratched her snout gratefully. "For one thing, you get the darnedest itches. What happened?"

I told her quickly, and when I was finished, she sighed. "Well, thank Heaven that's over."

"You think so?" I sat down beside her with Thorn upon my knees. "They say that peace is harder work than war."

And that was just about the last moment of privacy we were to have, because by then Lord Tower and the other court officials were fully restored and looking to us for answers.

I raised a tired paw. "If you're missing a king, it's us you can blame. If you're missing any silver cups, it's that fellow." I indicated Horn.

Lord Tower smoothed the yellow silk of his robe. "Then the King is really gone?"

Shimmer slid down beside us. "Yes. Do you want to make something out of it?"

However, Lord Tower knelt, and the others copied him. "You've saved us," he said, bowing.

As the others also began to bow, the Snail Woman stalked into the throne room. Her usual shiny shell was powdered with white dust from the statues, and her cheeks looked white as flour. In her hand she had a hammer. An exhausted Smith trailed after her. "Where is the King?" she demanded.

"Gone," Shimmer said, and explained quickly what had happened.

When she was barely finished, Lord Tower suddenly jumped to his feet. "Three cheers for the drag-ons," he cried. "Hip-hip . . ." And he lifted his arms exultantly.

"Hooray!" the crowd shouted in delight.

The cheering might have gone on indefinitely except that Shimmer held up a paw for peace. "We've also found the lost prince."

There are many people in Lord Tower's position who might have been greedy for power, but to give him his due, he seemed genuinely concerned. "This is wonderful news. Where is he?"

Shimmer indicated the cauldron. "His soul resides in there."

"Preposterous," said a voice from behind us. "*That* isn't the King."

"No, he looked exactly like one of the busts out in the lobby," Shimmer said, and turned to the Smith and the Snail Woman. "Did you see the bust? Doesn't he look like the boy called Thorn?"

"We did. It's true." The Snail Woman looked around as if daring anyone to contradict her.

When Lord Tower realized who the speaker was, he gaped for a moment and then again knelt and bowed even lower, so that his forehead touched the floor this time. "Lady, Lord, we are honored by your presence."

Shimmer put a paw on Thorn as she looked at the Snail Woman and the Smith. "You know so much about metal and magic—can anything be done to restore the prince?"

The Smith seemed embarrassed by all the attention. "Don't you want to restore your sea first?"

"If we may," Shimmer said.

The Snail Woman smiled, but there was an accusing tone in her voice. "The war is over, so you may use it as you see fit—just as we said originally."

I shrugged apologetically. "We couldn't be sure."

"Unlike that of certain apes"—she sniffed—"our word can be trusted." She turned to Lord Tower. "Her Highness intends to restore the Inland Sea with the help of the cauldron."

"Even if she had not earned our gratitude," Lord Tower promised, "we would pledge the resources of our kingdom to her enterprise. The clan of the Inland Sea has been sorely missed."

The Snail Woman turned back to Shimmer. "And after that we'll see what we can do for the boy."

The delighted Lord Tower jumped to his feet and led another round of cheers, drowning out what the Snail Woman was trying to say.

Since the cheering was likely to go on for a while, I slipped through the crowd.

The metal cranes were gathered in rows in the lobby, but though their eyes watched me as I passed, they did nothing. Outside, there were only a dozen or so statues still intact, the last bits of blue vapor escaping skyward. The other statues littered the garden grounds in an assortment of heads, torsos and limbs.

Here and there a small fire flared into life when one of the fire-rats scampered over a bit of lawn. However, since the fires died out on their own, I left them alone. The rats seemed to be having a high old time, exploring the garden and playing with the little monkeys.

"Children," I called. My little monkeys came scampering and chattering back to me. I had barely restored all my tail hairs when I heard a clanking behind me. Too late I tried to take to the air. A metal beak grasped my robe and held me dangling in the air while the Smith and the Snail Woman, followed by the rest of their cranes, sauntered out of the palace.

"You left quite a mess in our mountain. The next time you get an impulse to visit us"—the Smith snipped the tongs just before my nose—"take a deep breath, count to ten and let that thought pass." Then he went deeper into the garden, clinking his tongs together and calling to his pets. At the same time, the cranes picked up their small metal buckets again.

As the crane set me down on my feet, I looked over at the Snail Woman, who was washing her face in a fountain. "Lady, what were you trying to say to the others when the cheering drowned you out?"

She looked up, patting her hair back into place. "I was just trying to warn them that we might not be able to do very much for the boy. In fact," she said, glancing at a broken statue, "there may be only one thing we can do."

I knew she was talking about breaking the cauldron and releasing Thorn's soul. Rubbing my chin, I said, "Sambar isn't going to like that much."

She laughed as she headed for her chariot. "It wouldn't be the first time you had a dragon king mad at you."

"Thorn will come first anyway." I made a mental note to myself to stay away from the sea after that—assuming that Sambar survived his struggle with the krakens.

The Smith came back with a full bucket of fire-rats over one arm and a stone statue tucked under the other. "I'm ready, my dear. But I'm afraid our little pets will be up all night, what with all the air and the excitement they've had."

I watched the Snail Woman harness a team of cranes to her chariot. "Aren't you going to stay?"

"We've been through the celebrations for one war. We'll pass on this one." She jumped into her chariot. "Besides, it will take some study to help the boy."

"We also have a lot of cleaning up to do," the Smith said pointedly as he set the statue in the chariot.

I scratched my forehead. "That's a funny souvenir."

The Smith got up beside the statue. "We may be able to understand the spell on the cauldron better if I can examine another sample of the old magic."

Slipping her fan from her sleeve, the Snail Woman guided the chariot into the air. As it rose, the other cranes, with their loads of fire-rats, also soared into the air. "We'll see you by the Inland Sea," she shouted down to me.

As I sat down to enjoy the lovely—if slightly singed—garden, Indigo came out in her human form.

"I thought you liked being a dragon," I said.

"I do, but I asked Shimmer to change me back so I could go explore the kitchen." She held up a half-rotten apple. "The kitchen staff stole everything they could. This is all they left."

My own stomach had begun to growl. "I'm so hungry I could eat one of Sambar's snacks."

Indigo began to pare the rotten part from the apple with her dagger. "What do you think they'll do with the statues?"

"Make planters out of them. Let the ivy grow." I made a point of licking my lips as I gazed down at the apple. "Where's Shimmer?"

She cut the edible portion in half and held out part of it to me. "She's telling them about Thorn. He's a prince—fancy that." The jealousy seemed to have left her, to be replaced only by a sadness.

"Much good it's done him." I took it with a nod of thanks. "Do they believe her?"

"Well, the Snail Woman's word carries a lot of weight—especially with Lord Tower. And Lord Tower carries a lot of weight with the others." She began to nibble at her half of the apple. "I'd say at least half of them are willing to go along with the notion."

I finished my portion of our victory banquet with one chomp. "And the other half will suspect that the believers are up to something."

Indigo brushed off her hands. "There's just one thing that really bothers me. If there's a world for every possibility—"

"Almost every possibility," I corrected her.

"Then," she went on with a frown, "what about those worlds where the Boneless King rules?"

I rubbed my chin. "That notion used to bother my master too. And I know he intended to do something about it. In fact, he may be in one of them right now."

"There they are," an injured voice said from behind us.

I turned to see Lord Tower with a dozen servants with towels, basins of water, soap and silk robes to be tailored to our size.

And before we could object, we were literally picked up and carried back inside the palace to be pampered and fussed over. I tell you, it's hard to be a hero sometimes. There was nothing that the people of Ramsgate couldn't do for us. It got so that even a dedicated lazybones like me could barely stand it.

When Shimmer's clan brought in the human prisoners, the celebrations had to start over again because the war was over. With the prisoners the dragons brought word that Sambar had won a great victory over the krakens—which was welcome news, since I didn't relish the idea of having to fight a new war.

And when we finally tried to leave for River Glen, most of the palace insisted on escorting us. Now that the prince had been found, so to speak, Lord Tower vowed to stay with him. The rest of the court, too, accompanied us. If there were any skeptics about Thorn's authenticity left, they kept their doubts to themselves.

I was pleased, too, that the original occupants of River Glen had gathered in the surrounding mountains to see their home restored. It seemed so long ago that I had evacuated them before Civet could destroy their town with a flood.

As a result, between Shimmer's clan and our human escort there were probably more people in the mountains around River Glen than had ever lived in that unfortunate city, which now lay beneath the waters in that oval-shaped valley.

I had thought that once we were out in the wilds, the pampering would stop. But if anything it got worse, because each servant had to justify his or her existence.

I was standing on the shore, surveying River Glen and thinking of the fifth member of our party, Civet. The towers still rose forlornly from the water like the fingers of a drowning giant. There were dark patches of seaweed obscuring the buildings. I couldn't make out the spot where Civet the Witch had first loosed the sea to flood that poor city. Once the sea was gone, there would be a good deal of work restoring the city as well as Shimmer's home. And if Civet had been here, she might have pitched in to help. As it was, she had paid for her sins.

"No, no, no! Leave me alone." Indigo shoved away a maid who was trying shade her with a parasol. There were another half dozen with hair brushes, cushions and trays of snacks.

Indigo was dressed in an elegant robe of brocade

with felt boots and satin slacks. She no longer greased her hair blue but had it done up in black braids on either side of her head. "If you don't stop bothering me, I'll have Monkey bash in your heads."

I made a mental note to talk to Indigo about her language now that she was a court lady. "Don't look at me. You've always been pretty good at doing your own bashing."

Exasperated, Indigo bent, scooped up a palmful of seawater and splashed it over the maid. "Will you go away?"

However, the maid was used to royal tantrums, having survived the turbulent rule of the Butcher. Next to the Butcher's, Indigo's tantrums probably seemed like nothing. Holding out her hand, the maid received a silk handkerchief from another servant and calmly wiped off the fingers of the flabbergasted Indigo. "As it pleases you. But you only have to call." Still bowing, she withdrew some five meters to wait with the others.

"Temper, temper," I chided Indigo.

Indigo scowled. Speaking in a voice loud enough for the servant to hear, she said, "I liked it better when we were outlaws and on the run."

I looked around the army of tents on the hills surrounding the oval-shaped valley. They looked like thousands of fat, white pigeons roosting around a pond. "The only way I can get a nap is to sleep on some cloud," I said. "And even then you've got Shimmer's clan buzzing around." I nodded up at the sky, where Sergeant Chukar was trying to channel some of the young dragons' energy by drilling them in formation.

Indigo stuck a finger into the water and licked it cautiously. "It's not very salty, so once the water's drained, they should be able to bring the area back."

That kind of concern surprised me. "Are you thinking of settling here?"

She wiped her wet hand on her brocade robe—much to the distress of her servants, who tried to run forward with handkerchiefs until a glare from Indigo sent them scuttling back. "I go where Shimmer goes," she said to me. "It's just that people won't let me do anything. And it gets boring."

"Speaking of the queen lizard, where is she anyway?" I asked.

"She wanted to be alone." Indigo nodded to the lookout point that jutted out into the sea. "She's been awful funny lately—like her head was in the clouds."

I suspected what might be on Shimmer's mind. I just wished there were some way to prepare Indigo. To give myself some time for thought, I smoothed my hand over my new robe. They had wanted to give me a new tiger skin, but that wouldn't have been right. So I wore the old one even if the stains had not come out very well. "They say," I hinted, "that the worst curse in the world is to get what you wish for."

Thrush flew up to us. "Lord, Lady, it's almost time."

By the time we joined Shimmer, Chukar had

brought her charges down on a near shore. Shimmer, though, roused only when the last load of firewood was added to the pile. Then Storax, representing the dragon mages, and the chief human wizard set Thorn upon a spit beside the fire. (The whole ceremony had been worked out after deep, agonizing negotiations between Lord Tower and Lady Francolin.) Expectantly, Lord Tower and other notables stood near the edge of the reviewing platform while Shimmer joined the other dragons.

It was Indigo herself who poured the pail of water into Thorn. Then Shimmer swung Thorn over the wood, and Bulbul, as one of the oldest dragons, lit it.

While dragon mages and human wizards tended the cauldron anxiously, checking for cracks, the sea itself began to boil. In no time the vapor was rolling from the surface and into Thorn. By the end of the day, the sea had boiled away, leaving muddy streets, a few dead trees and a small forest of arrowweed. There hadn't been time for fish and other sea creatures to find their way to the new sea. There had just been ducks and other waterfowl, which had already been removed by Bombax and the minor mages to safer areas.

The next day Sergeant Chukar and her veterans and the human palace guard took turns carrying Thorn. (Lieutenant Crusher and his squad were there and properly apologetic for all they had done.) The long procession of dragons and humans followed the old road eastward up the slopes past the dry waterfalls to the site of the old Inland Sea. We had an easier time than Shimmer and Thorn had had, since Lord Tower had sent the army ahead to rebuild the road, and families were already begging to settle in the hills and restore the terrace gardens and orchards.

The Inland Sea was now no more than a flat white disk, shiny as a china plate, and I had to blink my eyes. The seabed was so vast, I found it hard to believe that an injured Shimmer had once crossed it on foot with Thorn. The ancient seafloor was so dazzling that I could barely make out the Weeping Mountain to the north, where Civet had once lived. To the east, the Desolate Mountains were just a faint smudge.

Climbing to a headland that overlooked the seafloor, Shimmer herself took Thorn. In that short time human artisans sent by Lord Tower had erected an elegantly carved and gold-leafed pavilion for the ceremony.

Marching to the very edge, Shimmer looked around. "Let us not forget the one who made this all possible," she said, and held Thorn up for all to see. And then she tipped Thorn over on his side, and the water began to flow, gushing down the sides of the headland and onto the seabed.

As the water began to spread outward, a cheer went up from the dragons, and even the humans got caught up in the celebration. And though the water seemed to pour out of Thorn no faster, the sea magically covered the salt bed, changing white to a light blue.

The sea filled its old bed so fast that it was like watching an artist paint a picture, a few deft brush-strokes filling in the entire canvas. As the waters rose, Shimmer's clan could no longer contain themselves but rose into the air to cut spirals and loops. The sea level rose with miraculous rapidity, and it was only when it was some two meters from the top of the headland that the water fell to a trickle from Thorn and then stopped.

As Shimmer righted Thorn, Storax solemnly announced, "The sea is restored."

CHAPTER TWENTY-FIVE

At that point a combined band of humans and dragons was supposed to strike up some sentimental tune, but suddenly a shining blue spot of light began to pulse before Shimmer.

"It's the Boneless King," Lord Tower cried. Many of the human dignitaries hiked up their robes, jumped down from the platform and tried to find a place to hide. However, the Lord himself clutched a chair as a weapon—though I doubted if the lord chancellor could actually have swung an object as heavy as that.

Shimmer crouched, ready to spring. "Monkey," she called.

"I'm right with you," I called, taking out my staff and leaping into the air. Had the Boneless King found a way out of chaos?

"Indigo?" Shimmer cried urgently, her eyes intent upon the light.

"I'm right here." Holding up her gown in one hand, Indigo pelted along on foot. The only weapon handy was a silver hair brush she had snatched from one of her maids. "I wish I were a dragon," she panted.

I was too caught up with the threat, though, to tease her. Then, as a hunting horn sounded a long, low note that rose quickly up the scale, the spot expanded, spreading outward rapidly to form a glowing oval with its base upon the rock. The light was now so bright that we could only see the silhouettes of slim hunting dogs and mounted riders with the helmets of flowers. As the hole spread into a glowing doorway, the Lord of the Flowers cantered onto the headland.

He was a short, squat creature with a pumpkin-shaped head and a face that would curdle milk. His leather hunting suit, cut into the shape of leaves, rustled as he rode forward. On his wrist was a hooded falcon.

He stared with satisfaction at the sea and then back at Shimmer. "So that old windbag of a Smith wasn't just bellowing. You disposed of the King and restored your sea. Good, good." His horse pranced as he turned to look at the sea.

"Yes, Lord," Shimmer said icily. "But I did not think you cared. You refused to come."

That was a dangerous thing to say to a creature as powerful and eccentric as the Lord of the Flowers. Once, when a fellow looked at the Lord the wrong way, the fellow had wound up with crabgrass sprouting from his scalp instead of hair. Quickly I bowed. "Please pay no attention to her, Lord. She's been under a good deal of strain."

The Lord of the Flowers leaned forward on his pommel. "Haven't you been hanged yet, ape?"

I doffed my cap and bowed low. "I've still managed to stay one step ahead of them, My Lord."

He looked back at Shimmer. "I thought you had better taste than to hang around with this reprobate."

"I take my friends where I can find them," Shimmer snapped.

The Lord smiled sadly. "A good philosophy." He straightened, the leather of his saddle creaking. "Don't judge me too harshly because I didn't come when the Smith snapped his fingers. I have fought my war; I have paid my price. And I was fairly sure you could deal with him yourselves."

Shimmer regarded Thorn sadly. "We have paid our own price, though."

"In any event, I have brought you a present, Your Highness." And with a little bow, he held out a slender stalk that held sprays of small white flowers shaped like pinwheels.

"Ebony's tears," Shimmer gasped.

The Lord of the Flowers passed it over to her. "The Inland Sea is not complete without these famous flowers growing along its shores."

Genuinely touched, Shimmer trembled as she held the delicate flower in one great paw. "I never thought any of us would see these again. You're too kind." We had used up what we thought was the very last flower to summon this master once before.

"Nonsense. I do this not for love of dragons but for love of this flower. Plant it," he urged.

Shimmer hesitated. "Shouldn't I dry it and save the seeds?"

"Plant it," the Lord urged.

"Don't argue with him," I whispered out of the side of my mouth.

"Also good philosophy," the Lord observed.

With a shrug Shimmer thrust the flower stalk into the soil. Almost instantly, more flowers sprouted from the dirt around it.

"It's magical, you see." The Lord raised an arm.

And the flower patch kept spreading outward from the first flower that Shimmer had planted. It was like watching a pool of milk cover the dirt, and the flowers kept widening in area until the flower patch raced away in either direction along the shore, sweeping around the edges of the sea and along the barren hills opposite us.

"It's like it was when a hunted Ebony wept by these shores and the flowers came into being." The Lord gazed at the scene with satisfaction.

Suddenly the earth looked as if it were covered with snow. When I looked down, I saw that I was ankle deep in stalks of the lovely little flowers, and the air was filled with their soft, sweet scent.

Lowering his hand, the Lord turned his horse's

head toward the hole. "Lose the ape, Your Highness. People will judge you by the company you keep."

However, before he could bolt back through the doorway, Shimmer spoke up. "My Lord, you've been more than generous. But if I could ask one more favor . . ."

He reined in his horse but did not look around. "That depends."

"In this cauldron is a soul." Shimmer's voice grew a little hoarse. "It was trapped by the old magic. Could you help us restore the prisoner?"

The Lord glanced over his shoulder. "That is more the Smith's magic than mine, but I'll find those who can help." And with a kick of his heels, his horse galloped through the hole and the hole itself winked out of existence.

I breathed a sigh of relief, because the Lord of the Flowers could be a double-edged sword as likely to cut as to help you. "You play a dangerous game," I said to Shimmer.

"I'm past caring." She set Thorn down among the flowers.

"Well, I'm not." Indigo flung her silver hair brush aside. "I'm tired of this shape. I liked it better when I was a dragon."

"She fought alongside us," Bulbul said encouragingly. "She's welcome in the clan."

Shimmer held a claw up to her lips with exaggerated care. "Quiet, Bulbul. By that thinking we'd have to accept that ape as well."

I wouldn't normally want to join the ranks of the ugly and hairless, but the princess—I mean queen— could use a little teasing. "Count me in, cousin."

Shimmer wagged a claw at me. "Don't presume too much. You'll only be honorary kin."

Indigo poked Shimmer. "Well, what about it?"

Shimmer blinked. "You're serious."

"Very," Indigo assured her. "My own clan's gone. And since I was raised in the dragon palace, humans are just as strange to me as creatures from the moon. From what I've seen of humanity, I don't have much use for it. And," she added, "I like the clan of the Inland Sea." She bowed when Bulbul roared his approval.

Shimmer scratched her snout. "Well, I suppose you can always change back if you get tired of it." She started to reach a paw to her forehead. "Botheration, I keep forgetting I don't have the pearl anymore."

Storax paraded forward smugly. "You'll have to learn some real spells, Your Highness."

"I'm too old to go back to school," Shimmer groaned.

"I want blue spikes," Indigo insisted.

His aesthetic principles offended, the Grand Mage appealed to Shimmer. "Your Highness . . . ?"

However, Storax found no sympathy in Shimmer. "Do as she says."

With a sigh Storax worked a quick spell. Immediately Indigo's nose and jaw began to stretch to a "proper" dragon size. Hunching forward, her fingers lengthened into claws. Brocade and skin merged into rainbow scales that slowly turned green.

And the next moment she was wagging a long tail as happily as a pup. "My back itches," she said with a wriggle of her shoulders. An instant later, wings sprouted and spread outward like two majestic sails.

"No more hair brushes," she whooped. "No more robes." She held up the claws of one paw admiringly. "And if one of those pesky maids bothers me, it's off with her head."

But that had given Shimmer an idea. She nodded to Thorn. "Could you transform him back into his original human form?"

Storax rubbed his chin. "And what of Sambar?"

"I'll answer to him with my head if I have to," Shimmer said.

Storax picked up Thorn and studied him from every angle. Then, with a sigh, he handed Thorn back to Shimmer. "There is a powerful magic on this cauldron—far too powerful for me."

By that time, most of the dignitaries had climbed back to the pavilion, and Lord Tower called over to Shimmer. "Your Highness, if we might go back to the schedule before the ceremonies get completely out of hand."

Right at that moment, though, a pebble dropped on my head. Putting out a paw, I felt dirt patter down. "The weather forecast is mountains in the sky and showers of pebbles." I motioned Indigo to put up one of her wings. When she did, I took shelter under it. "I don't see why that fool Smith can't park his mountain over the sea, where it wouldn't bother anyone right now."

As the sky began to glow red, dragons began to curl up against the dirt and pebbles raining down, while those humans not in the pavilion crouched with their hands over their heads.

Slowly the floating mountain materialized in the sky, blocking out the sun. With a glowing red top, it floated majestically overhead. As we gaped, a chariot flew from inside with the Smith and the Snail Woman in the vehicle.

People and dragons scattered to form an area for them to land on, but the Smith and the Snail Woman did not descend immediately. Instead, they circled around their mountain as if taking in the view of the sea. They must have liked what they saw, because when the chariot had rolled to a halt, the Smith and the Snail Woman were smiling.

"You've done well," the Smith said as he stepped down.

Shimmer regarded Thorn. "It's a hollow victory unless you can restore him."

The Snail Woman shook her head as she joined her husband. "We have been reading everything. We've even studied the residual magic in the Boneless King's old statue. That's impossible, I'm afraid."

Shimmer stood silently for a moment and then squared her shoulders. "Then there is only one thing to do. Let me take Thorn's place so he can be free."

Indigo stepped away from me and folded in her wing. "No," she protested.

Shimmer, though, was determined to settle this last and greatest debt. "This is the only way to satisfy Sambar and yet keep my obligation to Thorn," Shimmer said. "This way he will have his cauldron and Thorn will be free." She rested a paw upon Indigo's shoulder. "You have my clan now, and you have a home as fair as any—or it will be."

"But *you* won't be here," Indigo argued.

"Do you want him to be trapped inside the cauldron forever?" Shimmer demanded.

"No," Indigo admitted slowly. "But I don't want you trapped inside it either. Why can't we just break the cauldron? He'd have lost the cauldron anyway if you had managed to transform Thorn to human form."

"I was being cowardly." Shimmer indicated the blue, lifeless sea. "If I pay the price, my clan will have Sambar's help in restoring the sea to its former beauty."

"Now, now, that may not be necessary," the Smith said, and then hesitated.

The Snail Woman nudged him. "You started it. Go on."

The Smith tugged at his ear. "What I mean to say is that we can't restore him to a human form, but there's nothing that says he can't be in another shape."

"He could talk and walk," the Snail Woman added.

"Sambar will be interested in how well he boils water," I interjected.

The Smith looked at his wife and then shrugged. "I don't see why he couldn't. He'll be hollow inside."

Lord Tower jumped down from the pavilion. "You can restore the true King?"

"You'd want him as King?" I wondered.

"It is his right," Lord Tower insisted.

"And why not?" The Snail Woman tucked her folded fan into her sleeve. "We've seen how kind and noble he is. Part of the problem with human rulers is that they grow old and wear out."

I scratched my head. "But assuming they keep him polished, he could last forever. What if he changes later?"

Shimmer considered Thorn. "The real problem is Sambar. How can Thorn be a ruler and one of the treasures of the dragon kingdom as well?"

"That is a problem for lawyers and theoretical magicians," the Snail Woman said. "Do you want to give a shape to Thorn?"

Without hesitating, Shimmer said, "Yes. And let Sambar's wrath be upon my head." I think in the back of her mind she figured that if worst came to worst, she would carry out her original plan and free Thorn by taking his place.

I went over to Shimmer and placed a paw upon one of Thorn's carved sides. "What do you say?"

I felt the tingle against my paw. When I looked up, I saw that Shimmer had felt it too. "He says 'yes,'" I said.

"If we fail, it might be dangerous to him," the

Smith warned. "And there is no certainty we'll succeed."

Shimmer looked down at Thorn. "That's his decision as well." She left her paw there for a moment and then nodded her head. "I felt a tingle. He wants to try."

"One way or another he'll have peace," the Snail Woman observed.

As Shimmer handed Thorn to the Smith, Lord Tower strode forward. "May I accompany you?"

The Snail Woman glanced at me and then shook her head. "We're through having visitors in our forge."

With the Smith holding Thorn carefully, the two climbed back into the chariot. Taking out her fan, the Snail Woman guided the chariot back up to the mountain.

After that everyone gave up on the ceremonies altogether. While the dragons sported in their newly restored home, some of the humans found pleasant spots to picnic among the flowers. For once I had to admit that a dragon hadn't been exaggerating when she had boasted of her home: The Inland Sea was a lovely place. In fact, if things worked out, I decided, I might actually take Shimmer up on her offer of an honorary membership in her clan.

At the moment, though, only part of my mind was on the scenery. Just a small group of humans, led by Lord Tower, stayed with Shimmer and watched as the Smith fired up the forge. Red light and sparks spewed from the top of the mountain, making it look like a flying volcano.

It was about at that point that a group of guardsmen rode up. Lieutenant Crusher, acting as a guide, led them on foot. Saluting Lord Tower, he motioned behind him. "These men have brought the prisoner as you commanded, Lord."

Sitting miserably on one horse with his arms tied behind him was a fat man with a heavy ridge of a forehead, on which sat twin bushy eyebrows.

Shimmer seemed to know him. With a growl, she paced over to the man and smiled maliciously so she could show her fangs. "Hello, Knobby. Remember me?"

The man shrank back before the dragon. "I d-d-d-don't think I've had that pleasure," he stuttered.

Raising one paw, she studied her claws. "You once threatened me with a crossbow."

"No, no, it wasn't me," the man began to babble. "It must have been someone else. Or if it was me, I must have been drunk."

Lord Tower joined Shimmer and motioned for the guardsmen to help Knobby dismount. But faced with a dragon, Knobby sagged at the knees, and a guardsman had to stand on either side, holding him up. "So this is the man who raised the prince?"

"He beat that poor boy every chance he got," Shimmer snapped.

"Who? Who-o-o?" Knobby hooted hysterically.

"A boy called Thorn," Lord Tower informed him

sternly. "Now tell us how he came to you."

By then Knobby was so frightened that he became incoherent, and it took a good while before we could get any straight answers from him. As it turned out, it was some old man who had left the baby. Knobby didn't know who he was or where he had gone except that it was now almost thirteen years ago.

"I took him in out of the goodness of my heart," Knobby went on babbling. "There's many a person would not have given one hair about a poor orphan."

When Lord Tower had ordered Knobby to be taken away for later punishment, he turned to the rest of us with a sigh. "I sent those men to get some answers, but we still have as many questions as before."

At that moment, a shower of sparks rose from the mountain. "I do hope I made the right decision," Lord Tower muttered.

We were so busy watching the mountain, we didn't notice the blue speck of light appear in the air. But when I heard the sound of the hunting horn, I turned. Quickly the speck widened into a shining doorway again, through which I saw the silhouette of a galloping horse with two riders.

"It's the Lord of the Flowers," I said, backing up hurriedly.

The Lord raced onto the headland and circled. "Where is everyone?" He noticed the shadow covering the ground and looked up to see the mountain. "Ah, Old Windy's come to muddle up things as usual."

As he circled his horse, I saw the other rider more

clearly. He looked like a small boy of about ten, but he had white hair and white eyebrows. He was wearing a stained, patched robe of purple cotton and a sash of bright red. "Master," I cried joyfully, and ran to help him down.

Leaping down almost as nimbly as a monkey, the Old Boy shook his head. "I had no idea things were so bad here, or I would have come back sooner."

"How did you find him?" Shimmer asked the Lord of the Flowers.

The Lord of the Flowers held his reins tightly as another shower of sparks almost panicked his horse. "When I hunt someone, there is no escaping."

As I helped brush off my master, I couldn't help giving a shudder. "I remember," I murmured.

"And now if you'll excuse me, Your Highness, I'll leave. I have little taste for the Smith's artificial magic." With a nod, the Lord of the Flowers sent his horse racing back through the hole, and the air swallowed him up once again. However, as he disappeared from sight, we heard his voice faintly warn, "Get ride of the ape soon, or you'll be sorry."

"It's all . . . uh . . . a misunderstanding," I tried to explain to my master.

The Old Boy waved me away. "Well, I didn't get back any too soon. Look how scruffy and slipshod you've gotten without me around. Is that any way for a disciple to dress?"

The Old Boy was a master of magic, but he never could get to the point to save his life. I bowed several times. "Please, master. Can't you help the prince?"

"Perhaps. I certainly owe it to him to try. I got called away for an emergency—I just managed to solve it." The Old Boy turned to the others apologetically. "At any rate, I left the little prince in this quaint little village called . . . called . . . ?" He scratched his head. "Now what was that name?"

"Amity," Shimmer supplied.

"Ah, you've been there." He brightened.

I gently tried to keep him on track. "Master, the boy."

"Oh, yes." The Old Boy nodded. "Well, I left him there along with some money for his care, and—"

Remembering Knobby's protestations, I cleared my throat noisily. "I think you forgot again, master."

"Nonsense. I left a bag of gold just like this one." The Old Boy produced a small bag of gold from his sleeve. "Or was it *this* one?" he muttered as he stared at it. "Oh, dear. I should have come back a lot sooner to check on the boy."

"But how did you come by the baby?" Lord Tower prompted.

The Old Boy stowed the gold away again. "Do I know you?"

"Master," I suggested, " I can introduce you later."

"Yes, of course." While he went on speaking, the Old Boy absently began searching his other sleeve and his sash, producing several sets of keys, a small notebook, a ticket to the opera and a self-spinning top along with a number of objects that I didn't recognize because he must have picked them up on other worlds during his travels. "The assassins had brought the queen to the woods, where they left her to die of her wounds. They had also brought the baby to die of exposure. By that time there was nothing I could do for the poor woman, but I took the baby."

"It was probably some of the Butcher's men," Lord Tower said grimly.

The Old Boy redistributed his treasures to other spots in his clothes. "Quite probably. Now who are you?"

I made quick introductions and briefly told the story to my master. "Do you think you can help?" I finished. "They're trying to give him a human shape even if he has to stay bronze."

The Old Boy gazed up at the floating mountain. "The Smith and the Snail Woman are clever magicians, but I think I've learned a trick or two that they don't know. Together we might be able to do better than we could singly."

It was a measure of Shimmer's respect that she would be willing to be seen carrying a human. "May I fly you up to the mountain?"

"No, no need." He nodded, and a cloud appeared beneath the Old Boy and lifted him as easily as if he were on a dish. With his arms spread out for balance, he rose swiftly up to the mountain and disappeared into the side.

CHAPTER TWENTY-SIX

By now the whole affair had turned into a pleasant picnic by the newly restored sea. Human and dragon musicians took turns playing favorite tunes. There was one merry human song I recognized as "The Prince Diamond Jig," which was a lively tune with the dark humor that was typical of Ramsgate.

Jump, boy, jump—
There's a price upon your head.
Hide, boy, hide,
Or it's the knife instead.

And, of course, the dragons responded with a song that Shimmer identified as "The Ebony Caper."

The Serpent Lady speaks. Did he hear her?

Did he look into the mirror
And therein see his sorrow?
For him there is no tomorrow.

If I had just read the lyrics, I would have supposed this to be yet another one of their weepy songs, but the tune itself was even sprightlier than a jig and danced with a skipping step in two lines of dragons facing one another. The dragons had more of a sense of humor than I would have thought—though it could be just as dark as that of Ramsgate.

Of course, there were refreshments for both species.

After a few hours I noticed some of the dignitaries shedding their dignity along with their fancy robes and going swimming in their underwear. Even Lord Tower consented to do a stately dog paddle while Lady Francolin, with equal gravity and decorum, floated along beside him.

If Indigo had thought she could escape the attention of her servants by changing herself into a dragon, she was mistaken. If anything, they were twice as determined to be useful. The only way she could escape was to take flying lessons with Thrush.

Watching Indigo soar with the other young dragons over the sparkling sea, I turned to Shimmer. "I think Indigo just might fit in."

Shimmer barely glanced in Indigo's direction. Her eyes were on the floating mountain as she paced around in a circle. "She's my friend, and she's fought along with us. And she's known as much

301

hardship as we have."

I leaned forward and pressed my nose into some of the delicate little white flowers and then looked around the lovely scene. The sea was a bright, heart-stopping sapphire blue, and the sunlight reflected from the waves like little golden snakes wriggling around. "In this place they might all blossom and grow straight and true."

"But what about Thorn? I wonder how they're doing?" Shimmer paused and gazed up at the mountain. "Maybe I should go and check on their progress."

I lay down among the flowers and let the scent close all around me. "We're not exactly their favorite people."

"I think I will go." Shimmer was just about to spread her wings when a cloud of sparks flew from the top of the mountain and flames rolled skyward. All around the sea, humans and dragons paused to stare up at the spectacle as fire flew from the mountaintop.

Shimmer hastily sat down and gulped. "Or maybe I'll just stay here."

If the day was beautiful, the night was something to remember. The moon came out looking as bright and clear as a paper window behind which the biggest candle in the universe had been set. The surrounding hills, covered with Ebony's tears, seemed to glow a ghostly white, and the waters of the Inland Sea looked like black lacquer decorated with silver threads in an ever-changing pattern. And sea and sky seemed to blend together, so I couldn't tell where one ended and one began. Here Civet might have found the peace she had sought so long. And high overhead the flying mountain floated, hiding the stars in a lurid red light, its top periodically belching out flames.

The one thing that marred the entire occasion was that Thorn wasn't there to enjoy it.

The night was cool but pleasant, so few humans used their tents. I just lay down among the flowers. By day they had a faint scent, but the full moon seemed to draw the fragrance from Ebony's tears, and I felt like I could almost have wrapped it around myself like a blanket. Somewhere in the distance dragons were teaching humans how to play that lovely, sad song called "The Weaver's Lament," and somewhere else I could hear Indigo laughing. And I fell asleep thinking again that I might just take up Shimmer on her offer of an honorary membership in her clan—whether the overblown frog had meant it or not.

I woke the next morning to Indigo shaking my shoulder excitedly. "They're coming."

Shimmer was already hovering a meter off the ground, circling slowly. I sat up in time to see the Old Boy, his white hair gleaming, descend from the mountain on one of his clouds. The chariot, pulled by a team of cranes, followed him quickly. Angling down, it landed near Shimmer, the wheels crushing the flowers and filling the air with their delicate fragrance. Shimmer craned her long neck, trying to see behind the Smith and the Snail Woman. "Did you succeed?"

My master smoothed his robes calmly over his knees. "Of course we did."

Out from behind the Smith and the Snail Woman stepped a flesh-and-blood Thorn. Hopping off the chariot, he squatted and ran his hands through the flowers. "It's wonderful to be able to smell again." He rose and turned in a slow circle, gazing raptly at the hills and sea. "It's beautiful here."

Shimmer caught him up and rose on her hindlegs, sweeping him around in a circle. "Isn't it just like I told you?"

She had no sooner set him down on his feet when I hugged him next. "It's good to be holding flesh and bone again," I said.

When I had let go, Thorn squinted at the blue-spiked dragon. "Indigo?"

"I'll just shake your hand." Shyly Indigo extended a paw.

"We've been through too much together to stand on ceremony." The boy threw his arms around her neck and gave her a hug as well. "I'd like to see anyone push you around now."

"So would I." Indigo grinned.

Thorn turned and looked back at Shimmer and me. "I could see and hear everything. I tried to tell you, but I couldn't talk to you."

"We knew you were there," I assured him.

"I want to know all about your adventures," Thorn said, and raised his arms to put them around Shimmer and me. But then we heard a loud creak.

The Smith jumped down from the chariot. "Thunderation. I guess the conversion wasn't complete."

The Snail Woman followed her husband. "It's probably just a bone or two."

"It doesn't matter. Thank you." When Thorn bowed, we heard another creak.

I had to laugh. "I think you'll have to give up your plans to be a sneak thief."

"As if he ever was one," Lord Tower declared, and clapped his hands together. Instantly servants sprang forward and began to converge on Thorn with robes and jewelry. Civet's prophecy was doubly true—cauldron or human, people would bow to Thorn.

"Uh-oh," Indigo muttered. "He's going to get the treatment now."

Thorn, though, raised a hand and commanded, "Halt."

"The boy's learned something from jumping into a forge," I murmured to Shimmer.

"Or by having all that power," Shimmer whispered back.

Thorn sought out the lord chancellor. "I don't want to be the King."

I think Lord Tower had prepared for every eventuality except that. "But you must."

Thorn got a stubborn look. "I want to stay here, though."

"And I want you to stay too." Shimmer looked defiantly at Lord Tower. "The boy deserves a reward, not that mess back in the capital."

"The dragons could use a friend on the throne," Lord Tower suggested slyly.

Shimmer shot an angry glance at him and then argued softly with Thorn. "You've already done enough for us."

Thorn, though, was hesitating. "But if my mother and father really *were* the queen and King . . ."

The Old Boy had been following everything from a couple of meters up in the air. He floated in now on his cloudy perch. "The queen gave you to me. If anyone denies that, they'll have to answer to me. No one calls me a liar."

Shimmer could be just as stubborn as Thorn. "We're going to build a place for you right here."

"Your Majesty could use that when he visits," Lord Tower said diplomatically. "Affairs of state would often bring you here." He was a smooth one, all right. I could see how he had survived so many years under the half-mad Butcher.

Thorn plucked at his lip and then glanced at Shimmer. "I suppose it's another one of those times when you have to do the right thing."

Shimmer swallowed. "I suppose so."

"A wise choice," Lord Tower declared. When he clapped his hands, the servants again began to move toward Thorn.

"Hold it," Thorn said, and put up his hands again.

Lord Tower gave a respectful bow. "Your Majesty must dress according to his new rank."

Thorn looked down at his ragged old robe. "This served me well enough when I was a peasant. It will serve me well enough for a little longer." He patted his stomach. "Right now I'm hungry. What's there to eat?"

Lord Tower was wise enough not to argue this time.

There was still plenty of food left from the day before, and we sat down to yet another pleasant picnic while we filled Thorn in on our adventures trying to rescue him and the later battle at the Hundred Children. Since the Smith, the Snail Woman and my master had not been there either, they listened attentively. And Lord Tower made notes every now and then on his sleeve with a thin bit of charcoal. I thought he was going to pass them on to some historian, but as it subsequently turned out, he fancied himself a poet and balladeer and wanted the notes for his own epic. Well, I suppose even lord chancellors have to have a hobby.

We had just about finished up the meal as well as the stories when we heard a roaring sound. Indigo frowned. "It sounds like some big gust of wind sweeping in."

Shading my eyes, I peered at the sky. "In a way. It's Sambar." True to his word, the High King of the dragons had arrived.

In the distance, Sambar and his court looked like a huge flock of crows, but they kept growing as they came closer until we could see they were dragons. And they kept coming, pouring over the horizon in a river of green scales.

As they landed within the Inland Sea, I could see artisans with their tools to help build an underground palace, and there were hordes of servants and gardeners bearing baskets of coral worms, fish, sea kelp and just about anything else needed to reseed the sea. My favorites, though, were the singing sea lizards. I could hear them chirping inside jars of seawater. There were so many dragons, they filled the near sea from shore to shore.

"Ah, just in time for lunch," said Sambar. His huge frame swathed in silken bandages, the High King landed with all the gracefulness of a professional acrobat. Landing behind him was an escort of guard dragons, but their decorative plaques and helmets were gone and their hides were as scarred as those of Shimmer's clan. The victory over the krakens had not been an easy one.

With a bow, Shimmer nodded to the bandages. "You're hurt."

"I couldn't let you have all the glory." The High King of the dragons embraced his niece. "We drove the krakens back into the Abyss. They won't bother us for a very long time." He let go of her and looked around until he found me. "I was all set for a victory celebration, and guess what I found when I returned to my palace and saw the state of my larder? Did you have to take *everything*?"

I eyed the sky so I could be ready to escape. "It was all in a good cause. At least you still have a palace."

Shimmer bowed. "But the dream pearl was destroyed."

"Yes, Storax sent me word." Sambar puffed himself

up like a toad. "What are you going to do to make up for your broken vow?"

It crossed my mind that some of Sambar's escort could easily become our captors, and his huge army of soldiers and servants could overpower Shimmer's clan.

Shimmer straightened her neck proudly. "Let your punishment be on my head and on me alone."

Sambar gave a hearty laugh. He had only been pretending to be angry. "The worst punishment I could give you is to leave you right here. You'll find ruling a hard enough task. But," he said, holding out his paw, "I will take Baldy's bowl."

Thorn was still watching out for Shimmer. "I'm afraid that I am the cauldron," he said. "Or rather I was. If you'll forgive Shimmer, you can do what you want with me."

Sambar waved his paw indulgently. "Yes, yes, your jest is quite amusing." He looked again at Shimmer. "Now where is the cauldron?"

"The boy is speaking the truth." My master moved lower so he could stare Sambar straight in the eye. "It was his soul within the cauldron, and we changed him back. Would you have had him stay trapped inside for eternity?"

There aren't many who can stand eyeball to eyeball with the Old Boy. And the High King of the dragons wasn't one of them. He dropped his eyes and shuffled his forepaws uncomfortably. "Well, no, of course not. But"—his head shot up again—"what will compensate me for the loss of such a treasure?"

I spoke up before Shimmer could offer her head again. In the mood he was in, I was afraid that Sambar would accept her invitation this time and really take it. "I could say something about friendship being more valuable than treasure."

"You could," Sambar rumbled like a leathery volcano, "but you would be wise not to. I've no patience for platitudes at the moment."

However, I plowed on. "But a human king who is a dragon friend would be a true treasure." I doffed my cap and bowed. "And perhaps yours truly can find some treasure for you as great as the one you lost."

"I don't doubt you could, you little thief." Sambar sighed. "Well, since the deed seems to be done and can't be undone . . . ?" He cocked an eyebrow quizzically at the Old Boy. When my master shook his head, Sambar went on. "I suppose I might as well make a virtue of necessity."

Impulsively, Thorn extended his hand. "I pledge my friendship to the dragons, and anyone who does anything to harm that friendship will be outlawed."

Sambar hid his astonishment. Raising his great paw, he took the small human hand in his. "You know," he said thoughtfully, "this just might work out." He fixed me with a stern eye. "But I am holding you to your promise. I expect some kind of compensation."

"You shall have it." I bowed deeply to the High King.

"It's well you made that promise." Sambar held one paw behind his ear as a distant roaring filled the sky. "Because if you hadn't, I wouldn't have told you that I had sent for the King of the Golden Sea to replenish my larder. I believe he's coming right now. I wonder what treats he has for me?"

I saw the distant specks on the horizon coming in from the sea and then winked at Sambar. "And how could I keep my promise if I were in his prison?" Sambar was not as stupid as he looked.

Sambar winked back. "What a shame you have to go. The King wanted to talk to you about something you 'borrowed' a while ago."

My master's cloud bounced up and down as he leaned forward in distress. "You've been getting into bad habits again."

"Alas, master, it's the company I keep. But they're such brave and good and true companions that I forgive them their flaws." Nodding gratefully to Sambar for his warning, I started to give a hug to Indigo before I remembered how much she shied away from being touched. Instead, I contented myself with waving my cap at her. "We'll have a flying race when I get back."

To my surprise, though, she threw her forelegs around me and gave me a huge hug. "I'll be waiting." She laughed. I think being a dragon agreed with her.

Setting my cap on my head, I skipped over to Thorn. "Keep a room for me in the Dome." Not sure what to do with kings, I was only going to shake his hand, but he himself embraced me.

"You'll have the biggest and sunniest room," he promised.

"It better be one with a good view," Shimmer said, "so he can see his enemies sneaking up on him." She raised one foreleg to hug me, but I had a surprise in store for her.

"Let's have a fishing contest again." Jumping up in the air, I kissed one leathery cheek and added brightly, "Cousin."

Shimmer wiped her cheek in mock disgust, but I thought I detected the beginnings of a tear in her eye. "No, I take back any offer I ever made."

Hopping up again, I kissed her other cheek for good measure. "Too late. I have witnesses, cousin."

"I can almost see the King of the Golden Sea," Thorn warned. That also meant the King could almost see me.

With a skip and a hop, I leapt into the air. I paused long enough to take one look back at the Inland Sea, the prize for which we had all fought and for which one of us had died. The sunlight glittered on the surface like a golden net. Beneath me Indigo and Shimmer lifted their paws in farewell.

However, when Thorn raised his hand, he gave such a loud creak that everyone began to laugh. And the good-hearted boy laughed the loudest of all. A king who could laugh at himself would be a good ruler. Lord Tower had chosen wisely. So had Thorn.

I don't have the constitution to be sad, but as I

waved good-bye to them, I felt as if someone had hung weights upon me. If you were in a tough fight, you couldn't ask for better protection for your back. If you were in a tricky scrape, you couldn't ask for more resourceful companions. If you were in hard times, you couldn't ask for more loyal friends. On the long, lonely road ahead, I knew I would miss them.

And then I began to somersault away, their shouted farewells fading in the distance. But as I soared upward into the sky, I knew I'd be back.